FELLOW
MORTALS

FELLOW MORTALS

MORTALS

DENNIS MAHONEY

FARRAR, STRAUS AND GIROUX

NEW YORK

Farrar, Straus and Giroux
18 West 18th Street, New York 10011

Printed in the United States of America
First edition, 2013

Library of Congress Cataloging-in-Publication Data
Mahoney, Dennis.
    Fellow mortals / Dennis Mahoney. — 1st ed.
        p.   cm.
    ISBN 978-0-374-15406-6 (alk. paper)
    1. Dwellings—Fires and fire prevention—Fiction.
    2. Fires—Psychological aspects—Fiction.   3. Guilt—Fiction.
    4. Interpersonal relations—Fiction.   I. Title.

PS3613.A3493355 F46 2013
813'.6—dc23
                                                    2012028948

Designed by Jonathan D. Lippincott

www.fsgbooks.com
www.twitter.com/fsgbooks • www.facebook.com/fsgbooks

1   3   5   7   9   10   8   6   4   2

For Coley, Jack, Max, and Bones

PART ONE

I

The fire and the mailman, story of their life. It's all they ever talk about. He wishes it would end. But now it's in the news again—*Tonight, live at five*—as if he needs to be reminded how it happened, who's to blame.

Billy walks the lots between his place and the Carmichaels', where demolition crews have razed the two unsalvageable homes, hauling the wreckage off in dump trucks and leaving a gap, like knocked-out teeth, in the middle of the block. He smells the fire all the time, ashy in the sun, murky in the rain, and though the ground is level and clear where the basements have been filled, he can't take a step without discovering a piece of what was there. A curved shard of glass. A melted hairbrush. Nothing worth picking up but Billy always checks. The lawn is scorched dead along the sidewalk as if a giant magnifying glass had focused on the ground, burning two crisp holes with terrible precision. Arcadia Street has been desolately quiet ever since, and with the vacant lots affording a view of the woodland just behind the yards, the cul-de-sac feels closer to wilderness than any of the blocks between here and the center of town.

A trailer appeared today while Billy was out. Dull white

and unattached to any vehicle, it's twenty feet long and planted at the back of the Bailey property, right against the trees but glowing in the late-day sun. He had watched Sam Bailey, eerie in the half-light of dawn, enter the woods several days ago and stay there, out of sight and doing God knows what, for as long as Billy could wait before he had to go to work.

In the mornings, he's still surprised to look outside and see the Carmichaels' house instead of the Finns'. Just the other night he spotted Peg Carmichael in her bathroom, drying her hair like nobody could see her—fifteen minutes wearing nothing but a towel. It's been the only real perk of a bad situation. He and Sheri draw the blinds after dark. With Nan and Joan Finn they never had to. The Finns were old, it didn't matter, but he doesn't need Bob Carmichael eye-balling Sheri, the way she walks around the kitchen under-dressed. Or rather partway dressed, like she doesn't want to bother, wearing a big T-shirt without pants, too long to show any thigh, or the brown bathrobe she got ten years ago from her first husband.

"It's my favorite robe," Sheri tells Billy, case closed.

Not that Bob Carmichael strikes him as a peeper. He's a good guy, Billy likes him, low-key and easy to talk to. A weird fit for Peg. Bob's male-pattern bald and wears a lot of plaid shirts, and when he isn't playing ball with his two sons or working at the bank, he's usually wandering around, fixing old bikes in the yard and waving to every neighbor he sees. Peg's the CEO and principal broker of Carmichael Realty Company and looks it: a pantsuit-wearing woman who starts her day with a six-mile run and doesn't slow down until bedtime. She drives an Audi, whisks the kids from school to Little League and back, is rarely without her business portfolio, and treats Billy like a man who ought to be renting. He looked her up online and most of her listings weren't that hot, only one above $300,000. Their own house is only slightly better than Billy and Sheri's, but he guesses with the kids, the Audi, Peg's wardrobe, and Bob's mid-level bank job, Arcadia Street is the best that they can manage.

Peg pulls up and Billy walks over. It's Saturday afternoon but she's dressed like it's early Monday morning. She hops out without acknowledging he's there, opens the back door, and bends into the car to get a grocery bag. All her running's paid off. He stares the whole way over, watching when her back foot hovers off the ground.

"Need a hand?"

Peg shuts the door with her hip and looks him in the face. He's had a lazy eye since birth; it doesn't give him trouble but it's there in conversations.

"How's the roof coming along?" Billy asks.

Peg groans. The Carmichaels' southern exterior took the brunt of the damage. They had to replace the siding and four windows, and now a portion of the roof needs work, more than they anticipated. Billy's had similar woes, except that being downwind, he lost the siding and the underlying wall, and part of his roof actually collapsed. He's had the roof repaired and the wall rebuilt. The rest of it he plans to do himself. He had a list a mile long *before* the fire and can't get ahead, but a lot of his insurance went to preexisting debts, and labor costs are ludicrous. Just ask Peg.

"We're getting another estimate," she says. "It never ends. Look at this place." She scowls at the footprints of the two missing homes. "They could have at least seeded grass."

"I guess one of us could," Billy says.

"Do you know how expensive grass seed is?"

She looks at him and smiles, remembering he works at True Value.

"They ought to make Cooper do it," Billy says.

"He ought to be in jail."

"It was an accident."

"If I accidentally hit you with my car," Peg says, "wouldn't you still be mad?"

Billy laughs at her aggression, grinning at her pearls and buttoned-up collar.

"The big hero," Peg continues. "I talked to Joan Finn. She couldn't stop praising him. He burns their house down, offers them a guest room, snap, he's a saint. I wonder what he offered Sam Bailey."

"He called me up and offered to lend a hand with any repairs," Billy says. "I said thanks, we didn't need help."

"You thanked him?"

"I said it with a tone."

Peg rolls her eyes and keeps them up and off Billy.

"He called me, too. My lawyer said I shouldn't speak to him, but honestly," she says, "I couldn't stop myself. I mean the sheer audacity . . . as if apologizing makes it better for us!"

"How's your lawsuit moving?"

"Don't even get me started. Suing a government agency's like a suing a glacier. Even with a settlement it might take . . . what is *that*?"

She's finally seen the trailer in the Baileys' backyard.

"I guess it's Sam's," Billy says. "He must be planning to rebuild."

"No one told me."

"I saw him in the woods the other morning."

"Doing what?"

Billy shrugs, and that's about all Peg can stand by the look she fires back, like it's him who stuck a secondhand trailer in the yard.

"I've got to get this ice cream inside," she announces.

He can see through the shopping bag: celery, eggplant, bottle of juice. She leaves him there without saying goodbye and he watches her up the steps and into her house, where the screen door hisses on its pressurized tubes.

Billy walks across the lot, crackling over something so charred it's unrecognizable. TV remote? The sole of a shoe? He strolls around back and sizes up the trailer but it's nondescript in every way; even the dents and discoloration are generic. The Baileys' garden is still here, growing on its own, and Billy sees that the strawberry plants have already borne fruit. He checks to see if anyone's around and picks a handful. No sense leaving them to rot. He cuts across the Finns' and walks into his kitchen, where he puts the berries in a colander and hears Sheri coming downstairs, finally out of her nap. She works late at the diner Friday nights and sleeps past noon every Saturday, and now she shuffles into the kitchen wearing yesterday's blouse. There's a gravy stain right down the middle of her stomach. She hasn't showered or brushed, her hair's flat on one side, and she doesn't say "Hey" or acknowledge him at all. She finds the coffee pot empty and her face gets pissy, like every pot in America ought to be nonstop full, and then she dumps the basket into the trash, drizzling out a thin line of coffee on the floor.

"I've got to be out of here in thirty."

"I didn't want to wake you," Billy says.

He grabs a sponge and cleans the coffee off the floor. Sheri stands there waiting with a filter, sighing that she can't get around him to the counter.

"Beep," she says, and Billy moves aside.

He sees the garbage can, coffee grounds oozing down the side, and he's reminded of the fire-hose water and the soot. The house still stinks—smoke in the walls, in the mattress, in the ground outside, and not just wood smoke, either. Burnt tar. Melted siding. A headache stink that follows him around, in his clothing and his nose. He even smells it on Sheri.

"I talked to Peg," he says. "Henry Cooper called her, too."

"Good for Henry Cooper," Sheri mutters.

"Yeah, the big hero. Like apologizing makes it any better."

"Why wouldn't it?"

"If I didn't mean to punch you in the face, wouldn't you still be mad? He's sitting home getting paid, for Christ's sake. Meanwhile look at us. Look at how we're living."

"At least you still have a wife," Sheri says.

She won't stop harping on the fact.

"I got you something," Billy says, holding out the berries.

"Where'd you get those?"

"From the Baileys' backyard."

"Ew, creepy," Sheri says, pushing them away, and then she goes upstairs to get dressed without remembering her coffee.

Billy starts the pot and walks out back, where he stands with the colander and tries to spot Peg through one of her brand-new windows. The berries are redder than anything he's seen this spring, adorable and plump, like a basketful of hearts. He thinks of Henry Cooper when he pops one into his mouth, but it's sour and he spits it out bloody on the ground.

2

The grand jury had finally been impaneled early this week—thirty-two days after the fire—to decide upon the case of Henry Cooper's criminal indictment. The fire marshal, an investigator, and the elderly sisters, Nan and Joan Finn, had each given their testimony, but in spite of his eagerness to face the jury, Henry himself had been repeatedly dissuaded from appearing.

"It can't help," his lawyer said. "They aren't looking for remorse. They're looking for the slightest little evidence of crime."

"Doesn't hiding look bad?" Henry asked.

"They look at elements of guilt. The fewer elements the better. I advise you not to go."

Henry takes a shower now, starting out cold and dialing up to hot, even though he's barely broken a sweat today, and not the kind of sweat he'd get delivering mail. The soap is cucumber scent and has a few of Ava's hairs pressed into the soft white layer on the bottom. He lathers up and hums a jingle—*Ajax . . . Stronger than dirt!*—but immediately quits and bumps his head against the wall. The sound is echoey and hollow—one, two, three—and he stops this, too, so Ava doesn't hear.

"Are you all right?" she calls, muffled through the door.

"I'm okay!" Henry says.

He steps out, pouring water onto the floor, and pauses with his face in the fogged-out mirror.

Wingnut wags and licks Henry's toes. He's a plain brown mutt, fifty pounds and five years old, with a hound's bassoony bark and a long crooked tail—the kind of glad, generic dog kids doodle when they're four. Henry moves him off but then apologizes, summoning him back to pat his rump. He hangs the towel on the curtain rod, pees, and breaks wind. He wipes the splatter off the rim with a ball of toilet paper, lowers the seat, and forgets to flush, his mind racing ahead to brushing his teeth and talking with Ava, who's waiting out in the bedroom, folding laundry after a full day of work.

Flashes of the fire happen all the time, triggered by the plainest, most arbitrary things: the backs of Ava's knees, freshly brewed coffee. Memories of smoke, red and white lights out the corner of his eye. A body on fire and his sweater in the hedge. He remembers things he didn't even see, like now, when he's wiping off the mirror and imagines Laura Bailey shaking out her hair before she went to bed.

He pops a lid and takes his heart meds—Ava's sure to ask—though really he's been fine since the stent last summer. He opens the door and walks out naked, Wingnut padding at his heels, the two of them damp with steam and sniffing the cooler air.

Henry's forty-five years old, short and powerfully built, with forearms bigger than some men's calves and a paunch that makes him grand instead of flabby. His walrus mustache crinkles when he grins; he wipes it, top to bottom, watching Ava fold a sheet. She spreads her arms and snaps the cotton tight across her bosom. Any other month he'd have hugged her on the spot, wrapped her in the sheet, and bounced her on the bed. But the Finns are downstairs and so he helps her with the laundry, staring at the wall instead of what he's doing. He folds the same towel twice and even then it's unacceptable. Ava picks it up without a word and does it right. He lifts a pair of boxers from the heap and puts them on, tipping most of the pile off the mattress with a flump.

He lunges for the clothes and jabs her in the ribs.

"Sorry! Shoot—I'm sorry, Av. I didn't mean to get you there."

"Sit," she says, blowing up her bangs. "Let me do this."

He watches her. She's amply built, proud of her hips and breasts, and unafraid of wearing bathing suits. Her hands are like a milkmaid's, buttery and strong. She's a lab tech and Henry often views her as a nurse. He's seen her with a needle in a vein, all precision, but she's really at her best when she's tightening a tourniquet.

He sits and dips the bed. Ava stabilizes towels. He stands again and rearranges pictures on the dresser. Wing's at his heels, certain he can help. Henry hasn't worked his postal route in a month, the longest stretch of unemployment he's endured since the age of sixteen. They've suspended him with pay, though it may as well be jail, and he would get another job but Ava's certain he'd regret it.

"It's all you know," she says. "You'd have to work retail and stand all day."

"I could stand all week."

"You can't stand *still*," Ava tells him, and she's right.

He's pacing back and forth even as they talk. "They'll re-instate you," she insists. "They can't fire an employee with a single black mark on his record."

"It's a big mark."

"It was an accident," she says. "A terrible, mind-bogglingly stupid accident, but after twenty-one years they owe you better. Thank God for unions."

The union steward from the National Association of Letter Carriers was with him during the USPS disciplinary hearing, and although the fire occurred because of a bro-ken code, he's kept his job and is, in fact, liable to get his route back after months of union counterpressure.

Now today. Now the jury. Public opinion had swung in Henry's favor from the get-go, cameras having caught him at the scene, the sight of a crying mailman touching some sentimental nerve. The Finns were interviewed on the eve-ning news, Nan poised amid the ruins, Joan pitiful and tearstruck, the first of many to commend him for his quick-thinking rescue. People pitied the Finns and Henry, too, sorry for the tragedy, sorry for it all, absolving him in ways he couldn't understand. The district attorney took it easy and the jury no-billed the case.

"It means you're clear," the lawyer told him on the phone this afternoon. "No trial."

"That's it?"

"That's it," the lawyer said, and Henry closed his eyes, barely holding the receiver.

He was advised against contacting anyone from Arca-dia Street, but Henry took his chances and reached out to everyone. The Finns had been a no-brainer. Their insurance covered hotel expenses, but Henry and Ava agreed they needed an interim home instead of anonymous lodgings, and Nan and Joan accepted the offered guest room the very night of the fire. Henry's gotten used to the faster-emptying fridge, the public radio, the smell of medicated lotion, and the necessity—learned the hard way—of putting on pants before he saunters through the kitchen. He isn't used to tears, though, and Joan's been getting in a handful of serious cries every day for a month. Nan, on the other hand, has yet to cry once. They're weirdly good to Henry—Joan appreciative and childlike, Nan ironclad but temperate—as if he rescued them from something that he hadn't been the cause of.

Joan and Ava get along, comfortably imbalanced—a helpless little lady and the woman of the house. *Nan* and Ava, on the other hand, bristled from the start. They're electrically polite, vying for dominion, Nan asserting her rights within the boundaries of decorum, Ava mastering her home with limits and concessions. This morning they offered each other first use of the washing machine with so much crackling generosity that Wing tucked tail and hid beneath a table. Henry senses it whenever he walks up- or downstairs, right around step number eight, the invisible threshold between Ava's realm and Nan's.

He and Wing, more and more, spend their hours in the yard.

At least the Finns are here. Peg Carmichael said she wasn't allowed to speak to him, then chewed him out for five minutes, talking about her two sons' nightmares until he felt like the boogeyman himself. Billy Kane said thanks but declined any help.

As far as everyone's concerned, this is how it has to be. There's still the matter of civil suits from all the victims—the Carmichaels, the Kanes, Sam Bailey, and even the

Finns, who've been more or less strong-armed by their insurance company. Joan cried when Nan informed her, but Henry and Ava understood it wasn't personal and didn't worry about the money, since all fees and settlements were to be handled by the postal insurer and USPS-retained legal firms, the fire having occurred with Henry on duty as a government employee. Incredible but true, he won't pay a penny out of pocket, win or lose.

Ava folds the laundry heap and puts it all away, sock balls and underwear, shirts with the arms crossed over like mummies. She turns her back and Henry watches how she crooks an arm and unzips her dress, dropping her shoulders—left, right—so it slips to her waist. She unclasps her bra, hunching it forward onto her arms, and with another couple tugs, her dress is at her ankles and she steps out, one foot at a time, like she's stepping from a puddle. He sees the side of one breast, then the underside of both when she bends down low to get her panties off her heels. Her legs have gotten softer, her skin less resilient, and her moles too numerous count. She walks into the bathroom, running her fingers through her hair so it falls back messy to her shoulders, and when she shuts the door behind her, Henry slumps to the floor, and he doesn't start to cry until he's positive she's standing in the shower.

Ava pauses in the bathroom, breathing easy after fifteen hours in a bra. She pulls Henry's towel off the rod and wipes the floor. The shower mat's soaked; she'll have to wash that before it molds. The toilet water's yellow. She considers letting him know but she can feel him out there, dwelling on the accidental rib shot he gave her. Everything

he does since the fire weighs him down. She sends him to
the market and he buys the wrong peppers. Has him mop
the kitchen and he blinds them with ammonia. She tries to
give him jobs that she can fix or doesn't care about, anything to make him feel useful for a while.

She's nostalgic for the summer like it's already gone,
missing the board games and wine on Friday nights, the
regular beach trips, Henry mowing the lawn, copper-
shouldered in the heat. Every now and then, she even misses
his cigars.

She showers and her hair disentangles in the rinse. The
soap is slippery in her hands, softening her skin, down in
all the right places with her fingers and her palms. She
thinks of being younger, barely out of school, diving underwater with a boy she doesn't know, and yet her evening in
the bathroom—this particular moment, with the warm
scent of phlox on the outdoor breeze—is the closest Ava
comes anymore to rolling unbuttoned in the sun.

Stepping out, there's Henry in the bathroom door. Ava
jumps a quarter inch, only partially surprised. The knot
beneath her shoulder blade doubles up tight. He stands
with a tilt from carrying mailbags and has a permanent
furrow on his shoulder from the strap. His mustache is
tidy but his hair's all mussed. He's strong enough to lift
her and she wishes that he would—just grab her in a bear
hug and hold her in the air.

"I ought to call the Carmichaels again."

"Henry . . ."

"I know, I know. They want to be left alone. I didn't
talk to Bob, though," he says, referring to Peg's husband.
"And the Kanes . . ."

Ava sighs extra long.

"All right," he says. "Forget it. I'm worried about Joan, though."

"Joan has Nan."

"She started crying after *Wheel of Fortune*."

"You can't expect people to bounce right back, even when you're helping."

"How come Nan never cries?"

"Because her sister does," Ava says. "Maybe she cries in bed."

She rolls up the mat and puts a dry towel in its place. Henry leans against the sink, ear cocked toward the floor, as if he's listening for Nan's faint sobbing in the distance.

"We could buy a swing set for the Carmichael boys."

"Henry."

"Anonymously," he says. "Like the big turkey in *A Christmas Carol*."

"They send their kids to Dunne Keating. They're richer than we are. Plus they already have insurance and they're sure to get a bundle from the civil suit."

"But this'd come from me."

"Anonymously."

"It'd still be from me," he says, lowering his head, his hair a bit thinner at the crown than several months ago.

She moisturizes her face and fires up the hair dryer, cutting him off so matter-of-factly that he doesn't take it personally. He's standing too close; she can barely move her elbow. She gives him a warning blast with the dryer and backs him out of the doorway.

Wingnut stands at the bed, unsure of what to do. He doesn't wag a lot these days, tuned as he is to Henry's over-all mood, and even though he's finally adapting to the changes, he keeps hoping Henry'll make Ava laugh and they'll relax, maybe let him snuggle in the middle of the bed. He's gotten used to Nan, who likes him more than anyone expected, Nan herself included. She sneaks him toast dipped in coffee, compliments his smile. All Wing wants to do is see people happy. He smells the hamper and the hair dryer, comforting and warm, and can't imagine why the house feels so bad.

Ava combs her hair, raising heat along her scalp, and then she brushes her teeth and rinses, prickling from her soles to the bottom of her tongue. Henry follows her to bed, where she sits and pats the quilt, and then he joins her, hip to hip, and Wing flops down around their feet.

"I need you to pull yourself together," Ava tells him.

He looks at his hands as if the pulling-together's real, something he can physically accomplish if he tries.

She touches Wingnut's head as if to grant a benediction. Henry lies back, breathing at the ceiling. There's only one cricket outside, and the air's so humid it's congesting in the window screen.

"We can't go on like this," Ava says. "Don't apologize— stop. If I hear you say 'Sorry' one more time I'm going to light *myself* on fire."

She turns and holds a palm to each of Henry's cheeks.

"You're the best man I know," she says. "But helping the Carmichael boys won't work. You need to find Sam."

"I don't know where he is."

"Ask Nan. She knows about everything."

Oatmeal cookies, vegetable shortening, ironing, bleaching, fiber, dogs—all of her knowledge slightly out-of-date but basically correct, like one of those old Funk & Wagnalls encyclopedia sets they come across at yard sales. But Ava asked for help today and Nan's been making calls.

It's the first thing the two of them have thoroughly agreed upon.

"You think he wants to see me?" Henry asks.

"He probably wants to kill you. But it's that or killing yourself for the rest of your life."

She pecks him on the lips, pressing into his mustache, and then she holds him there and opens her mouth, kissing him for real. Henry kisses back and yet he's hesitant, submissive. She straddles him and sits, reaching into his boxers.

"Ava."

"Shh."

She squeezes for effect. He's strong enough to throw her off but never to resist her, and he stares up, teary for a whole new reason.

"We need this," she says.

"It doesn't feel right."

"That's the problem," Ava whispers.

"Nan and Joan . . ."

"They're asleep."

"What if they wake up?"

"They're old enough to understand."

She guides him in and plants her weight. Henry holds her hips.

"You took your pill?" she asks, tensing for a moment in his lap.

Henry nods. Ava moves, leaning forward till her hair's in his eyes and then she hugs him up close, with his face between her breasts, smothering the fire just like that.

Joan Finn is unsettled by the creaks overhead. She's sitting in a small upholstered chair, wearing rose pajamas and a bathrobe and reading *People* under a lamp. The guest room is crowded with a bureau, a separate nightstand for each sister, and a bed that Henry bought so they wouldn't have to sleep on a pullout. There's a single window out the side that Nan keeps open for the air, but anyone could break through a screen, Joan thinks, here at ground level after dark. She waits for Nan to return from the bathroom and says:

"I hear something."

Nan puts a glass of water next to her rosary beads. She pulls a single dead leaf off a marigold she rescued from their yard, listens for a spell, and says, "It's nothing to worry about. Read your *People*."

Fifty years ago, Joan had boyfriends—she was briefly engaged once upon a time—but she's been living with her sister so long, it takes an extra minute for the lightbulb to finally flicker on. Once it does, she rustles through her magazine, trying to mask the sound, as if by hearing them together she's infringing on their privacy. She's seen plenty of lovemaking in movies and did, in fact, have sex with a man half a century ago, but the intervening drought, deepened by religion, has resulted in what her sister calls secondary virginity. It's a true state of grace, listed in the catechism.

"They're married," Nan reminds her. "They'll be done in a few minutes."

Joan's impressed that Nan can estimate a time frame. Her sister seems privy to a universe of secrets, even though Nan herself retained her primary virginity and was rarely attached to a boy longer than a high-school prom.

The creaks finally stop and Nan prays the rosary, counting Hail Marys briskly and efficiently, the words so ingrained they form a kind of silence in her mind. She

prays for Sam and Laura Bailey, the Kanes and Carmichaels, the man who cut her off at Stop & Shop, the sick
of the parish, the obituary names from the morning paper,
Wingnut, and most of all Henry. Bearing one's cross is a
much-neglected art, she thinks, glancing up at Joan, and
then she says a prayer for Ava, her own private thorn, a good
woman whose only serious fault—domestic inflexibility—
irritates Nan because it's her fault, too.

With the Hail Holy Queen, she wishes for a home, and
then she lays her beads on the nightstand, takes a sip of
water, and settles into bed with the latest issue of O.

3

Laura's wardrobe burned. The funeral home provided clothes—or had it been him?—but Sam Bailey spent most of last night remembering the wake, unsure if she'd been buried in a dress or a skirt, unable to visualize the style of her hair. Eventually it struck him: she was out there, right that minute, in a coffin underground less than twenty minutes from the motel, her clothes and hair all perfectly arranged and it was possible—unthinkable but possible—to see her face and even hold her hand. And there he sat, sipping soda, flipping back and forth between several different movies, and he couldn't shake it off until he finally grabbed his keys and got in the car. He drove in a daze, at the very least determined to see her grave—he had no memory of the headstone, either—until the bustle of the town, the high-school students playing music in their cars, the neon colors of a normal Friday night, brought him back to his senses and he skipped the cemetery altogether, returning once again to his room at the motel.

He's been staying at the Chalet Motor Inn for nearly a month, long enough to feel at home with the green telephone, the wood veneer on the walls, the carpet stain shaped like the birthmark on Laura's right thigh. The first night of his stay, he found a bat clinging to the air conditioner. He told the owner but the bat disappeared. He's called the place the Bat Chalet ever since and often remembers the first night in bed, when he was scared he'd feel a flutter if he drifted off to sleep.

He hears a Johnny Cash ringtone playing through the wall, enough to get the song looping in his head, and when a motorcycle roars, he opens his eyes, sees the daylight, and groans out of bed. He walks into the bathroom and the toilet seat's up. He puts it down, bothered that he's already lost the habit, then raises it and pees and puts it down a second time. He brushes his teeth, wets his hair, and dresses in the same clothes he wore yesterday.

"No," he says.

He dresses in a fresh shirt and jeans, takes an awl from his toolbox, and pokes a new hole into his belt. He's lost close to fifteen pounds and his skin is too pale, but even though his appetite's been iffy, he decides he ought to treat himself to breakfast, something to commemorate the day.

He packs his knapsack, heaps the bedsheets and pillowcases by the door, ties the garbage bag, and wipes down the counter of the sink. He does a final check for the bat in the air conditioner, and then he takes his bag and leaves, closing the door and squinting in the light. There's no one at the checkout office. He realizes that he hasn't seen the owner since he prepaid early in the week—that from now on, he really won't be around people anymore.

He takes a notebook out of his bag, writes *Thanks. Sam Bailey*, and folds the paper and key into the drop slot before driving off. He orders two egg sandwiches, coffee, juice, and a bag of crullers at a drive-thru and takes his time going to Arcadia Street. He listens to a male and female

DJ team, their banter both confident and desperate in its humor, like they know there's something shameful in their own forced cheer. He turns them off and rolls down the windows, trying to pretend that it's an ordinary drive.

When he reaches the old neighborhood he parks around the corner and walks the rest of the way, checking each house for signs of life, but he slept so late that it's already midday and everyone's at work. He's so intent on reaching the woods that he's oblivious to fragments of his home underfoot. Looking back from the trailer, he's reminded more of anonymous construction sites than any place he once lived, until he notices a seltzer can—one of Laura's—that must have fallen out of the old recycling bin. He leaves it there and checks the trailer door, where Peg has left a note asking if there's anything he needs. Wait until she hears he used another real estate agent.

He shoulders his bag and hikes into the woods. There's no trace of the path he beat the previous day, but he follows the terrain and recognizes garbage: a snack-size bag of Wise potato chips, the heel of a bottle, a forty-gallon oil drum, empty and graffitied with a penis. Several minutes walking and the trash disappears. The trees smell richer and the weeds thicken up. Here and there it's so dense he has to fight his way through, tripping on the roots and getting lashed around the face, and when he stops to take a breath he can't see the trailer anymore.

The woods back here used to scare him in the dark. He and Laura hiked it several times and they'd considered—in a playful, mostly Laura-driven way—camping this spring before the bugs got bad. But he had planned to build a fence like the Carmichaels have because at night, when he stood in the yard and looked toward the trees, he often heard sounds and wasn't sure if they were animal or human. Now the woods are his: thirty acres of undevelopable land, surrounded by hundreds more that may as well belong to him, too, all of it sprawling backwards from Arcadia Street and off toward the long, rolling hills around town.

The land and the trailer cost him most of his homeowner's policy, but with Laura's life insurance he won't have to work for upwards of a year, longer if he's frugal. He's been an art teacher at the high school for half a decade, but now a substitute is finishing his classes and he's glad to put it behind him. It isn't the kids. He likes quite a few and he's relatively popular, but he couldn't bear the adults lurking in the teachers' lounge, asking how he is and second-guessing all his answers. How's he doing, is he eating. Is he getting any rest.

"Laura would want you to smile," a colleague told him at the burial.

He'd always liked this woman, a soft-spoken social studies teacher with a lisp.

"No, you're right," he said. "I'll rent a comedy or something," and the woman went away looking glad that she had helped. He remembers it now whenever he watches TV. He wouldn't mind trying a comedy some nights except he always pictures her, sitting with her husband, laughing at a show with her tongue between her teeth.

He reaches a clearing in the trees, a quarter-acre plot of grass and wildflowers with a small, lumpy hillock in the rear. Sunlight flickers through the leaves, dappling the ground with a thousand moving shadows. He can see the open sky directly overhead. On the hill there's an outcrop of shale, mossy at the base and dampened by a freshwater trickle. Sam sits and eats one of his egg sandwiches, watching titmice and tossing pieces of croissant to some of the squirrels. Minutes pass, possibly an hour, enough to move the angle of the light upon his face. He takes his time standing up, unsure if he's been dozing. The squirrels are gone. His legs are pins and needles so he tries to walk it off, hiking back farther than he did the day before, looking for the tree he needs so desperately to find.

He has an Audubon guide and spends the day exploring and identifying species. Cedar, birch, elm. Tamarack and ash. He sees fewer and fewer promising shapes the longer he looks until eventually he can't see the forest for the trees, or the trees for the forest, or a single good reason to have purchased thirty acres. He's tired from the hike, out of shape and out of food. He left the crullers at the trailer but he can't bear the thought of walking out without a nap, so he settles on the ground and sleeps much longer than he means to.

When he wakes it's already evening—an evening much darker in the woods than in the town. He's up right away, heart jolting in alarm. The rushing in his ears is like the rustles of the leaves. He can't remember which way is out. It's got to be less than half a mile west, but he can't quite determine the direction of the sunset. He rummages around to find the flashlight buried in his bag, thinking to himself, *It's all right, it's all right*, because he doesn't want to say it out loud.

There were times he lost his mother as a child, at the beach or at the park, and he'd been told he once went missing thirty minutes in a corn maze. He can't remember this—wouldn't that have traumatized a child, just a little?—any more than he can remember his father, who died in a crash when Sam was only two. But hiking in the dark now, trying not to panic, he's reminded of the year he lost his mother to an aneurysm. She'd been relatively young and reasonably healthy, and quick as a phone call he didn't have a parent in the world. If he hadn't had Laura to support him when it happened . . . well, he really doesn't know. But he hadn't been alone.

The flashlight only makes the situation worse, the focused beam pointing out the darkness all around him, threatening to find something fearsome in the trees. One set of trunks looks the same as any other, but he thinks he knows the way and follows anything that strikes him as familiar. He's aware of every sound: swishes, snaps, whippoorwills, and insects. A blood-chilling squall he hopes is only a fox. The clouds are breaking up, and now and then he sees the moon passing in the gaps. It's arresting as it always is, common but surprising, like his own pale face shining in a glass. He thinks of Laura on a moonlit pillow on their bed. On a pillow in her coffin. At the wake and underground.

He sees a maple in the dark, giant and profound. It's shaped like a Y but the wind has cracked half of it away. The remainder of the left-hand fork juts up, six feet tall and pointing at a bough. At the bottom of the bough, there's a tiny sprig of leaves. It hovers only inches from the jagged piece of trunk; he can feel it in his fingers, how they almost seem to touch. This is it—how'd he miss it during hours of exploring? Through a thicket up ahead, he spies the clearing where he sat and ate lunch, but he doesn't want to leave anymore and turns the flashlight off, waiting for his eyes to readjust so he can watch the little sprig when it lowers in the breeze.

4

Henry's reading the paper out in the yard, a well-groomed lawn with a vegetable garden and watermelon vines. Earlier this morning there was tension over tomato paste, Nan favoring a high-sodium classic and Ava holding firmly to the no-salt variety. Henry was called upon to settle the debate. He knew that Ava's choice was for the benefit of his own blood pressure, but how could he of all people deny the Finns their favorite—and, it must be said, more flavorful—tomato sauce recipe? Ava left for work in a snit and Henry's been hiding outside ever since, and despite having sided with Nan, he cowers when the elderly sister opens the door and joins him and Wingnut on the steps.

"Sam Bailey bought the woods behind his property," Nan says. "My friend Louise plays bingo with a woman whose niece works for a lawyer. The lawyer handled the closing. He's been staying at the Chalet Motor Inn but checked out early this week. He's living in a trailer on Arcadia Street."

"Wow," Henry says, looking up to see her. Sun glints off the door and forces him to squint. He massages newspaper ink around his neck and feels a clenching in his chest, a physical awareness of the trailer, and the man, less than fifteen minutes from his own backyard.

Nan bends as if her body is a well-made hinge, leaning down to pet Wing without compromising her posture. Henry breathes until the pressure near his heart begins to dissipate. He listens to a chickadee singing from a tree.

"It's the right thing to do," Nan says, cleaning another smudge of newsprint off the side of Henry's forehead. "If you don't see him now, you'll both keep dreading it will happen accidentally. You'll look for him at gas stations, supermarkets, everywhere you go, and when you see him you'll remember that you never made an effort."

"What do I say?"

"Say you're sorry. After that, you'll have to feel it out. But say and do whatever you have to say and do, because you might not get a second conversation."

He shuts his eyes and tries to picture it—a trailer on the plot—and then imagines pulling up and knocking on the door. He stands and locks his knees and feels a tingle in his thighs. Nan hugs him with a pat and Wingnut wags, intuiting a car trip entirely from Henry's body language, and they all go inside and feel refreshed by the coolness of the kitchen.

Joan's sitting at the table with a thousand-piece jigsaw, a recent gift from Henry, who's convinced that old ladies love doing puzzles. He set it up this morning right in the kitchen—another thing that irritated Ava, who uses the table more than Henry realized—and then he hovered there and cheered when Joan made her first tentative connection. She checks the picture on the box, a hedge maze with a fountain in the center, mostly shadow, leaf, and sky—a puzzle for legitimate fanatics.

"Look," Joan says, showing him the six-piece fountain.

"Hey, you're doing great! You'll have it done in no time."

She smiles at his smile, says it's "wonderfully green," and recommits with a tremor and a small, fragile sigh.

Henry calls Ava at the lab.

"Lindt Diagnostics."

"Good morning," Henry says, thrown as always by his wife's professional voice. "May I please speak to Ava Cooper?"

"What," she says.

"Av?"

"It's me. What do you need?"

"Oh, it's you!" he says. "Hey. How's your morn—"

"I can't talk. Ruby called out and there's a half-dozen patients in the waiting room."

"Nan found Sam," Henry says. "He's living in a trailer on Arcadia. I'm heading over now. I'll be home before dinner. If I'm late, start without me."

"You're going now?"

"You said—"

"I said you ought to find him. I don't know if suddenly showing up . . . How do you know he's living in the trailer? Maybe it's construction. He's probably rebuilding."

"No, he's living there. Nan's friend plays bingo . . ." and he tells her all he knows, looking up at Nan to verify the facts.

"I don't know, I don't know."

Henry listens closely for the sound of her expression. She only gets this tone with a certain kind of face, like when he's fiddling with an outlet or balancing a ladder.

"What am I doing wrong?" he asks.

"Put Nan on."

Henry hands her the receiver, glad of further input. Nan listens for a moment, then turns to him and says, "I forgot about the wash."

"I'll put it in the dryer," Henry says, sure thing, and then he walks downstairs on a clear, simple mission.

"He's gone," Nan says.

"Is this a mistake?" Ava asks.

"No."

"It made a lot of sense last night," Ava tells her. "But Henry doesn't think. What if Sam snaps?"

"Sam Bailey isn't a violent man. It might be ugly but it won't be dangerous."

"Henry doesn't know when to quit."

"That's how he got me out of the shower," Nan reminds her.

Joan looks up, bewildered by the talk, and looks back down, bewildered by the puzzle.

"He's coming upstairs," Nan whispers. "Say a prayer."

Before Ava has a second to respond, Henry's back in the kitchen. He's forgotten to add a dryer sheet but gives Nan a big thumbs-up: mission accomplished. She hands the telephone back and walks downstairs, intuiting his oversight and heading for the dryer.

"Don't talk too much," Ava tells Henry. "And don't expect too much. He doesn't owe you anything, remember."

"Geez, Av. I'm not going there for me."

"I wish you had a phone."

"It's only fifteen min—"

"Call me when you're home," she says.

"I will."

"Don't be pushy."

"Av . . ."

"All right. I love you," Ava says.

He warms his ear against the phone, the softness of her breath so close he almost smells it.

"This is good," Henry says. "Something's dropping into place."

5

It had been a warm, blustery day in a spring without rain. Henry lit a match. The fire looked clear in the sun and he threw it down, thinking the wind had blown it out and not thinking twice, despite the drought, despite the mulch under the boxwood hedge.

He struck another match, fresh cigar clamped in his teeth, mailbag swaying off his shoulder. He wasn't allowed to smoke on the route. He wasn't allowed at all, having promised it to Ava, married all these years and there it was, she put her foot down. But it was such a fine day with the leaves sashaying in the trees, he told himself the smell wouldn't linger in his clothes—that a few quick puffs were a very small betrayal. The flavor made him salivate. He'd found it in the truck, a single White Owl that had rolled behind the clutch, and when he finally got a light, puffed big, and sniffed it in, he drifted to a thousand other spring afternoons. He thought of Ava in a sundress, twenty years younger and firm as a plum, and then he pictured her expression if she smelled stale cigar. He saw his uniform reflected in the window of a car—gray pants with vertical stripes, collared shirt, blue sweater with the streamlined eagle on the breast. A uniform of dignity, a uniform he loved. He licked tobacco off his lip and contemplated the ember, and then he crushed the whole cigar underfoot, smiled, and continued on his way, walking to the door at 6 Arcadia Street.

It was Sam and Laura Bailey: married, late twenties, childless, and relatively new to the block, still getting junk addressed to the previous owners. They got a water bill, a medical journal for Laura, and a sculpture magazine for Sam. He guessed that Laura was a doctor, having seen her a few times in the early afternoon, as if her shifts were different hours than a regular person's hours. She was willowy and pale with warm, smoky eyes, as if he'd woken her from dreaming or she hadn't yet slept. He handed her the mail one day and felt transfixed, comfortable but weirdly self-conscious in her gaze. She was quiet in a way that made her seem smart, and when she turned, he saw the beautiful knot that she had fashioned in her hair.

Turning from the Bailey house, he caught a whiff of smoke. It was one of his favorite parts of spring, everything fragrant for the first time in months—grass, dirt, tulips, sunlight softening the asphalt. All he missed was rain, though as a mailman he hadn't begrudged so many weeks of dry weather. He'd been a carrier for two decades but only had his current route a handful of months. Arcadia was one of the smaller streets, a cul-de-sac with sixteen houses, tightly packed Capes with long backyards, the east-side homes bordering the woods and giving the block a special kind of privacy—rural and remote, separate from the town.

Everybody worked except for Nan and Joan Finn, there at number eight with the floral lace curtains flapping at the screens.

Five catalogs, a Medicare notice, a handwritten letter, several flyers, something from the bank, an envelope of seeds, and more junk mail than anyone under eighty was liable to get in a week: a typical day for Nan and Joan. They were both skinny and tall, with noses so hooked he once saw a pair of umbrellas hanging on a rail and thought of the Finns.

He found Joan sitting in the living room, surrounded by shelf upon shelf of figurines: songbirds, saints, miniature trees.

"Afternoon," he said. "Beaut of a day."

She smiled and looked around like maybe Jesus had addressed her. Then she noticed Henry standing there and smiled just as warmly. He thought of her hair as butterscotch-gray, same as her teeth and skin, but her sweater and her eyes were cornflower blue.

"Spring has sprung!" Joan said.

"It sure has. You have some letters here."

"Thank you!" she said, not getting up. "The weather's saying rain tomorrow."

"April showers," Henry answered, sending her into ecstasy. "Say hi to your sister."

"I will!"

Henry walked off, admiring the sky. He cut across the lawn and prechecked the mail for number ten: Billy and Sheri Kane. Power bill, phone bill, credit report, and something from the courthouse: a black-letter day. The grass turned scrabbly right at the property line. There was a band of dirt that led to a newly poured sidewalk square, another span of dirt, and finally a road patch—probably the scars of a dug-up sewer pipe. The house itself looked worse.

Cockeyed steps, decrepit siding, an American flag so grubby Henry felt they ought to burn it out of respect.

He left their mail inside the screen door, which was so badly dented that it wouldn't fully shut. Kicked, Henry thought, and then he registered a sound—a crackling he'd been hearing for a while unaware. He looked up the street and there was fire in the bushes—in the little group of boxwoods at Sam and Laura Bailey's—sending smoke and orange flames into a hedgerow of yews. The yews were burning, too, right against the house.

"Holy shit," Henry said.

He dropped the mailbag and ran. It must have been a match, he thought, remembering the mulch, but even with the drought he couldn't believe how ferociously it spread. He squinted at the heat from several feet away, moved closer upwind, and beat the fire with his sweater, but the sweater caught, too, and he was forced to let it go. The boxwoods vanished in a flare. Then the fire caught the yew and really cut wild, covering the wall like water rushing up.

He ran to number eight and looked for Joan, who was exactly where he had left her, smiling in her chair.

"Oh!" she said, surprised to see him back.

Henry glanced next door, dizzy at the sight.

"I need your phone."

He banged the door and strode halfway into the living room before noticing her face. Joan backed away, smiling but alarmed, growing smaller by the second near a shelf of figurines.

"There's a fire," Henry said. "You got to leave. Where's your sister?"

"In the shower."

"Where—"

"There's a fire?"

"Where's the shower!?" Henry yelled. She pointed up. "Call 911," he said.

He took the stairs two at a time and stumbled at the top, slipping three steps and murdering his shin. He found the bathroom door and knocked with his fist.

"Nan!"

"Who's there?"

"It's Henry Cooper . . . the mailman. You got to come out."

The hall was narrow and dim. Smoke drifted in—he could feel it in his eyes. The window by the stairs darkened intermittently. He leaned against the door and heard the shower curtain slide.

"Who's there?" Nan said, closer to his ear.

"You got to get dressed, we got to go."

A smoke alarm tripped. He heard Joan calling from below, and when he hurried to the stairs and leaned over the rail, she was looking up and quaking like a child he'd forgotten.

"Did you call the fire department?"

"Where's Nan?"

"Did you call 911?"

She clasped her hands and nodded.

"Get out of the house," he said.

"The porch . . . ," she answered, looking out front. He ran downstairs. Fire rippled at the door, billowing the curtains, more than he expected. Another smoke alarm blew, right above his ear.

"Wait in the yard," he said, moving her along. "Go, I'll get your sister."

He ran back up and checked the window at the top. The Baileys' whole wall was hidden by the smoke. He returned to the bathroom and rattled the knob.

"Miss *Finn*."

"Go away!" Nan said. "Joan? Joan!"

"Back up!" Henry yelled.

He rammed against the door.

It was flimsy hollow-core and fractured when he hit it. Screws and bits of wood skittered off the sink. Nan trembled in a robe, hair raggedy and wet, all collarbone and eyeball and wispy in the steam. She aimed a hair dryer level to his head, like a gun.

"Whoa," he said, showing her his palms.

The window up the hall trembled at the heat. He moved fast, stooping low to get his arm around her hips, and then he tipped her up and hauled her out the bathroom on his shoulder. She hit him with the dryer, hard enough to hurt. He thumped downstairs as quickly as he could, trying to catch the dryer with his free hand and getting rapped on the knuckles and the wrist.

At the bottom of the stairs, she quit attacking him and sagged. He took her out back, where the smoke had risen high enough to shadow out the sun. Joan, waiting helpless in the corner of the yard, thought her sister had collapsed and started sobbing.

"She's okay," Henry said, standing them together.

Nan turned and saw the Bailey house, heavily aflame. She hugged the dryer to her breast and wobbled on her heels.

"Don't move," Henry said.

He ran around the house toward the sirens out front. A crosswind of fire hit him at the porch. He wasn't seriously burned, only flashed on the cheek, but he staggered with his hand clapped to his face.

Fire in and out the windows, flaring up the eaves, roaring with a sound like wind through a tunnel. The flames had jumped a hedge to number ten—Billy Kane—where he noticed that the flag had withered on the pole.

Trucks jammed around the road but no one seemed to rush. Firefighters walked instead of ran, their lack of energy surreal but almost comforting to see. Henry found his mailbag lying on the ground. He grabbed it out of instinct and ran toward the Baileys' house, stepping on a fire hose and awed by the colors.

Number four had started burning: the Carmichael family—Peg and Bob, *two young boys*. Someone yanked him by the arm until he stood across the street, where his bowels turned feeble at the full panorama. Henry clenched tight, scared he'd have an accident, jellied in the legs and fighting for a breath. He didn't recognize the neighborhood. Red and white lights, fire in the windows, diesel fuel blowing off the engines of the trucks. Smoke towered up and carried for a mile, tall enough for anyone in town to see it rise.

An ambulance arrived, police and paramedics. Henry took a firefighter roughly by the arm. He was young, just a rookie with a red goatee.

"There's two ladies in the yard at number eight," Henry yelled.

"Where's eight?"

Something terrible collapsed, an entire piece of roof, sending sparks sky-high from the Baileys' second floor. Out the corner of his eye he saw the window of the dormer, and a *person* at the glass, barely real, like a mannequin.

"There!" he yelled. "Upstairs, number six!"

"What . . ."

"Someone in the dormer!"

The rookie hesitated, frazzled by the extra information. He sent a firefighter after the Finns and ran to the Baileys' with another pair of men. Henry followed them, adrenalized and charging at the flames. He stumbled on a hose and landed on his palms, mailbag spilling out before him in the road. A gust of wind picked a letter up and took it to the flames. Henry gathered up the rest and crammed it into his bag. A policewoman pulled him off the ground with a jerk, swearing in his ear and telling him to *go*.

Henry checked the dormer but the figure wasn't there. He moved away, searching every window of the house. The fire shifted and he saw her—there, downstairs. A woman, like a sculpture, burning in the living room, standing with her arm raised gracefully above her. She was beautiful aflame and Henry almost swooned.

Then he took another look—it really *was* a sculpture, and it must have been a statue he had spotted upstairs. Everyone was out. Everyone was safe. But he staggered once more just looking at the damage, sitting on the ground and seeing what he'd done. The water barely helped. They'd be fighting it for hours. He tottered back and forth, clutching at his hair, staring at the flames until his eyes went dry.

Nan and Joan Finn joined him at the curb. They were small and holding hands, kid sisters in a storm, oblivious and trusting him, believing he had saved them. Joan was right beside him, wearing slippers in the grass. The hem of Nan's bathrobe swayed near his leg. Pain like a hammer claw mounted in his chest, squeezing in deep and prying up his ribs.

He constricted there, airless, at the sight of Laura Bailey.

The rookie hauled her out, bowed across his arms, in a rainfall of water from an upturned hose. Mouth open, eyes closed, wearing nothing but a nightgown. The fabric of the gown clung tightly to her breast, and her head hung limp, and her hair unspooled. She was sooty from the bottoms of her feet to her throat but her face looked rinsed and immaculately pale.

Henry tipped to his knees and Laura vanished, blocked by the medics and a pop-up stretcher. All around him it was dark—nightlike and evil—and the Finns pressed close and put their hands on his back. They were holding him. Their fingertips were skeletal and real.

6

Henry pulls around the corner onto Arcadia Street and has to roll the windows down because the car's a thousand degrees and full of dog breath. Nan insisted that he eat before he left—"to buck you up," she had said—but then instead of sitting down and offering advice, she'd made him a turkey sandwich and retreated to her room, leaving him to eat and brood about the trip. Now he wishes that he didn't have a morsel in his gut. He hasn't returned to the block since the fire and braced for something else—not the char-blackened ruins of his memory, of course, but not the plain drab neatness of the neighborhood, either. The homes are just gone. The Carmichaels' house looks the way it always did except for a plastic tarp covering a section of the roof, and even that looks crisp and kindergarten blue. Billy and Sheri's house is worse for wear, lacking siding on the wall that used to face the Finns', but the underlying wood is new and nobody would guess how close it had come to burning down.

The trailer's at the trees, farther back than he expected. He turns around to park and brakes too hard. Wing jerks against the dash, nose smearing up the glass: he doesn't know this place and wants to check it out. Peg's Audi isn't here. Billy's car is parked in front of his house but that's it. There's not a single other vehicle that might belong to Sam.

Henry rolls up the windows and takes a double breath, leaning on the wheel before he unclicks the belt.

"Okay," he says. "Okay." And then to Wing: "I'll be back."

Wingnut answers with a wag, but when Henry steps out and shuts him into the car, he cocks his head and stares in disbelief: surely not. His confusion only grows watching Henry walk away, his desperation rising to a high-strung whine.

Henry doesn't hear it. The fresh-laid dirt is dry and uncompressed, picking up prints like he's walking on the moon. He's sensitive to places, a walker by profession, able to read the safety of surroundings, sometimes even a resident's personality, merely by intuiting the nature of the property. Here the lack of *anything* is difficult to gauge.

The trailer fronts the woods instead of the street and Henry walks around it, onto the narrow span of grass hidden in the shade. No one answers when he knocks, so he knocks a second time. The thought of going home and coming back is too disheartening. His only other choice is waiting here awhile. He notices a very faint trail into the woods. Worth a shot, Henry thinks, peering into the trees, listening for any kind of movement in the depths.

He can't leave Wing stranded in the car and wouldn't mind the company anyway, so he walks back and leashes him up, aware of how brazen it'll look if someone sees him walking his dog around the property. He doesn't feel safe until they're entering the woods, where a different strain of fear comes with every step. Branches, twigs, and roots crackle all the way; he's as subtle as a Sasquatch tromping in the wild. The trees buttress one another, meshing overhead and struck, now and then, by kaleidoscopes of sun. Wing's so excited he's choking himself with the collar. There must be animals around, there behind the tree, behind the bush, there behind *that* tree. Mud and birds, scat, things rotting in the understory. Smells on smells and everything alive.

They come upon a clearing—goldenrod, leaves, thick green ferns massing at the border. It's sunny here but shady in the back, where the rock face trickles on a small, mossy hill. Dead center is a bag and a Styrofoam cup. Henry hesitates, pondering the evidence before him, till he notices that Wingnut's staring farther off.

Sam partially emerges from the corner of the clearing. He's carrying an ax and stands behind a maple, wary of the visitors and ready to defend himself.

"Hello?" Henry calls.

Sam reveals himself and stares. He's wearing work boots and dungarees and doesn't have a shirt. Dirty sweat accentuates his muscles and his bones, and his hair's unkempt and shadowing his eyes. He has a feral, almost mystical appearance in the trees, like a reindeer standing on his two hind legs.

Wingnut barks and it's embarrassing, offensive.

"Quiet," Henry says. "Stop. Settle down."

He ties the leash around a tree and walks across the clearing. Sam advances several steps but doesn't leave the shade.

Henry greets him with a nod, moving in a hunch. When he's close enough to talk, he draws a breath and straightens up, lungs so full he feels the pressure in his ribs. They've never met before—Henry always missed him on the route—and it suddenly occurs to him that Sam might be wondering who he is. He'd gone to Laura's funeral and sat in the back with Ava, convinced he ought to be there but terrified he'd make matters worse if people noticed. He snuck out early, having stared throughout the service at the back of Sam's head until the light played tricks and he could almost see an aura.

"I'm Henry Cooper."

Sam blinks but the blink looks purposeful and slow. "What do you want?"

Henry's at a loss. He's been picturing the pale young man that he remembered, scorched around the eyes and fragile to the touch, but here he is now, vigorous and lean, with a strong, ruddy sweat and brandishing an ax.

What's the question? What does he *want*? Henry shakes his head until he can't really see and says, "I'm sorry. I'm so sorry. I had to see you, I had to say that, I could kill myself, I'm so sorry."

Sam retreats half a step, leery of the outburst. He double-grips the ax, opening his stance. Wingnut barks, only once but with a comical effect, like a hiccup, and yet it doesn't seem to register with Sam, not at all.

"Was it an accident?" he asks.

"Was it . . . my God, of course it was," Henry says. "I didn't know she was home. I'd have run right in. I tried to and fell, they wouldn't let me . . ." and he stops, looking down at the dark crust of mud ruining his sneakers.

"You'll have to live with it," Sam says.

A cicada buzzes, right in Henry's brain, followed by the far-off stutter of a nuthatch. Ten or twenty seconds and the lull could be forever, stronger than whatever they could do to break away.

"What are you doing out here?" Henry asks, so faintly that he wonders if his words are even audible. When Sam doesn't answer, Henry looks at him and says, "I'll do anything you need. Anything at all."

"I want you to go."

Henry slumps from the inside out. It's like his blood's given up, barely pumping anymore. He reaches into his pocket and hands Sam a card with his phone number written in permanent marker.

"Call me day or night," he says. "Even if it's twenty years from now."

Sam takes the card and holds it at his side, looking like he might just drop it in the leaves. Henry starts to go.

Sam says, "Wait," and then he pauses there, expressionless, long after Henry turns to look at him again.

"Did you see her?" Sam asks.

Henry nods, feeling ill.

"Was she still alive?"

"I don't know," Henry says. There's a fracture in his voice. He coughs and says, "They carried her out. She wasn't moving."

"What did she look like?"

"I can't . . ."

"You told me anything I need."

Henry looks down and wrestles with his hands, wishing he could sit and seeing, for an instant, Ava's face instead of Laura's. He concentrates, focusing the picture in his mind.

"She was soaked from the hose. Her nightgown was sooty but her skin looked clean. She was pale. Not a mark . . . she was perfect. Her eyes were closed. Her hair was loose. She didn't look hurt."

Sam's eyelids sag. He looks more drained than confrontational, a man who hasn't slept well in weeks, almost too exhausted to sustain a real emotion.

Henry gets a long, fine prickle up his arm. Once again they're in a lull and he's afraid of staying put, scared to make a sound, and scared to move away. He's just about to turn but sees something odd and does a double take, staring over Sam's left shoulder. Off behind them in the woods, maybe forty yards away, there's a long, pale arm rising in the shade. It appears to be a branch, vertical and thin, but the top of it is clearly, unmistakably a hand. It reminds him of the sculpture on fire in the living room. All except the arm is hidden by a thicket.

"Is that . . . ?"

Sam's face pinches at the center. He takes a step, one step so menacingly quick that Henry flinches and his hands shudder up to come between them. The look on Sam's face—the glare, the wooden jaw, the first expression that he's shown throughout the conversation—sends Henry in reverse and makes him want to run.

"I'll go," he says, backing up more, but then it's Sam who turns away and leaves him in the clearing.

Henry watches him retreat toward the thicket with the ax, where he lifts it overhead and thumps it in the ground. The soil's so soft, the blade disappears. Sam ignores him and attempts to move a weather-downed tree, a twenty-foot birch with most of the branches still attached. He lifts it with a grunt and tries dragging it along, but the tree's so heavy that it doesn't move at all.

Henry waits another minute, flexing out his arms, and then he frowns, rubs his eyes, and leaves him there alone. Wing's straining at his collar hard enough to wheeze. Sam struggles with the birch and there's a great crash of branches—just the kind of sound Wing's dying to investigate. Henry halts in front of him and doesn't take the leash. Wing wags more emphatically and happy-whines a little, but instead of coming closer, Henry holds up a finger, says, "One more minute," and departs, yet again, for the stranger in the trees.

The scored bark is easy to grip. Sam is able to lift one end of the birch off the ground, but the tree won't budge no matter what he tries. He moved the tree this morning, just enough to get it started, and he doesn't understand why it isn't moving now. He's underfed and underslept but can't accept that he simply isn't strong enough. The branches must be snagged. He tries to shimmy it around. It's a stupid piece of wood, hardly taller than himself, and yet it may as well be iron given the effort he's expending. He could go and get the chain saw but all he has to do is move the goddamn thing thirty feet. He can still feel Henry right across the clearing, but instead of looking over he commits himself again, digs his boots more firmly in the dirt, and pulls until his biceps burn. His toes begin to slip; he has to walk without moving just to keep purchase on the ground, and he growls with his eyes shut, breathing through his teeth, straining like he's tearing someone's arm from its socket.

Suddenly it floats, magical and airy. Instead of feeling satisfied he pulls it even harder. He could lift it, he could swing it, he could throw it in the air. He's tremendous in his fury, monstrously endowed, ripping up the forest with his own bare hands. When he finally has to quit and drop it to the ground, it wobbles there and hovers, eerily aloft.

He turns and finds Henry right behind him in the weeds, grimacing and huffing, trunk balanced on his shoulder.

"Give me room," Henry grunts. "I don't want to hit you with the end there."

Sam backs up, trembling from the work, out of air and too delirious to fully comprehend.

Henry readjusts and lets the back of the tree totter to the ground. He gets a grip and plods ahead, dragging it with ease, whipping Sam's shins with the branches when he passes. He's early middle age and dressed like a retired gym teacher: golf shirt tucked into his shorts, belt way above the navel, lots of hairy thigh, and tube socks stretched to his calves. It's a fifty-dollar outfit, plain white sneakers included, tidy as the haircut squaring off his head.

"Where do you want it?" Henry asks.

Sam's looking at his face but doesn't hear the question, too preoccupied with Henry shouldering the weight.

"Over here or over there?"

"I just wanted it out of the way so I could walk . . ."

Back to the sculptures, Sam nearly says, but the partial answer's good enough for Henry, who nods and says, "Right," and sets to work dragging the tree so far beyond any conceivable footpath that Sam begins to wonder if he plans to take it home. He finally puts it down and readjusts it where it lies, as if he means to build a wall and needs the bottom just so.

"What else?"

"That's enough," Sam says.

"What about that one?"

Henry strides toward another fallen tree, a shagbark hickory that's quite a bit thicker than the birch. Sam follows him along as if magnetically attached. He hadn't dreamed of moving that one, not without a saw.

"I've got to cut that first."

"Nah, I can move it," Henry says, straddling the hickory to pull it off the ground.

Sam allows it just to see if he can move it. Up it goes.

Halfway out of the thickest vegetation, Henry meets his stare, gives him a kind of quick thumbs-up with his eyebrows, and keeps working through the bracken, bandy-legged and snorting through his mustache. It takes him ten minutes to get the hickory halfway to the birch, and then he turns around to Sam and says, "You mind if I let my dog off the leash?"

Sam checks the dog, who's been sitting there in silence, panting in the sun. He wags when Sam regards him, raising up a faint poof of soil with his tail.

"Just go," Sam insists, meaning he should leave.

Henry takes it as a green light and smiles at his dog. He drops the tree—it quakes the ground at Sam's feet, a serious piece of wood—and jogs across the way to fiddle with the collar.

"His name's Wingnut!"

The dog comes bounding like a lunatic, thrilled to be out and looking everywhere at once. He zeroes in on Sam, who backs away alarmed, but the dog runs past and sniffs him on the fly, capering off and wagging his rump, reaching all four borders of the clearing in a single mad dash. When he finally slows down, he trots over, licks Sam's hand, and does exploratory laps around the woods. Henry's back at the hickory tree, hauling it over a shrub.

Sam wanders to the clearing, where the sun is so abrupt he closes both eyes. It softens him and tires him, its gentleness and color too alluring to resist, and so he sits and feels it pulsing on his shoulders and his neck, how it smells so familiar in a way that makes him weary of the day. He thinks of Laura's feet, pale white, with cozy arches and her toes like buds. For the life of him he can't recall the color of her nightgown. Henry didn't say—only sooty. Only soaked. But he's certain Henry's memory is vivid as a mural.

Wing jumps a fern and vanishes into the trees.

"Your dog ran off."

"He'll be back!" Henry says, closer than expected.

Sam turns and there he is, finished with the tree, heart-attack red and veiny at the temples. He cups his hands to his knees and waits for something else.

"That one," Sam says, picking out a log a hundred feet distant in the shade, nowhere near the sculpture or the path he meant to forge.

Henry doesn't question it or hesitate at all.

Sam thinks about the nightgown and pops himself a soda, sugary and warm from the bottom of his bag. As long as Henry's game, he finds another and another: idiotic labor in the afternoon sun. Was it white? Was it blue? How could he forget? He thinks until his memory dissolves altogether and he can't remember anything about her with precision. He checks a pair of wallet photos, all he has left. She's laughing in the first, freckle-tan from their honeymoon and naked at the shoulders. The second one's a profile, Laura with a book. She's wearing a turtleneck. Her eyes look strained, almost sad, and he can't remember when or where he took the picture.

He saw the smoke driving home that afternoon, a black plume rising in the distance, and it didn't cross his mind that he should worry, not about the house and not about her. But the closer he came, the more his blood pressure rose, until he had to roll the window down and try to cool his face. A neighbor's house, he figured, something on the block. Even when he stopped and saw where the fire was, he didn't believe that Laura was in danger. She was a grown woman, wide-awake at that hour. Only kids and old people got caught in house fires, he thought to himself, remembering the Carmichael boys and the Finns.

He parked on the side street and ran along the road, never noticing the mailman, wondering where she was amid the cavalcade of trucks. There was fire and light and sprays of mist, long jets of water flopping in the air. He saw his own burning house, vacuous and black; she wouldn't be standing that close to the flames so he looked across the street and checked the onlookers standing near the unburned homes, where the windowpanes flashed with reflections of the fire. He passed a dozen different firemen who paid him no attention. He thought an officer or *somebody* would lead him off the road, but he carried on, invisible, entirely alone, shouting "Laura!" very flatly, scanning everywhere at once.

He started back and met a cop who took him by the arm, and even then he called her name, certain she was safe. Finally Nan Finn approached him in a robe. She was hesitant and stiff, rough-hewn around the eyes, but it wasn't until he recognized Joan, twenty feet away and scared of seeing *him*, that he first understood something terrible had happened.

"What next?" Henry asks.

Sam jolts at the voice and wipes sweat around his eyes. He looks at Henry, stupefied, recalling what he'd read in the paper—that it must have been a match or a half-lit cigar, that he'd carried out the Finns and now they're living in his house. That he hadn't lost his job—it was only a suspension—and the jury let him off as if he'd dented Laura's car.

"That one over there," Sam says, very low. He points

where he means, far across the clearing, to a thick white pine fully rooted in the ground. He picked the tree at random, one of many big trees, fifty feet tall and solid as a barrel.

Henry rubs his jaw, gazing all the way up, but instead of saying "That?" or even "What?" he says, "Right. You got a chain saw?"

"No."

"I'll get the ax."

He frees it from the ground and strides across the clearing. Then he spits on his palms—really spits on his palms—squares up true, and starts chopping at the pine.

Sam sits for a while watching Henry work, prickling when the sweat starts drying on his back. The afternoon light flutters through the leaves, and the shadows and the colors intermingle like flames. The thumping of the ax grows monotonous and thick. A trace of nutmeg wafts up gently from the ground. He thinks of Laura in the kitchen, crimping dough around a pie dish, skinny in her dress. *No . . . jeans*, Sam decides. The oven smells warm; it makes the kitchen like a bedroom. Evaporated milk cans open with a kiss. There's a little spot of pumpkin at the button of her cuff and a faint taste of flour when he pecks her on the neck.

Wing gambols from the woods, covered in burrs. He rolls in the one rank puddle of the clearing, raising a mosquito cloud before drying his fur in the dirt. He looks delighted when he stands, steaming with fulfillment. Sam smiles—almost smiles—for the first time in ages. The sun is noticeably lower and he wonders if he dozed; his thoughts about Laura had the color of a dream. Henry hasn't slowed or broken rhythm all the while.

There's a popcorn sound and the pine tips away, lean-

ing into the woods and swishing off the nearby trees. Wing
snaps to his feet.

Henry backs off, stumbling with the ax, saying "*Whoa*"
at the fractures and the great deep whump. Then he bounces,
like the shock wave's bumped him off the ground. Sam feels
it where he sits, from his shoes to his hair.

The forest falls still, birdless and astounded.

"I need it over there," Sam says.

Henry slumps. "What time is it?" he asks.

Sam checks the sun.

"Maybe six."

"Shit. You got a phone?"

"No."

"My wife," Henry says, wincing at the word. "I've got
to go."

Sam wishes he could smirk but he's drained by the sun.
It's the light of going home for ordinary people.

"I'll finish up tomorrow," Henry says. His cheeks are red
but under the flush he looks sallow, probably dehydrated,
definitely shot. "You got my number there," he adds, as if
he hasn't just declared he's planning to return.

Sam walks away without a gesture of goodbye. Henry
has the sense to let him go without a word and Sam lingers
in the trees, out of sight, until he can't hear the jingle of
the dog's collar and he's positive they're gone.

Evening's coming in, the shadows of the woods long and
unavoidable, the last glowing bars subtly diffused. Once
again he smells nutmeg faintly on the breeze. There must
be some plant with a similar aroma. Then it fades and he's
alone, totally alone.

And that's the end, Sam thinks. The last he'll hear of
Henry Cooper.

7

Billy saw Henry in the early afternoon. He had just stepped out to take a breather in the yard and pulled his ventilator off when the Buick caught his eye. At first it idled at the curb, an ordinary car, but Billy grew suspicious when the engine stopped and no one opened the door. Window glare prevented him from seeing who it was, so he ducked inside and watched from the living room, where he'd spent the whole the day breaking things apart.

Peg had warned him: hire pros to handle the water damage. Billy had rented fans and kept the circulation flowing, but although the house had seemed completely dry, moisture from the fire hoses lingered out of sight, softening the walls and building up mold. Everything was rotting from the inside out, and so he'd taken today off work, dragged the furniture out, pried the molding up, and torn the damp drywall away, piling all the wreckage in the yard until at last, only fifteen minutes ago, he'd gotten the entire living room down to the studs. He'd been sweeping up debris when he walked out back and saw the car, and now he's standing in amazement, eyes burning from the dust, watching Henry from the window of his dark, stripped room.

Henry walks behind the trailer, where he knocks: no one's there. And then, to Billy's surprise, he goes all the way back to the car, gets his dog, and hikes into the woods.

"What balls," Billy says.

He finishes sweeping up and Shop-Vacs the crud from the newly opened walls. There's a nickel, which he keeps, and a vintage playing card—four of hearts—which he cleans off gently with a cloth to give to Sheri. Then he opens both doors to get a better flow of air and uses half a can of Lysol, proud of the room's refreshing orange scent. No mold, no rot, clean wooden floor, and so much space with all the furniture removed.

Half an hour has passed and the Buick's still there. Billy showers upstairs and changes all his clothes and suddenly he's starving from the long day's work. He decides to get a sub—Sheri's working late tonight—and walks outside to look at Henry's car. Billy loiters out front, staring into the trees, but there isn't any sound and nothing he can see. Whatever Sam's doing back there, he's doing it way back, and it's strange, very strange, that he hasn't driven Henry straight back out.

Billy's seen him with an ax. What if something happened? Dead dog, Sam bloody—Henry Cooper with the blade half buried in his skull. "No, his chest," Billy thinks, picturing the scene, holding for a moment the imaginary ax and knowing how he'd swing it with an overhead chop. Henry would defend himself, putting up his hands, but the blade wouldn't stop—it'd cut right through, maybe cleaving through his chin before it got him in the heart.

He considers staying put or walking back to see, except whatever's going on, it isn't his concern. He'll either get himself in trouble or be forced to make excuses. So he drives to get a sub and breathes through his nose, trying to clear away the lingering stink of the mold.

He takes the long way home past the Cooper house. He got the address from the phone book and checked it out last week, and now he parks across the street and spies Nan Finn for just a moment in the living room. But he's determined to get a look at Henry's wife—Ava, Billy learned—and cranks the hand brake tight as it'll go. He stares for so long in the same crooked hunch that his neck grows stiff, threatening a knot. Ten minutes later, Ava's on the porch. She wears a pale blue dress, fitted at the top and airy at the knees, with bare feet and soft brown hair below her shoulders. She's a full-bodied woman, the opposite of Sheri, round in all the right ways and easy in her movements. She puts her hands to her hips and glances up the street. Eager, Billy thinks. Happy in her skin.

He could go and introduce himself. *Hi, I'm Billy Kane— I talked to your husband on the phone. Thanks, thanks. We're doing okay. Far as I'm concerned, what's done is done. I appreciate the offer, Mrs. Cooper.*

Call me Ava.

"If there's anything you need," Billy whispers to himself.

When he makes it back to Arcadia Street, Henry's car is gone but Sheri's is parked in front of the house. He's disappointed: he didn't expect her home before ten and wanted to surprise her with the living room.

Bob Carmichael's throwing a Nerf football with his boys on the sidewalk. He has a dopey grin whenever Billy sees him, as if he couldn't ask for more than two skinny sons, a fire-damaged house, and a wife who looks fresher going out than coming in. He throws a high, wobbly pass that bounces near the car.

"Afternoon!" Bob yells.

"Hey. How's it going?"

"Good, good," Bob says, grabbing a pass with an awkward clap of his hands. "You say hi to Mr. Kane?" he hollers to his sons, seven and nine, with names Billy never quite remembers. The younger one is quiet but generally friendly. The older one's more talkative except when Billy's around, at which point he clams up as if encountering a stranger.

"Hey, guys," Billy says.

"Hey, hi," they mumble, turning back to Bob, who in spite of his womanly arms, high voice, and partial balding, is an automatic hero to his sons. They'll hate him when they're older, Billy thinks. They'll avoid him.

"Go long!" Bob yells, and throws a blooper right to Billy.

Billy catches it and wrings it like a sponge. He fits his fingers into the grooves and fires it back, but it slips off his hand and flies into the Bailey lot.

"Shit, sorry!"

Bob winces at the curse and glances at the boys, who look at Billy with disdain, less for swearing than for throwing the football like a spaz. The older boy runs across the lot to pick it up. Peg emerges from the house, ignoring Billy and talking straight at Bob.

"I told you I don't want them playing in the dirt," Peg says. "There's glass in there."

"My fault!" Billy waves. "The ball got away from me."

Peg rolls her eyes.

Billy goes inside and he's in luck—Sheri just got home and went straight upstairs to shower. She meets him in a robe with a towel on her head and says her friend agreed to finish out the end of her shift.

"You see the living room?" he asks.

"Why?"

He grins and says, "Follow me."

"What?"

"Come on, I'll show you."

He leads her by the hand all the way down the stairs and makes her close her eyes until they come around the corner.

"What the hell *happened*?" Sheri asks.

"I ripped the drywall out."

"I can see that. Was it really that bad?"

"You should have smelled it."

"I can smell it right now. Jesus, Billy . . ."

"It had to be done. Half the wall was so bad you could have put your hand right through. It's gonna be great," he says. "This is just the necessary wreckage."

"This whole place is necessary wreckage."

"Here," he says, handing her the old four of hearts. "I got it from the wall."

"Thanks." She frowns, unsure of what to do with it.

He follows her into the kitchen, where she notices the sub and says, "You bought yourself dinner?"

"I didn't expect you home this early," Billy said.

"I left you a message."

"My cell died."

"I left a message here. You told me you'd be home all afternoon."

"I went out for a sub."

"Obviously," Sheri says, opening the fridge and scowling at the week-old Tupperware bowls.

"Have mine," Billy says.

"I'm not *that* much of a bitch," she says.

"We'll share it. It's a foot-long."

She smiles at him now, softening enough to take the towel off her hair and shake them out, hair and towel, like she's shaking off her day. They grab a couple beers and eat together at the table.

Once her hunger wears off and the beer relaxes her a bit, she says, "I'm sorry, all right? I'm just sick of coming home to such a mess."

"I know," he says. "That's why I'm trying to fix it."

"I think we ought to bite the bullet and hire a contractor," she tells him for the umpteenth time.

He wants to say it's too expensive but he's tried that before, over and over, and she doesn't want to hear about the mortgage, the credit cards, the car insurance payment, and the stack of other bills that never seems to shrink. Instead she acts like do-it-yourself is the cheapskate's way of dealing with a problem.

"We'll take another loan," she says.

Billy shakes his head. Sheri opens a second beer and lights a cigarette—more smoke, Billy thinks—and something in the twilight catches in her face. She's beautiful, her haggardness disguised by the glow. A year ago they sat in the yard every weekend, sipping drinks and listening to music after dark, getting drunk and acting flirty till she led him upstairs and, more often than not, pushed *him* onto the bed. Now he has to bring it up or nothing ever happens. Half the time she does it like a job, late at night when both of them are tired: two minutes on her knees, three minutes on her stomach, reaching over when he's done to set the clock like she's punching out at work.

Billy stands and puts his arms around her, kissing at her throat. She holds her beer and cigarette out of the way and says, "Billy," leaning back until her bathrobe opens at the neck. He's about to reach inside when Sheri notices the drywall piled in the yard and says, "Ugh," which Billy assumes is her reaction to his kissing.

He doesn't stop but holds her even tighter. Sheri loses balance, just enough to flail and touch him with her cigarette. Billy jumps away, swatting at his arm. He's mad enough to yell but tries to keep it in.

"Well, what did you expect?" Sheri says.

He doesn't know.

"It's guacamole," Peg tells Danny, the younger of her sons.

They're together in the dining room, parents on the one side, children on the other. She was late coming home because the order wasn't ready and the credit-card machine had "started acting up." Now she's sitting in her work clothes, barely out of the car, and the meal feels rushed before they even settle in.

"What are the chunks?" Danny asks.

"That's guacamole, too." She scoops some onto a chip to set a good example, but they've overdone the lime again and Danny sees her grimace. "It's good for your cholesterol."

"That's okay," Bob says, shrugging at his wife. "They don't have to worry about cholesterol yet."

"That's because I feed them well."

Takeout every night. It's a fortune but she never has time to cook dinner. She forgives herself. She always buys organic at the market. Greek yogurt with granola. Juice for antioxidants. Bob likes to joke about her cage-free eggs, how they love to roll around when nobody can see.

"It's iguana," Ethan says, savoring the guac.

"The cheaper places use frog," Bob says. "They have deals with the local biology labs."

"It's avocado," Peg says, as if it's seriously in doubt.

She's so annoyed she fails to notice Danny loading up a chip; he's not convinced to try it yet but closer than he was. Bob begins to concentrate closely on his food, acting like it's something genuinely foreign. He does it every meal, be it Mexican or pasta, and it drives her up the wall to see him furrowing his brow.

"Did you get the right order?"

Bob nods in affirmation, shattering his taco with the very first bite.

"I wanted refried beans," Ethan tells his mother.

"They're with the rice in your burrito."

"These are pinto beans."

"Here," she says, sliding him a dish.

She makes him wait until she's rolled another place mat down because she doesn't want lid steam dripping on the table. Danny spills milk and everybody jumps, backing up before the puddle starts pouring in their laps.

"Paper towels!" Peg yells.

Bob hustles to the kitchen. Danny's goggle-eyed in fear because it isn't just the milk. The guacamole fell, too, face-down on the carpet. Ethan sees it while their mother's still distracted by the drink. He takes a round paper lid, slips it underneath the Styrofoam, and puts it on the table virtually intact. They rub the rest of it away with the bottoms of their feet and Danny smiles at his brother, terribly relieved.

Half a roll of paper towels and the table's back in order, though it takes Peg and Bob a few more minutes to clean the dribbles between the dining room and the kitchen, wash their hands, and get the boys settled in their seats. Peg doesn't lecture when she pours another milk, but she puts it in a sippy cup and Danny's forced to use it.

They sit and try the meal again and no one says a word.

Except Peg. "I'm sorry. I was just trying to have a nice dinner for a change. I remembered that we all liked Mexican the last time we got it."

"It's great." Bob smiles.

The boys nod in agreement, though it all feels obligatory to Peg, who finds a little bone inside her *enchilada verde.*

"Looks like Billy's hard at work," Bob ventures through a bite.

"He had better clean it up before it rains," Peg says, referring to the drywall piled out back. "It's bad enough he hasn't finished with the siding or the lawn. At least before the fire they were hidden up the block. Honestly," she says, "between the damage and the two empty lots, I couldn't move a property in this neighborhood if they were giving it away."

"Sam bought land."

"And if he'd gone with me instead of Marcie Ross, he would have saved five hundred dollars an acre."

The family falls silent at the name Marcie Ross—a nemesis of Peg's, rosy and repellent. Bob will never be forgiven for the time he complimented Marcie's billboard near the CITGO station, and all he really said was that her hair looked better than it used to.

"And remember what I told you," Peg says to Danny and Ethan. "You're not to go anywhere near the trailer or the woods."

"Why?" Danny asks.

"I'm not comfortable having you talk to Mr. Bailey."

"Your mother doesn't mean that Sam's a bad person," Bob says. "He just wants some privacy."

"Which I would give him," Peg insists, "if I could *talk* to him a minute. But he's always in the woods doing who knows what. I keep leaving notes. He's never there—he's like a ghost."

"He was there before dinner."

"What, where?"

"In the trailer."

Peg stands up and marches to the door, still in motion when she bends to get her pumps—hop, pop, double hop—and off she goes, into the darkly falling evening and across the barren plot. She keeps her eyes upon the trailer, moving at a clip, half expecting Sam'll spot her and rabbit into the trees. When she makes it to the door, she doesn't hear a thing. There's not a glimmer of light from either set of blinds. But the strangeness is the reason that she soldiered out at all, and she's about to follow through when Sam emerges from the door.

Peg retreats until the streetlights are visible again.

"Hi," she says, frightened of his tall silhouette.

She doesn't say more until he's lit enough to recognize. He's skinnier and browner with a two-day beard; it occurs to Peg she hasn't really seen him since the fire, that she can't talk trailer straightaway without condolences.

"I'm sorry," she says. She really truly is.

"Thanks," Sam says. "I got your notes. I should have said hello."

"No, please. We were worried, that was all."

"How are your boys?"

"They're fine, they're shaken up. It scared them."

"I know."

He keeps looking eerier the better her eyes become, dangerous and lank, wearing dirty jeans and flannel. There was style to his hair but now it's scruffy. She can smell him. He reminds her of a homeless man who used to be a student, someone in the very early stages of addiction.

"I heard you bought the land back here," Peg says. "I wish I'd known. Are you planning to rebuild?"

"No."

"You're staying in the trailer, then?"

"I haven't worked it out," he says. "It's only been a month."

"No, of course," Peg says. "I only meant to say . . ."

"Thanks for coming by."

He turns toward the door, finished with the talk.

"Sam," Peg says, stepping forward inadvertently.

He stops and they're together, closer in the dark, in the very tight gap between the trailer and the trees. She can hardly see his eyes but feels the way he's looking at her, staring down and using all his height to make her small.

"May I ask you a personal question?" Peg says.

He doesn't tell her no.

"What are you doing for a bathroom?"

"There's a tank," Sam says, and she imagines it beside her, there beneath the floor in the damp, muddy gloom.

"It isn't any of my business . . ."

"I'm asking you to go," Sam says.

She doesn't have a breath, never mind an answer. He leaves her there abruptly, goes inside, and shuts the door. It's as if he's really vanished, how she's instantly alone.

8

"There wasn't a phone," Henry tells Ava at the door, panting like he's jogged the whole way home. Before he says more, Wing's jumping up between them, Nan's calling them to eat, and Henry's kicking off his shoes and walking to the bathroom. He's muddy, with a crust of dried blood along his forearm.

"Henry . . ."

"Just a sec, I've got to whiz like the devil."

"You were bleeding."

"What? Whoop, look at that. I didn't even feel it. It's the blood thinners, babe. Lemme wash, just a minute. Start without me," Henry says, leaving Ava, Nan, and Joan to listen to his stream.

They've waited up to eat, growing antsy when he didn't arrive by six o'clock, and they're all privately starving except for Henry, who's drawn and openly starving, so much so that Ava stops herself from questioning him fully until he's eaten. He marches out of the bathroom and animates the room, more vigorous than all three women put together. He stretches and groans and wipes his face, rocks the chair, clatters silverware, and shifts the whole table when he moves, and even in the dining room the air feels open and the birds outside sound a little more alive. He cuts a piece of meatball and palms it out for Wing, who wolfs it with a smack and grumbles for another. Henry wipes his hand and balls the napkin on the table, then digs into his food with his head mere inches from the plate.

"We didn't say grace," Joan reminds them, awed by the suddenness and speed of Henry's eating. They're serious meatballs; Joan herself can handle only one.

Henry says the prayer with his mouth full, mumbling under Nan's crisp enunciation, and then he's all about the meal, making it look more physical than ordinary eating, bolting it down and smearing the rim of his milk glass with tomato sauce. Nan winds spaghetti very tightly on a fork. Joan cuts her meatball into quarters with a butter knife. Ava's appetite grows after three or four bites, several hours' worth of stomach acid blanketed with pasta.

"So he didn't chase you off," she finally says.

"He tried to at first," Henry tells her. "Then he needed help dragging logs off the footpath."

"Logs?" Ava says, brandishing her fork.

"Well not *logs*," Henry says. "Just branches and sticks," and she can see the little man cycling in his head, trying desperately to brake and pedal in reverse.

"The poor guy's living in a trailer. He's sculpting whole *trees*. He's got a sculpture out there . . . I couldn't really see it but the arm was sticking up. You'd have sworn that it was real."

"He's very talented," Nan declares. "He sculpted every day."

"Yeah, it's good he's staying busy, right? I guess he bought the land for all the wood. It's something back there, but man, that trailer's really small."

"What did he say?" Ava asks.

"Not a lot. I apologized as much as I could, told him anything he needed . . ." Henry pauses for a second, glancing up at Ava. "He asked about the fire. He wanted to know what Laura looked like. I almost couldn't answer but I had to, you know?"

Ava thinks of Laura, whom she never once saw, the woman with the hair Henry openly admired. She didn't seem real when she was actually alive but Ava senses her tonight, like a presence in the room. Henry withers in his chair and lays his fork beside his plate. She leans across the tabletop and takes him by the hand.

"He didn't seem to want me there." Henry sighs.

"You ought to respect his wishes."

"I don't know," Nan says. She folds her napkin into a triangle and looks at Ava. "What if Henry is the person Sam really needs?"

"Or the only one he doesn't need," Ava says. "Isn't that up to Sam?"

"Of course it is," Henry tells her. "I just can't tell what he wants."

"He let Henry stay there for hours," Nan says. "That doesn't sound like a man who wants to be alone."

"It sounds like a man who doesn't know when to *leave*," Ava says, sharply enough for Joan—still working on her meatball—to put her knife down and glance around the table in alarm.

"I think it's up to Henry," Nan says.

"Are you going there for him or for yourself?" Ava asks him.

"Why's it got to be one or the other? Look at us. We're married, you and me," Henry says, making a you-and-me gesture with his hand.

"You and I," Nan whispers.

"We love each other, back and forth," Henry says. "We can't be selfless all the time or the other person'd get gypped out of *their* being selfless."

"What does that even mean?" Ava asks.

The light's turned purple outside, dusky warm and giving the room a saturated hue. A phoebe cheeps. Ava squeaks her chair without moving and the Finns, stock-still, make no sound at all.

"Joan," Henry says. "What do *you* think he needs?"

She looks up spooked, shaken by her name, having sat there comfortably forgotten with her meal. Henry stares at her with open-faced sincerity and hope.

"A friend?" Joan asks.

Ava sighs and shakes her head.

"Absolutely right," he says, drumming on the table. "It's exactly that simple."

Joan looks relieved.

Ava's ready to sleep at nine o'clock, the arches of her feet full of buckshot and thorns. Before they go upstairs, Joan leads Henry into the kitchen. She's been working on her puzzle all afternoon and has the border and the lower-left corner nearly done. Henry laughs, assuming she's been having a marvelous time, and his laughter automatically convinces Joan she has. They all say good night and go their separate ways, Nan and Joan with cups of tea and a criminal forensics show, Ava to the bedroom with Henry at her heels.

"Tell me the truth," she says, stopping him the second he's in the room.

"What?"

"You pushed yourself today."

"He needed help to clear a path. It wasn't *dangerous*."

"You promised me a year ago. You promised not to push . . ."

"I know, I know," Henry says, defeated far too easily for Ava to pursue a proper argument. "I promise . . ."

"Don't," she says. "Don't."

He had promised with cigars.

"I didn't mean to worry you," he says. "Ava, look at me. I didn't—"

"Let it go. I'm glad it went well, I'm glad you're okay. But I'm really too exhausted for a long conversation," and with that she turns away and leaves him at the door.

It feels later than it is, deeper into summer—almost like fall is right around the bend. The room's muggy and she can't raise the window any higher. She would like nothing better than to sleep outdoors with the June constellations moving overhead and the grass still warm from the afternoon sun. The room's cramped and the ceiling's too low to hang a fan. She's tired of the wall paint—gingerbread tan—more suitable for winter when it cozies up the bed. She can't stop yawning and her eyes have a leak. She sits and feels the mattress sag. They ought to flip it, ought to buy a new box spring. She wonders how it feels starting over altogether. Brand-new wardrobe. Bright white sheets. Working with an architect, drawing up plans.

Wingnut pauses in the middle of the room, neither wagging nor alert but lazily content. He's filthy from the woods and needs a bath. So does Henry, who has the pine-sapped look of someone who's sweat and dried several times in one afternoon. He peels off his shirt and stretches out his arms, works a rotator cuff and groans when it pops.

"He isn't living very good," Henry says. "I think I ought to bring him something."

"We have enough to pay for already, feeding two extra mouths."

"They barely eat."

"And only one of us is working."

"I'm still getting paid."

"But only one of us is *working*," Ava says, and shuts her eyes.

She's noticed how he looks when he riffles through the mail, separating bills like a cardsharp handling a deck, knowing all his pals are out delivering their routes. Even his body misses work; he's gained ten pounds since the fire, and it's taken an afternoon of threatening his heart to make him look spent instead of restless.

"Did I do something wrong? Aside from moving logs?"

"I'm tired and my feet hurt."

"Give me those."

He kneels and rubs his hands together, building up heat.

"You're exhausted," Ava says. "I ought to be giving *you* a massage."

"I'm fine," he says. "I told you—it was really easy work."

He lifts her foot, intuiting the one that hurts most, and tips her back gently onto the bed. Ava props on her elbows, just to show resistance, but the pressure of his thumb immediately glows. Henry hums at her foot, near enough to kiss it, his mustache not quite tickling her sole.

Mr. Clean gets rid of dirt and grime and grease in just a minute . . . She's never decided if it's worse that he hums old commercials, or that she always hears the lyric bouncing in her head. But she's happy they're in tune, that his hands are on her foot, and that he really did survive the visit out to Sam's. He hits a spot along her arch that prickles up her thigh. She settles back and hears maple leaves swishing in the yard. She thinks of fireflies bobbing outside, gold-green, and it's almost like dozing in a hammock in the breeze.

"I'll tell you," Henry says. "Seeing him alone out there, living in a trailer . . ."

"Shh," Ava says, opening her toes.

Henry and Wing drive back to Arcadia Street the next morning. They follow Ava going to work until she turns her own way and blows them a kiss out the window, more professional and beautiful than Henry's used to seeing her at home. She's a woman he'd admire if he passed her on the road, and he thinks of other people that'll see her this way—patients at the lab, businessmen and doctors—when her smile is directed at the world instead of him.

For days and days she swaddled him up, petting his hair and bringing him drinks, calling him from work every two or three hours just to see if he was doing okay. But when the newness of the fire wore off, when the aftermath and living with the Finns grew familiar, he began to feel a starchiness in all her ministrations. He'd sensed a similar detachment from a surgeon last summer when he had to get a coronary stent. The surgery itself had gone as well as they had hoped, but the artery they'd pierced to get the catheter inside kept bleeding, just a little, when it should have knit together. Each day, Henry's surgeon grew increasingly annoyed, subtly at first and openly at last, as if the bleeding were a voluntary failure of his patient.

Wing tracks Ava for as long as he can see her. Then he's back, eyes ahead, remembering the way and sniffing in the wind. Henry's eager, too. He's in agony from yesterday, sore at every joint, but Ava's kiss pepped him up and what's a little rain? He's brought along a thermos and a bag full of sandwiches and pears. He could haul a whole forest. It's a wide-open day.

He parks in front of the Bailey lot and double-toots the horn.

Like a shot, there's Sam striding at the car. He's wearing long johns and socks without shoes, pounding into puddles and electrically awake. Henry steps out, shutting Wingnut in.

"Get out of here!" Sam yells, ten feet away and bearing down fast.

Henry backs up and stumbles off the curb. Sam shoves him in the chest.

"*Whoa . . . ,*" Henry says.

Sam pushes him again. They tangle at the feet and topple in the road. Wing snarls in the car, scratching at the door. Henry gasps and doesn't move. Sam grabs him by the neck, kneeling on his stomach, and his face is inescapable and near enough to blur. There's banana on his breath and mud below his eye, and Henry has a feeling like he's staring at a relative, everything familiar from the oil on his nose to the one stray whisker he neglected when he shaved.

"I'm sorry, I'm sorry," Henry stammers.

"You killed her," Sam says. "Understand? *Understand?*" punctuating each with a jostle and a bump.

"I'm sorry," Henry moans, incapable of stopping. He's shaken by a sob. Snot bubbles from his nostril.

Sam is catatonic when he wobbles to his feet. He walks away, leaving Henry like he isn't even there. Wing's stopped barking but he presses at the glass. Henry stands and has to catch himself; he might have sprained an ankle. He watches Sam trudge toward the trailer, where he walks around back and shuts the door too quietly to hear. Henry wipes his hands, conscious of his heart and of the rainfall just now beating on his head.

He slumps into the car, holding Wingnut back with an outstretched arm. Wing's beside himself and jumps around, front seat, backseat. The air smells heavily of overwrought dog.

"Settle down," Henry says.

The engine sounds offensive and he stalls when he turns. He starts the car again, grinds a gear, and drives away, clipping the curb and squealing when he jerks around the corner. Wing jostles up against him.

"Sit!" Henry yells, frightening him down.

He clears the neighborhood and drives toward the busier part of town, unaware he's doing fifty till he skids to meet a red light. He's pretty sure he jumped a couple of stop signs, too, and when he turns to park the car, once again too abruptly, Wing topples in his seat and thumps against the door. A truck hisses by, buffeting the car. Henry shuts his eyes and breathes through his nose, smelling water and exhaust, remembering the fire trucks and craving a cigar, imagining the taste until his heart feels clenched.

He fumbles in the glove box, pops a jar, and chews three aspirin as quickly as he can.

He turns to look at Wing.

"I'm sorry. You're a good dog. Good dog. Come here, you're a very good dog."

Wing licks him on the mouth. Henry pets him up and down, trying not to cry, and then he reaches into the bag and offers him a sandwich. He can barely see the road through the fogged-up glass and his head's still roaring like he's revving up the engine.

Sam trembles on the flip-down bedding of the trailer and the rain ticks metallically above him. He can't sleep, can't sit, can't go out or walk around, and when he punches the wall, harder than he means, it leaves a two-foot fracture in the cheap wood veneer. He opens a can of chicken noodle soup and eats it cold. The oil in the broth reminds him of Laura but he can't remember why—some memory of winter and the clink of metal spoons. It's a terrible meal even by nonperishable standards, and he reminds himself he has to call the power company and see about electric. Peg was right: he needs a better plan than living like this, especially with everybody knocking on the door. He makes a shopping list: batteries, a radio, sanding cloth, rope. Another round of groceries and a few more books. He could really use beer, now instead of later, but he can't imagine driving into town right now.

To hell with the weather. He grabs his backpack and a cooler full of hot dogs, soda, and potato chips and hikes into the trees. They swallow him at once, branches sagging down, leaves reaching out and clinging to his clothes. It's

damper in the shade where the ground stays cool. Little
molecules of fog hover in the air. He has a memory of
driving up a mountainside with Laura—Mount Paradox,
a tourist peak with a paved road and a restaurant waiting
at the top, spectacular in leaf season, scarier going up than
coming down, the backward pull more insistently alarming. He white-knuckled the ascent but Laura didn't mind,
not until the summit, where they had to turn around. That
was when it got her, on the long drive down. She kept her
hand against the dash and wouldn't speak until the bottom, whereas Sam preferred to know that gravity was driving. He can feel it right now—the sense of nature taking
over, the inevitable tug of moving in the wild. This is where
he doesn't have to fight to stay in motion. This is where he
feels more solid on the ground.

The weather settles down by the time he's in the clearing. He looks directly up and can't see the rain, just a bright
gray sky and mist around the leaves. The place has grown
familiar, and despite being soaked he's happy that he's
come, safe from any visitors and bigger, more at ease, in
the broadness of the woods. If only he could pull the trailer
out here, but he's something like a quarter mile in without
a road. He notices the logs that Henry piled yesterday. The
notion isn't new: build a cabin, settle in. He could clear the
way enough to get an ATV and then deliver what he needed.
Keep it simple, off the grid.

He finds the ax where he left it and continues past the
clearing to an elm tree looming in the shade. He rejected it
the first few times he came across it. The trunk has a hole
too pronounced for him to work around, an oblong pit,
deep black, full of rot. It's the hole that draws him in today,
focusing his thoughts. It reminds him of the burned-out

window of the dormer, and he swings the ax with terrible precision at a limb. Everything dissolves in the action of the cuts—Henry and his dog, Peg and her concern—and he picks another limb and hacks that, too. His blood warms up and pretty soon he's settling into shorter cuts, aiming them at angles. After that he takes his chisels and a mallet from his bag, concentrating closely, roughing out the form. His nerves begin to settle like he's had a couple drinks and he continues for an hour, maybe two, maybe more.

He started working with wood in eleventh grade, whittling sticks with a pocketknife he'd gotten for his birthday, just trying out the blade by shaving bark and chipping knots off the side. Later he began to carve symbols and designs, and after the knife snapped shut and almost severed a fingertip, he bought a proper carving set with chisels, gouges, and a fixed-blade knife.

He moved to songbirds and people but he'd always liked mythology, and before long he was carving nothing but monsters and female nudes. He made a three-headed dog that was crude but recognizable, a minotaur, a winged man, and every nymph or goddess he could find a good picture of. After high school he earned his MFA, tried a few small gallery shows, and had a sculpture, *Death of Hercules*, featured in an issue of *Woodcarving Illustrated*.

Laura liked his work but struggled with his *working*, especially once she took an overnight shift at the hospital pharmacy. She went to her job at eight p.m. and left Sam sculpting in the basement, hour after hour, until he finally went to bed at one or two in the morning. He'd wake the next day underslept and noncommunicative, just as Laura was getting home, ready to talk and share a meal, and after that she'd go to sleep and Sam would teach lithography and watercolor at the high school. Their schedules aligned on afternoons and weekends. Laura would be up and fully slept when Sam returned from teaching. They would talk and watch the news and go for walks after dinner. They liked making love in the five-o'clock light, right when half the town was buried in commute. But after a while, Sam's eagerness to sculpt preoccupied his thoughts and he found himself waiting for the hour she would leave.

Laura sensed it. Now and then, when the work seemed important, she encouraged him to head downstairs right away. He could tell it disappointed her and tried to stick around, but Laura noticed that, too, and it was easier to go. Walks became requirements. Meals were more efficient. Laura just assumed that he would sculpt after dinner. She would garden, she would read, she would fill her time alone, and Sam would do his thing, not wanting to disturb her. In the last few months, he'd been going downstairs earlier and earlier. Weekends were daylong versions of the same.

It had gone that way the night before the fire. Sam sculpted after dinner. Laura weeded in the garden, showered and dressed, packed her midnight lunch, and called his name from the top of the basement stairs. He put the chisel down long enough to see her. She mentioned some trifle, a door hinge he needed to fix or one of the other chores he'd been neglecting all season. They smiled goodbye without a kiss and went about their nights.

He finished after one and slouched upstairs, massaging his neck and passing a sculpture in the living room, the only life-size piece he'd done all year. He'd cut her out of pine, a beauty in her youth. Her body curved upward like a vine or a shoot, one arm raised high above her head. Her upturned eyes gave balance to her frown. Flowers twined around her waist, clinging to her hips, and a long gnarled hand held tightly to her calf—a monstrous hand, something that would never let her go. She might have been sinking into the ground or rising into the sun, and though he'd striven for exactly that effect when he conceived her, the sculpture didn't work as fully as he'd hoped, as if he hadn't really caught the tension of the struggle.

Laura wanted it out of the living room—he wasn't sure she liked the piece at all—but he needed someone's help to move it into the yard. It was one more thing he hadn't yet done, like staining the deck and finding time to build the table she'd been asking for. When he woke the next day, she was sleeping at his side. He wasn't used to that. Most mornings, she'd be waiting in the kitchen, where they'd eat and say goodbye before she finally went to bed. He'd forgotten how adorable she was when she was sleeping, hair covering her cheek, hand tucked below her chin. She sighed and cuddled over, sweaty in her gown, and he spooned her with a palm cupped gently to her breast. When her breathing felt deep, he raised the sheet above her waist, admiring her knees and the bottoms of her feet, more familiar with her shape than anything he'd ever tried to sculpt. He thought to wake her up but she was sleeping too smoothly; she was perfect there without him, better untouched. Instead he took a shower, missing her more than usual, and when he passed the nude sculpture in the living room he noticed every flaw, every accident of form.

He puts the chisel down now and shivers in the mist. It isn't raining but the clouds are here to stay. He hasn't eaten and his skin feels cold beneath his clothes. Yesterday he gathered dry wood beneath a tarp. He gets it now and takes it to the clearing, along with a bagful of shavings from the elm to use for tinder. He sets the first log and splits it with the ax. The inner wood's clean, like a new bar of soap. He chops until he has a good pile for a fire, makes a teepee of kindling on a loose mound of shavings, takes the hot dogs out of the cooler, and fishes a box of matches out of his bag.

He pauses with a match pressed against the box. He scrapes the tip. The fire flares, glowing open in the gloom. Then the flame looks delicate and neat, like a seed. He watches how it moves, how it bends when he breathes. Pinpricks of Laura sparkle up around him. Dried paste on her toothbrush, crusty in the bristles. Half snores. How she drooled on her pillow like a child. He holds the fire in his fingertips, squeezing at the sting. The blisters are immediate, the pain so intense he can think of little else. From his *fingers*. From a tiny pair of millimeter burns.

He kicks the kindling in a scatter, eats a hot dog raw and drowns it with a full can of cold 7-Up. The carbonation hurts, building in his chest. He screams around the clearing, just to let it out, and then he thinks of Henry Cooper lying on his back. How he sobbed out loud, guileless and small. *He didn't mean it*, Sam thinks. Doesn't matter. *Yes it does*. He imagines taking off—shutting his eyes and running full tilt until his forehead bangs off a trunk. Instead he wanders back toward his first finished sculpture.

He gazes at his work, feeling it anew—an emaciated man reaching overhead. Sam worked it from the bottom of a great cracked fork, but he only carved the torso, leaving out the legs, as if the body had been left partly buried in the maple. There's bark along his hips and nearly to his navel, where his skin begins to lighten with the soft inner wood. The rib cage is skeletal and hacked, almost crude, and his abdomen is twisted with impossible severity. His neck is long and striated, showing every tendon, and his head is like a skull wrapped tight in old skin. The figure gazes upward and his mouth hangs horrifically ajar—unhinged, bare-toothed, with a low, crooked jaw. He stretches for a bough with an overlong arm. His finger bones are delicate. His nails are bitten raw. The bough is just above him, dipping to his hand, with a tiny bunch of key-leaves floating out of reach.

Sam stares for many minutes with his hands in his jeans, shivering and wishing there were someone he could call. He feels something damp in the bottom of his pocket, takes it out, and sees a little piece of paper in a ball. It's a credit-card receipt from the owner of the Bat Chalet, the last person he intentionally spoke to. Fourteen days ago, according to the date. For a second he'd been certain it was Henry Cooper's number.

PART TWO

9

Nan and Joan seriously consider rebuilding their house, but after daily conversations, prayer, and sleeping in the Coopers' cozy, lived-in home for so many nights, their hearts turn reluctantly to facts. They would have to build cheaper, maybe smaller, maybe uglier, and even for a house with no personality, most time frames were over half a year. They're also forced to admit that Arcadia Street changed long before the fire, as most of their older friends died or moved to retirement communities, their vacant homes filled by strangers or the likes of Billy and Sheri Kane, whose fights were often loud enough to overcome the Finns' storm windows and air conditioners.

Sam and Laura were the notable exception. In the short year the Baileys lived on Arcadia, they had fixed the picket fence, spruced up the yard, and painted most of the house from the inside out. Sam shoveled the Finns' walk after every winter storm and Laura liked to bake and bring them slices of her pies. They were good for the neighborhood, openly affectionate and balancing the Kanes, although the Finns had often wondered if the marriage might be strained. Laura was frequently out in the yard, growing vegetables and trading almanac strategies with Nan—giving milk to pumpkins, feeding cornmeal to cutworms to make them explode—whereas Sam was always hidden in the house, friendly but aloof, the two of them increasingly apart when they were home.

Now, with little chance of Sam reclaiming the lot next door, they're all but guaranteed a new-construction family, the kind who puts tiki torches in the yard and has parties after eight. It simply won't do.

They choose Peg Carmichael as their agent. She mailed the Finns a packet of listings shortly after the fire, and while she isn't quite a star of the Waterbury real estate firmament, she's familiar to them and has, strictly speaking, been a neighbor.

"I've known a lot of good agents," Nan says one night over lasagna. "Some of them have a true passion for finding people the right home. Peg isn't one of them. She wants to find a house that's five to ten percent above its true worth and keep it there."

"She works for you," Henry says. "It's in the agent's best interest to lower the asking price."

"She works for half of the final commission. It's in Peg's best interest to close the deal at the highest price her client will accept."

"That's got to be unethical."

"It certainly is."

"Pick another agent," Ava tells her.

"I can handle Peg Carmichael," Nan says, and no one at the table disagrees.

"I still want to offer those boys a swing set," Henry says.

He's crushed when Joan informs him that they had one several years ago. Peg donated it to a local school after Ethan sprained a wrist.

"You can help," Ava says, "by finding Nan and Joan a house. Am I right?" she asks, deferring to the Finns with a bright, unchallengeable edge.

"You've been so good to us," Joan says, touching Henry's hand.

"That's right," Nan declares. "We need you now. And if you want to help the Carmichaels, you're better off speaking to Bob."

The Finns don't drive anymore, and in spite of Peg's offer to pick them up herself, they insist on Henry being their chauffeur—Joan because it seems like a wonderful idea, Nan for reasons of her own.

"Frankly," Peg told her on the phone, "I'm uncomfortable letting him into other people's homes."

"He isn't a wood bee," Nan assured her.

"He's an arsonist."

"Not according to the Waterbury County grand jury."

"You have to understand my point of view . . ."

"I do," Nan said. "We'll see you tomorrow morning."

Nine o'clock the next day, Henry drives them to the first of four prospective houses. Nan watches Henry out of the corner of her eye, how he never once glances at the dash but holds a perfect legal speed, talking like a tour guide driving in his own hometown. He has a comment for everything they pass, facts about this billiard hall and that gas station, how the owner of Tom's Diner is a man named Bob, how *green* the park grass has finally gotten, and look: there's Mary Robeson—she used to give him bourbon on his route every Christmas. For all his nonstop talk, the most he's said about his second trip to Sam's is that "it didn't go so hot." Even Ava couldn't wheedle any details, but Joan had caught him off guard by noticing he'd changed his pants as soon as he made it home. How had he gotten dirty on a five-minute visit?

"Ahh, the woods . . . you know," Henry told them, like he'd just spent a week in the primeval forest.

"Watch your speed," Nan says.

Henry nods, easing off the gas and slowing the car to twenty-nine, still without checking the speedometer and pointing out a dentist's office where he once found a molar under the mailbox.

"This is a great neighborhood," he says, turning onto Winterbourne.

Nan hones her eye. The trees are short, the houses all a decade old, the hedgerows . . . was that a *football flag* hanging off a porch?

"Lot of young people," Henry says. "College grads, couples just starting out. People like the Baileys," he adds with a sigh.

"It's pretty," Joan says. "It doesn't look like Arcadia, though."

"Of course it doesn't," Nan says.

They all spot Peg in her buttercream suit. She's standing at the curb as only a real estate agent is able to do, all business on a residential street, both belonging there and not quite part of the environment. She gestures with her hand, meaning *here* instead of *hi*.

"I shouldn't have come," Henry says.

They park and meet Peg along the sidewalk. She greets the Finns but doesn't acknowledge Henry, not so much snubbing him as acting like he truly isn't there.

"Here we are," Peg says, unclasping her portfolio and not bothering to look at the actual house.

It's a plain little Cape with beige siding, vinyl windows, and PVC fencing, the whole place reminding Nan of Home Depot circulars, right down to the bushes out front, the kind of squat generic landscaping typically seen on parking-lot islands at the mall.

"It has a lot of charm," Peg reads.

Nan looks at Joan, whose smile glazes over with her eyes, noticing the charm now that Peg's pointed it out. Joan would rather be charmed than saddened by an undistinguished home, and her effort to stay positive fills Nan with a deep rush of love. She remembers the year Joan struggled with anxiety, the night she called from her apartment in a panic, convinced she had a prowler in the kitchen. She'd heard footsteps, silverware shifting in the drawers—all of it imagined, possibly a dream—and when Nan later asked her why she hadn't called 911, Joan admitted she had only hoped to hear Nan's voice. Her escalating fears, born of loneliness and winter, culminated in a near-fatal month of pneumonia. Nan remained at her side throughout the hospital stay, determined to be there, voice and all, even when Joan's health began to stabilize again, and when she was finally strong enough to go home, there was never any question of where that home needed to be. Nan ended Joan's apartment lease, hired movers to bring her belongings to Arcadia Street, and spent a whole Saturday arranging her sister's collectible figurines around the living room. Joan's expression when she saw the figurines was unforgettable, a vision Nan has frequently recalled ever since.

The four of them go inside and when the door shuts, it

sounds like the seal of a new refrigerator. There's no furniture. The carpeting's clean, the walls are freshly primed, and the living room, despite its emptiness, has a plush, unnatural lack of echo. Nan and Joan continue to the kitchen. Henry and Peg reach the doorway simultaneously, bottle-necked and waiting for each other to proceed. Henry steps aside with an after-you flourish.

"There's a lot of light in the morning," Peg says, but the sun is already high above the house and the Finns are forced to visualize how it looked a few hours earlier. "The oven's new, replaced last summer. Scratch that," she says, consulting her notes. "The dishwasher's new. You could angle a table into the corner for a breakfast nook, and the—"

Peg's interrupted by a knocking in the living room. Henry's hung back and rapped the wall with his knuckles, head tipped in concentration. He notices the women staring from the kitchen.

"Sounds like quarter-inch drywall. Better hope you don't snore," he tells them with a chuckle.

"Is quarter-inch bad?" Joan asks.

"It's not unusual in newer houses," Peg says. "Let's look at the bathroom. It's beautiful tile work," she notes, referring to the green checkered walls that remind Nan of the hospital where Joan nearly died. The shower looks exposed without a curtain and it's strange to see the toilet-paper holder hanging empty. Nan tries the sink. The water pressure's strong; the drain runs clear. She can hear the water trickling in the pipes downstairs.

"Ask her how old the furnace is," Henry whispers to Joan, ridiculously loud.

"Peg?" Joan says. "How old is the furnace?"

Peg checks her papers, continuing to flip even as she

answers. "It's original. But the house is only twelve years old."

"Most furnaces conk out around fifteen years," Henry says, again to Joan and speaking like he can't be overheard.

"This particular model lasts twenty," Peg replies. "That's average. With regular maintenance, you shouldn't have to worry for a long time."

"Did the previous owners maintain it?" Nan asks.

"I couldn't say. Considering the overall condition of the house, I would assume they did. Here's my favorite room," Peg declares, real enthusiasm rising in her voice.

She leads them into a sunroom that none of them expected. Big enough for two easy chairs and a coffee table, with hardwood floors and recessed shelving on the inner wall, the room faces the yard with floor-to-ceiling windows in dozens of individual panes. A heating stove, elegant and small, stands in the corner. Nan can picture it—summer with her spider plants dangling in the sun, winter with the fire and her chamomile tea. She could buy a little feeder, sit and watch the cardinals. Maybe grow an orchid. Feel the January sun.

"The sink leaks!" Henry yells from out in the bathroom.

Peg's portfolio creaks in her grip. When she turns to walk back, she stumbles on the riser. Nan follows her into the bathroom, where a small pool of water's spread around the floor.

"Do you need to be here?" Peg demands.

"I'm sorry," Henry says, cornered at the toilet. "I can wait outside . . ."

"Henry stays," Nan says. "He has nothing to apologize for."

"Can we talk?" Peg asks.

"Yes we may," Nan replies.

Peg leads the sisters to the middle of the kitchen. Her body language grows more flexible and folksy. "I'm only trying to make this easier for you."

"So is Henry," Nan says. "We need his objectivity."

"Objectivity's essential—that's my bread and butter—but fault-finding is better left to me, professional inspectors, and most of all you. It's your home. You have to live here," she says, as if the paperwork's already signed and she'll be handing them a key. "You need to trust your own impressions of a home's true potential. I once had a couple pass on a dream house because the young woman's mother objected to cloth wiring. What an outside observer sees as a deal-breaker, we might see as an opportunity. But letting you see the opportunity is impossible if a third party—whose motives aren't entirely clear—is determined to find problems. There's no such thing as a perfect house. Not until someone gives it a heart."

"What was the hidden opportunity of cloth wiring?"

"Nan." Peg sighs, reaching to her elbow. "I'm on your side. I need you to trust that my advice comes from close, often painful experience. If you want the best I have to offer, I can't allow Mr. Cooper to interfere at every stage."

Henry's standing in the bathroom, fumbling with his hands, looking like they're choosing which punishment will suit him.

"Are you willing to work with me or not?" Peg asks.

"You work for us," Joan says.

Peg's startled; she's been dealing with the tiger in the room and never saw the mouse coming at her heel. The sisters stand together, indivisible and firm.

"Henry stays," Nan says. "He's also right. We'd like a house with potential that's a little less hidden."

Peg stares at them in turn and finally at the wall. Nan and Joan look at Henry with a reassuring smile and he swells, growing several inches taller at the sight.

"Fine," Peg says. "Fine, that's fine," opening her notes and writing something minuscule inside. "It's just a difficult market in your range right now."

"We can make this work," Nan says, confident it's true, seeing Peg more distinctly as a real fixer-upper.

"It's part of the process," Peg assures them after three more houses fail to wow.

She says she'll be in touch, checks her phone, checks her hair, and speeds away to the office, hell-bent on finding them an upkept, gas-heated house with thick walls, snug pipes, a solarium, and real personality. Back at home, Nan takes a nap and Joan shows Henry her puzzle, the giant hedge maze she finished after dawn and hid beneath a tablecloth, hoping to surprise him. It's taken all week, her earlier frustration growing, piece by piece, into confidence, delight, and finally obsession.

"I'm gonna glue it up and frame it," Henry tells her. "You can hang it in your brand-new house."

"I'd love another one," she says, sounding like she's asking for some liquor in her coffee.

"I'll be back in half an hour."

"Henry," Joan says.

He pauses at the door, worried by her tone.

"Make it a hard one."

"Okey-doke." Henry grins.

He's gone for over an hour, checking two or three shops until he finds a real monster: a thousand-piece snowscape with evergreens and mountains, essentially monochromatic, even the trees powdery white. Joan meets him at the door, expectant as a girl, and smiles at the puzzle with a keen, religious fervor.

"*Snow*," she says, mostly to herself, and then she thanks him with a squeeze and sits at a table she's prepared in the living room, another part of the home the Finns have gradually taken over.

Ava greets Henry with a kiss, having made it home from work and prepped chicken for the grill. She smells like seasoning and talc and light summer ale. Something's new in her today—a playfulness of tongue, a silkiness he doesn't have a proper explanation for.

"How'd it go today?" she asks.

"Peg's a hard nut," Henry says. "Nan's a real nutcracker."

"No surprises, then. C'mere," she says, leading him into the kitchen. She hands him a bottle of beer and Henry takes a sip, trying to guess the cause of her mysterious expression.

"Sam Bailey called."

"What? When?"

"Twenty minutes ago. We had a whole conversation. Sort of," she admits. "I got the impression it was a long talk for him."

"What'd he want?"

"He wants to see you," Ava says. "He says he understands if you don't want to go, considering what happened when you went the other morning."

Henry wipes the bottle on his neck. Jig is up.

"He knocked me down and started yelling. He didn't mean it," Henry says. "He was running and he fell, we tangled up. I guess he lost his head. The guy's a wreck. It's like you said, he hasn't had a regular talk with anyone in weeks, and here comes me of all people. It wasn't that bad. I didn't want to scare you."

Ava doesn't like it. He can see it in her shoulders, in the way the sweaty bottle isn't slipping in her hand.

"I don't have to go," he says, feeling for his keys.

"No, I think you should."

"If it worries you . . ."

"He sounded really normal," Ava tells him. "I've been picturing this cold, dark woodsman with an ax. But you can't go now—you'll have to go tomorrow. We're having chicken and for once you're going to sit with us at dinner."

"I always sit—"

"You're going to sit *with* us."

Henry takes a seat to prove he gets the point. He watches Ava's jeans while she moves around the kitchen, how her back keeps showing in the gap below her shirt. Her hips seem perfectly designed for his lap, and the bottle warms him up with a nice, sunny fizz. Joan's busy with her puzzle. Nan's sleeping in her room. Even Wing is out of sight and they're together in the kitchen. He's attentive when she talks, hearing everything she says, and then she's balancing a tray full of drinks near the screen.

"Little help?" Ava asks.

Henry's up and at the door. He holds it open right beside her, conscious of her eyes and of the keys in his pocket, tempting him to drive off to Sam's straightaway.

10

Henry reaches Arcadia Street at 8:16 a.m., having risen predawn and paced the house until Nan required him to sit, Joan encouraged him to eat, and Ava finally let him go at the reasonable workday hour of eight o'clock. Wing's alertness has an edge, a memory of danger and a spirit of defense.

Henry parks and says, "Relax. He invited us today."

Sam saunters from the trailer. Henry takes his foot off the clutch without shifting into neutral and the car bucks forward.

"Damn it," he says, blushing from the jolt; he hasn't stalled that badly since he learned how to drive.

Sam lifts a hand, not quite waving as he walks toward the car. Wing snarls at the sight, lunging for the road as soon as Henry flips up the lock.

"No," he says. "Sit. Knock it off, Wing. Sit!"

He squeezes out and shuts the door, shaken by the fury of the barks. Sam halts where he is, back beyond the walk, but when Henry gets close enough he offers him a hand. Henry shakes it too emphatically and cracks Sam's knuckles.

"I guess your dog hates me now," Sam says.

Wing grows far more insistent when they turn. He's impressive with his bare teeth flashing at the glass and yet his voice keeps breaking, like an angry adolescent.

"He'll get over it," Henry says. "You got any junk food?"

"I have a couple of old donuts."

"That'll work."

Sam gets the donuts from the trailer, a pair of stiff crullers in a wax paper bag.

"Give me the first one," Henry says. He waggles it back and forth and opens the door the width of one cruller, slipping it in for Wingnut to sniff. "Look what Sam has. That's for you. Go ahead, good dog. That's from *Sam*."

Wing takes the donut in a one-two bite and lifts his head, first to Henry, then to Sam's paper bag.

"You want me to open the door?" Henry asks.

Sam nods, firming up his stance as if preparing to kick.

Wing hops out and tentatively sits, waiting like the world's most well-behaved dog. Sam holds the cruller down low and doesn't move.

"Go ahead." Henry nods. "There you go. That's for you."

Wing takes it with his ears back and eats it with a snap.

"Atta boy," Henry says, and Sam glances up, looking pleased as if it's him and not the dog being praised.

Wingnut wags, gentle-eyed now, sniffing Sam's boot and eventually smiling, much like Henry, with enough easy mirth for Sam to pet his head.

"You up for a walk?" Sam asks. "Everyone can see us out here."

Henry says sure and looks at all the houses, where the windowpanes are glaring in the early-morning sun. They walk across the dirt, off the grass, and into the dark seclusion of trees. Henry wonders why they can't just talk inside the trailer but he doesn't want to ask and doesn't need to know. The back of Sam's head is maddeningly blank and the hike feels longer than it did the week before. Wing hears a crack and races through the trees, startling a wood thrush and promptly disappearing.

"Does he ever catch anything?" Sam asks.

"Nah," Henry says. "It'd probably scare him to death if he did."

They reach the clearing and the pine that Henry felled the other morning. The wide-open light is like a huge breath of air. It's neater than before—Sam's been tearing up weeds—and the ground has a quality of careful preparation. There's a weatherproof chest, far in the back and secured to a tree with a bicycle chain.

Sam drops his head, shadowing his face, and mutters something brief and difficult to hear. He takes a key from his pocket—he's subtle about it; Henry would have missed it if the metal hadn't glinted—and walks toward the chest without a word of explanation. He kneels and pops a padlock, swinging up the lid, and hesitates a minute like he's having second thoughts.

When he turns, Henry flinches in the middle of his chest.

But it's nothing but a notebook dangling from his hand, pale blue with a little metal spiral up the side. Sam returns and holds it open to sketches of a small log cabin. He has five or six pages carefully designed—several different views, neatly measured and refined.

"I need your help," Sam says.

"You're building a house?"

"You offered . . ."

"No, of course!" Henry says, snapping to his wits. "I

don't get it, though. Why a little cabin? This is only one room."

"I can't stay in the trailer," Sam says. "Not with half the neighborhood knocking on the door."

"You want to build it out *here*?"

"What." Sam coughs. "You thought I meant to build it out there? Next to Peg?"

They picture it and can't help smiling at the thought: a cabin on the roadside, puffing out smoke. But at least Sam's trailer has water and electric. Henry tries to sort it out, looking up at Sam as if he's told him, very gravely, that he plans to raise a unicorn.

"If you want to be left alone," Henry says, "why don't you just get a house away from Arcadia?"

"Follow me," Sam says, heading for the trees.

They hike the woods beyond the clearing, moving slowly in the brush, watching out along the way for thorns and poison ivy. The soil feels rich and fertile underfoot, the kind of ground that you could flip and find a handful of worms, antique coins, centipedes, and bones. *Old growth*, Henry thinks, mindful of his steps, and then they pass through a grove and there's a body in the shade.

Henry stops as if they've come upon a white-tailed deer, a figure unexpected but entirely at home. He holds his breath and stares, admiring the sight. It's a man Sam fashioned from the bottom of an elm—seven feet of trunk, the remainder of the tree chopped away, branches stacked chaotically behind it and the ground soft beige with the shavings and the chips. The man is muscular and broad, powerfully kinetic, chained to a boulder by his elbows and his neck. He has a broad, open face and a long grizzled beard, and his body looks pained, writhing on the rock.

Henry gazes at the hole in the middle of his chest.

"That's . . . how do you *do* that?"

"I used to have to model them in clay before I started," Sam says, but that's as far as he'll explain. He might have answered, *Magic*.

There's a breeze in the uppermost branches of the trees—rustling overhead, buds falling at their feet—but the air isn't moving on the ground around the sculpture and it's strange, how it feels like they're standing indoors.

"I plan on putting suet in the hole to draw the birds."

"Ha!" Henry says, wishing Ava were here to see it.

"So the cabin," Sam says, "keeps me closer to the work."

Henry coughs. Something gummy leaves the bottom of his throat, but he can't spit it out and has to swallow it again. "I don't know the first thing about building a cabin."

"I only need your strength," Sam says.

Henry thinks of Ava's face when she found him at the fire. All she'd heard at that point was somebody had died, not the way the fire started, not the fact of the cigar. He'd been terrified to tell her and had fought to get it out, blubbering and thinking she would leave him on the spot. But she only drew him closer with her fingers on his back, squeezing hard as if the only real victim were him.

"We'd start by cutting a path out to the trailer," Sam says. "I'll need to get an ATV to bring supplies into the clearing. You'll help me gather rocks and carry concrete to lay the foundation, but the harder part is dragging all the logs from the woods."

Henry could tell her about the path and he could tell her about the sculptures, but the rest of it would have to be a secret. Not a word.

"If you're going to stay and help," Sam says, "we need some rules. First is no more apologizing."

"That's gonna be hard," Henry says.

"It's the only one I really care about."

"Okay."

"I don't want to talk when I'm sculpting."

"I wouldn't talk at all."

"No," Sam says. "It's fine if we're doing something together. But I really have to focus when I'm working."

Henry nods.

"I'll resent you if you treat me like a pity case. That's it for now. I might think of more," Sam says. "Is it a deal?"

All the blood in Henry's head settles to his feet until the weight is so profound he isn't sure that he can move. The hole inside the sculpture looks deeper than before, the tension in the chains more tangibly severe. He can feel the seconds passing, very slowly, very quickly, and it's Ava more than Sam who seems immediately real.

"If you don't want to help . . ." Sam says, growing cold.

"No, God, it isn't that," Henry says. "I'll definitely help. I was just . . . nothing. I was trying not to apologize again. I want to do this. Wait till Wing finds out. Assuming that's okay . . ."

"Sure," Sam agrees. "As long as he isn't running around the neighborhood. You don't want Peg calling Animal Control."

"Right," Henry says, freeing up his feet. "When do you want to start?"

"Now," Sam says.

II

Billy Kane's worked at True Value for three years and bets that he could build a house from scratch, given money and time and no distractions, same as he could get in shape if he didn't work forty hours a week and the gym fees weren't so offensive. His entire life boils down to organizing screw drawers and mowing dandelion heads; next week it's like he didn't do a thing, and his manager and Sheri only notice that the screws are intermixed and the backyard's a weed farm. Work leads to work, not some fantasy reward, and if his current income is any indication of the future, he'll be working past retirement, right until he's dead.

He's been stocking pesticide and fungicide this morning—he can almost taste the chemicals and feels a little poisoned. Cleary's, Compass, Merit. Toxic, every one. There's a satisfying name for everything he knows—gainful employment, home insurance, helpmate—and they all leave residues and odors in his nose.

It's dead in here today, nobody but pros who know exactly what they need and where to find it. They intimidate Billy, men with pipe dope in their fingernails and muscles you can only get at work sites, but then he notices a woman in the fertilizer aisle.

"Can I help you find something?" Billy asks.

She smiles up and shrugs—kind of yes, kind of no. She's short and wearing office clothes, clearly on her lunch, and he can almost see a gap between the buttons of her blouse. She reads a pair of labels and compares them very closely.

"This one's popular," he says, picking up a box.

She shakes her head politely. "I need a lot of phosphorus."

"This one has it," Billy says, pointing at the word.

"No, it's too much nitrogen. I need a better mix."

He laughs and puts the box away. "You really know your stuff."

She chuckles at the compliment and shows a pair of dimples. "I'm sort of a fanatic," she confesses. "I spend an hour every day tending flowers in my yard."

"You smell like it," Billy says.

The dimples disappear.

"I mean the flowers," Billy stammers, "like you smell really nice."

She tightens up crisp, focusing on the shelf, and then she finishes comparisons and quickens her selection.

"That's a good one," Billy says. "Let me carry that up for you."

"I think I've got it," she decides. It's an eight-ounce box.

He watches her the whole way up toward the register and finally has to wave because she looks back and catches him. It's right around lunch; he could linger in the break room, anywhere but here with the woman glancing over like she's ready to report him.

Billy's walking to the back, jingling nails in his pocket—a handful he took, nothing anyone'll miss—when he spots Henry Cooper up an aisle with a chain saw. Billy's eyelid flickers and his groin goes soft, but before he has a chance to hustle out of sight, Henry turns around and brightens up in recognition. They're the only people standing in the power tool department, just the two of them surrounded by the nailers and the drills.

"Billy," Henry says, like a long-lost pal.

He ambles with the chain saw cradled in his arm. In a moment they're together, shaking hands, face-to-face, Henry talking too insistently to fully comprehend.

"I mean it, Bill," he says. "If there's something I can do for you and Sheri . . . ," and his own wife's name, so affectionately spoken, makes the whole conversation feel private and familial.

"And about that civil suit," Henry says, "I understand completely. No hard feelings. You have every right to get what's coming to you."

"Thanks," Billy says. "No hard feelings either way."

He studies Henry carefully—bright teeth, good shave, a picture of health from his haircut to his tube socks, the kind of guy who doesn't get drunk and never dreams of cheating on his wife.

"I'm getting this for Sam Bailey," Henry says. "He's working in the woods . . . Of course you live right there. He's got another saw except it isn't very good."

"What's he doing?"

"Oh, you know," Henry says, now evasive. "Cutting wood, keeping busy."

"That's good," Billy says. *Kill his wife, buy him a saw.* "If he needs something else, tell him I'm around."

"I'll let him know." Henry beams. "Listen, though, I'd better get going. It was great seeing you, Billy. Give my best to Sheri, and best of luck with all your renovations."

"You bet. Brandon up there can ring you out."

"Thanks!" Henry says, a regular VIP with the cashier's name in his head, and he shakes Billy's hand a second time and walks away satisfied and flush.

Billy stands there, staring at the back of Henry's scalp, right where the barber leveled off his hair. Plenty more time to chase him up the aisle. Plenty more to say, things occurring to him now. Instead he holds the nails in the bottom of his pocket, squeezing till it feels like a real man's pain.

In the late afternoon after Billy's out of work, he looks for Henry's car but doesn't see it on Arcadia Street. Sam's trailer seems abandoned but beside it, near the trees, there's an ATV that Billy's never seen. It's a hauler with a cargo bed, obviously used, with a drab orange body and a big set of wheels. Billy parks the car and saunters back to have a look. There's a trail through the woods—when did *that* get cleared?—but it curves out of sight less than thirty yards in. He checks the ATV again. The engine feels warm and Henry's chain saw is resting in the middle of the bed. He thinks of hopping on to get a feel of what it's like but suddenly the trailer bangs open right behind him.

"Sam," Billy says, jerking up straight.

Sam freezes at the door, watching him intently.

"I came to say hello. I was looking at your ride. Really sweet," Billy says, checking out the tires. He smiles at the chain saw and says, "I sold this to Henry at the store. Just this morning. If you need to swap it out . . ."

"That's the one I wanted."

"Great," he says. "You can always change your mind. I've got to say, I can't believe you're talking to the guy."

"Who?"

"Henry Cooper," Billy says, lowering his voice. He

walks a little closer to the trailer, man-to-man. "If he's giving you any trouble . . ."

"I asked him here," Sam says. He steps down to the ground, locks the door, and walks past Billy to the ATV, where he lays a heavy backpack snug against the chain saw.

"Why?" Billy asks. "He killed your fucking wife."

Sam answers but he fires up the engine when he speaks, drowning out the words and kicking up exhaust. Then he rumbles up the path, leaving Billy on his own. *Go home*, he might have said, or *go to hell*. Either way.

Billy doesn't talk much before and during dinner. When Sheri doesn't ask, he finally has to tell her.

"You'll never believe who came in the store."

"Who," Sheri answers, deadening the question. She's preoccupied with dolloping Cool Whip onto her berries.

"Henry Cooper," Billy says.

She sucks her finger with a *snick*.

"He apologized again. Walked right up and tried to shake my hand. Can you believe this guy? He said no hard feelings about the lawsuit, like he's *letting* us sue his ass into the ground. He was buying a chain saw for Sam Bailey. I talked to Sam tonight. He got an ATV."

"What does that have to do with anything?"

Now he's lost his train of thought because she couldn't follow along. He plays it backward in his head: dinner, *go to hell*, sweet ride, Henry Cooper.

"I don't get it," Billy says. "Sam told *me* he wants to be alone but now the two of them are clearing an ATV trail together? I mean, Jesus."

"What did you say?"

"When?"

"To Henry. At the store."

"I turned and walked away."

Sheri closes up the fridge. "That's it?"

"What was I supposed to do? Punch him in the nose?"

Sheri looks at him and blinks and twists a button on her blouse. "You didn't say anything?"

"I guess I could have shared my feelings," Billy says. "It's tougher when the other guy's holding a chain saw."

Sheri laughs out loud. It's like the bark of a Chihuahua. "Did you think he'd fire it up and chase you through the aisles?" Then she loses it completely, picturing the scene. Billy scowls at his hand where he pricked it with the nails. "I'm sorry," Sheri says, noticing he's mad, pinker than a girl being tickled in the ribs. She finally simmers down, looking ravaged and relieved.

"What would you have said?" Billy asks.

"I'm not the one who's crucified him every day since it happened."

"Which I've never understood."

"It was an accident!" she says. "I could see if you were Sam . . ."

What a broken record. He wouldn't trade places with the guy, not at all, but at least Sam Bailey has a real fresh start. He can buy a new house, find a woman when he's ready. Everybody else has to fix what's left, doing all this work and spending all this money, just to get back to where they already were.

She turns away and eats her berries at the counter. Billy scans the news and finds some interesting stories, but before he has a chance to make nice and change the subject, Sheri's heading upstairs.

"Leave the dishes," she instructs.

He waits until she's gone and gets another beer. The second-floor bathroom's directly overhead, and when the water starts flowing through the pipes in the wall, he knows she's in the shower and it wrings Billy's stomach, thinking that she's naked up there. Out of reach. He considers going up and standing at the door, but he smells his own armpits and really needs a shave. Sheri wouldn't touch him, let alone enjoy it. So he stands on the chair and puts his hand against the ceiling, picturing her foot mere inches from his palm, and then he walks out back and listens to the trees—land he might have bought if he had known that it was selling.

12

"Careful over here," Sam says.

He's standing with a log balanced on a pair of saw-horses. They laid it there to notch it, sixteen feet of solid pine, easier to cut when he doesn't have to stoop.

"It'll stay," Henry says, dismissing it like every other danger in the woods.

"I mean it," Sam tells him. "This one's barely staying put."

They'd cleared a path fairly quickly for the ATV and by the end of the first week, Sam was driving tools and bags of concrete into the clearing. After that they cut, delimbed, and dragged more than sixty young pines out of the woods, beginning with the nearest trees but roaming ever farther in the search for arrow-straight, eight- to ten-inch diameter trunks. A number had been cut a half mile out and there were days when all they got were three or four logs. In addition to the wood, they also gathered rocks. Sam built a two-man sling to carry them out and it was backbreaking work, hiking through the forest with a hundred pounds of weight swaying in between them. They built the foundation early this week but skipped proper footings; there was simply no way to bring enough concrete to pour below the frost line. Henry isn't worried—pioneers did without—but Sam keeps thinking that it might become a problem. Too late now, Henry told him, and he's right: the mortar's set and they've begun to place the logs.

The flat-cut sills are in position on the stones, fastened tight with anchor bolts and ready for the walls. They've set the girder on the piers, laid the joists, and nailed the flooring. It's a satisfying platform, ten feet wide and fourteen long, its newness in the clearing seeming natural and clean.

"Taking a leak," Henry says.

The two of them have found an easy rhythm in the work, most of their exchanges practical and brief. *Turkey or bologna? Watch your head there. Stop.* On the very rare days when Henry doesn't visit, Sam sculpts from dawn to dusk, knowing if he doesn't, then he'll never leave the trailer. He's gotten more muscular and calloused from the labor, able to exert himself for hours and rejuvenate fully overnight. He has energy to burn, a healthy spring he hasn't felt since high school. He eats because he needs it, falls asleep fast, and wakes without cobwebs, but standing here now with the cabin floor completed, he begins to see the permanence of all his recent whims.

Henry zips up and says, "I brought meatball sandwiches and coleslaw."

"I got that beer you like."

"Great."

Wing flounders in the weeds. He tries to bite a wasp and runs toward the cabin, where he basks in a sunny patch of flooring while they eat.

"How are Nan and Joan?" Sam asks.

"They're okay," Henry says. "Settled in. They're looking for a house."

"Must be tough."

"I don't think their hearts are really in it."

"I mean about sharing your home," Sam says. "How big's your place?"

It's the most they've openly talked in one continuous shot and Henry puts his sandwich down, a move more instinctual than courteous, it seems, with his stomach rumbling audibly and coleslaw sticking to his mustache.

"Fifteen hundred and thirty square feet, give or take," Henry says. "That's according to the public record but it feels a lot bigger, more like sixteen or seventeen hundred."

Sam's amused by his precision and his willingness to share. He'd likely tell him anything without reservation.

"What's your credit card number?"

"Why?" Henry asks. "You need supplies?"

Sam shakes his head and takes a long sip of beer. "I was looking at my card the other day and noticed that the numbers made a pattern."

Henry reaches into his pocket and surrenders his entire wallet. Sam plays along, reads the card, and says, "No, it must be nothing."

"Check the other cards."

Even after Sam empties out the wallet, Henry doesn't ask him what the pattern might have been. Sam reads his driver's license. Organ donor: check. He has twenty-seven dollars and a photo of his wife.

"How's Ava holding up?"

Henry glances at his sandwich. "She's fine. She's great. It was oil and water with her and Nan but things are getting better. Thanks for asking, though. I'll tell her you were wondering."

"She doesn't mind you being here?"

"No, of course not," Henry says. "She encouraged it. I wasn't sure I should . . . I mean, the first time I came, before we met . . ."

He trails away, lost, both hands on his beer. Sam continues watching him and eating in the lull.

"She worries," Henry says, pressured to continue. "Ever since my surgery . . ."

"What surgery?"

"I got a coronary stent last year. I'm still on Coumadin. It's why I bleed like a hog with every little scratch."

"Is it serious?" Sam asks, twisting his bottle into the dirt.

"Nah, it's no big deal," Henry says. "Everybody has stents."

"I wouldn't have had you help . . ."

"Stop—you sound like Ava," Henry laughs, looking panicked. "I had to fight three months before she let me use the mower. I shouldn't have brought it up. It's not an issue. That's the truth."

He picks his sandwich up and finally takes a good round bite. Sam reclines on his elbows, looking overhead, following the pixilated motion of the leaves.

"You fight a lot?" Sam asks.

Henry makes a noise swallowing his food.

"Me and Ava? No, you know . . . just married-couple stuff." He puts his wallet back together, studying the picture. "I try to keep her happy so we're always pretty good. I used to get her a flower every Friday after finishing my route. You'd be surprised how nice the roses at the Pump-n-Go are."

Sam thinks of how he used to leave Laura little notes, scraps of paper in her coat or in the visor of her car—anywhere she'd find them when he wasn't right beside her.

They were short, like a lyric or a weird phrase they'd laughed about together. Maybe just *hello* or a drawing of a bird. He did it all the time the year that they were dating. Laura teased him for it, calling him the sensitive *artiste*, but that was half the charm—the element of play. Eventually he stopped. She mentioned it the month she accepted the late shift at the hospital pharmacy. They struggled with the rhythm of their separated days and he began to write her notes again, tucking them into her pockets and under the cap of her thermos, knowing she would find them in the middle of the night. But it wasn't the same. He was too self-conscious, too aware he would have skipped it if she hadn't brought it up. He finally let it go. It seemed a lot of work. He's thought about it often in the weeks since the fire, how it could have been the last thing he said before she died instead of *bye* or *see you later* from the bottom of the stairs.

"What are you sculpting next?" Henry asks.

"I don't know."

He's completed three more figures since *The Reacher* and *The Prisoner* with the wound—a man below an outcrop, pushing up the rock; another man shouldering the whole upper tree; and his favorite of them all, the one he calls *The Gazer*, hidden farther back above a clearwater brook. It's a sugar maple, fallen horizontal like a bridge, with its uprooted trunk settled on the bank. He cut the tree in half, leaving just enough wood to form the shoulders and the head. The figure is a youth gazing down at his reflection, one hand clasping at his heart, the other reaching down toward a pool ringed with stones. In the evenings, Sam's been covering the trunk in dirt and moss. Now it blends like it's always been a feature of the bank, as if a boy had really stared until the forest overgrew him.

"You ought to try an animal," Henry says. He settles back and chews his food, pondering the notion, looking like a man feigning inspiration. "At least get off the torture kick you're on. Your stuff's great—don't get me wrong, you're better than what's-his-name . . . the really famous sculptor." He snaps a couple times, trying to remember. "Doesn't matter," Henry says. "I'm just thinking that you might shift gears to something else. What about a bear—"

"I don't need suggestions."

"Yeah, no. I wasn't trying—"

"Then don't," Sam says.

"Sam, I'm sorry," Henry says, hives rushing up his neck. "Shoot, damn it. I didn't mean to apologize, either. I know I promised—"

"I want to finish this wall before you go. We need the first four logs ready on the sides."

Henry goes without a second's hesitation, sneaker untied and threatening to trip him. There's a cowlick on his crown and when he jogs, it's with the jerkiness of someone playing dodgeball.

Sam keeps relaxing in the sun, sipping beer. He watches Henry wrestle with the logs on the pile. He's lifted plenty worse but the morning's worn him out and Henry's skin begins to mottle as he's scraping it along.

Wingnut stands, looking back and forth between them. Sam gets up and strolls around the platform, trying to imagine where the furniture will go. He'll have a table and a chair, a loft to lay a mattress, and a woodstove back against the innermost wall. He'll need to get a water tank and hook it to a sink. He'll have to dig an outhouse and pile up supplies.

Henry struggles on, crimson to the ears—probably the color of a Pump-n-Go rose. Nobody would harbor a suspicion if he dropped, if he buckled from a heart attack and didn't make it out.

Sam's walking with his beer, looking up to see the leaves again, and suddenly he's bending at the waist around a log. It's the one they raised to cut, balanced on the horses, and he's walked directly into it and moved it with his gut. He drops the beer and pulls the log back, trying to arrest it, but he pulls too hard and rolls it into his hips.

He stumbles in reverse, knocked beneath it with a bump. The horses start to tip and Sam tries holding up the log, but it's all too rapid and impossible to stabilize. He and the horses topple down together. Now he's lying on his back with the log across his chest. It rolls along his palms, moving to his neck. He wants to shout except the weight of it is resting on his diaphragm, squeezing out his breath and scraping at his chin. He can still hear Henry pulling wood across the clearing, too preoccupied to notice. Wing's barking at the birds. The sun is overhead and there's a bright-white cloud, like a rabbit or a lamb, shining in his eyes. He locks his jaw and pushes with everything he's got, imagining a bench press, lifting it a foot. Once it's up, he can't sustain it and the log begins to fall. In a moment it'll drop directly on his throat.

Henry finally notices and runs to pick it up. He cups his hands beneath the end of the log and orders him to go. Sam shimmies in the dirt until he's clear of it completely. Henry drops it and the two of them are still, breathing heavy.

"Holy shit," Henry says.

Sam trembles there awhile, staring at the log. His beer has left a small dark puddle where it fell. Wing waggles up between them, thinking it was fun, lapping at the beer from the puddle and the spout. The little bright cloud covers up the sun and suddenly it's dark and even chilly on the ground. Sam can see it in the shade without looking up, an afterglow that never quite settles in his eyes.

"You should have let it fall," he says.

The red in Henry's face darkens like a stain. He grabs Sam's arm and says, "Knock it off."

"Let me go."

"Hey . . . *look*." Henry's eyes are so blue, they're difficult to bear. "I don't want to hear that crap. Understand?"

"You don't have the right—"

"The hell I don't," Henry says.

He loosens his grip and Sam escapes it with a flourish, shaking out his arm as if he's broken free alone. Henry gets up. Sam walks away and stands aloof, not enough to look defeated, but his breathing comes in shudders and he wishes he could sit again. The sun returns, deepening his shadow on the ground, and he starts to think of Laura when he hears:

"Come and help me with the log."

He tries ignoring it at first and yet he can't, he really can't. Henry's standing like he always does, spitting on his hands, so insistent in his energy that Sam begins to move.

"Why don't you just go."

"Come on," Henry says. "Over here. Chop-chop." He lifts the end of it and holds it there, waiting for assistance.

Sam approaches it with caution; it's the log that almost killed him. Then he's lifting it with Henry, which they do in perfect sync. He's distracted by the weight and by the shudder in his arms. They have to feel it out and move at equal speed, careful of their footing on the uneven ground. Soon they reach the pile and the satisfaction's mutual. They lower it in unison and gently put it down.

13

Saturday morning, mid-July, a salad of a day enticing Ava out—farm stands, flea markets, barbecues, lakes, fifteen hours of sunlight and everything in play. She's slept late and feels both languorous and rushed, satiny with sleep but eager to begin. Henry's up and dressed and packing a cooler in the kitchen, and at first she almost wonders if he's filling it for them.

"She's awake!" Henry says.

He hugs her so emphatically her breasts jelly up. She holds him in a cling and doesn't let go. He's gotten noticeably firmer in a few short weeks, widening his back and rounding out his biceps, and even though his appetite has steadily increased, his stomach is tight and he has more definition to his jaw. All from pulling weeds and clearing up a trail. She suspects he doesn't eat half of what he packs, finding some excuse to give it all to Sam.

"Let's swim today," she says, talking so close their mouths intermingle.

"I promised Sam . . . I'm already late," he says, lazy and aroused by the sugar of her breath.

She slips a hand up his shirt and rubs the middle of his back while her hips sway counterrevolutions lower down.

"Ava . . ."

"Mmm."

"Babe, I got to go."

"Right," she says, pushing him away.

He kisses her, a quick little peck atop the head. She may as well start breakfast—it's an hour past dawn—but when she opens up the fridge they're out of orange juice and cheese. She makes a mental shopping list, adding tile scrub and dryer sheets, remembering the mildew in the shower, and the laundry, and a promise to the Finns that she would drive them to the mall. Before she cracks an egg, her day is cut in stone.

"Good morning," Nan says, walking into the kitchen.

Ava greets her with a smile, especially when Nan holds the newspaper up. The paperboy's lateness is a shared consternation: they've been phoning in complaints as a team for several weeks, increasingly aware of their united sensibilities. With Henry off at Sam's and Joan doing puzzles, they've spent the last few weekends cleaning, shopping, cooking, and landscaping together. They're growing peppers, squash, berries, peas, and heirloom tomatoes—the garden, and the home, cooperatively cultivated.

"Sam says hi," Henry tells Nan. "You wouldn't believe those sculptures," he adds for maybe the fiftieth time that week. "I hope you get to see them someday. You too, Av."

Nan and Ava trade a look about the rank of invitation. He'll do anything for Nan, he'll speed right off to buy Joan another puzzle, and whatever's going on, he's always there for Sam.

"I'll come today," Ava says, turning from the stove.

Henry holds the cooler like she's threatening to snatch it. "I don't know," he says. "He wouldn't know you're coming. We should tell him. But he doesn't have a phone and really, either way, he's still pretty fragile."

"Then why invite us out?"

"I didn't mean *today*. I thought you had to shop."

"You can drop me at the market," Nan says, picking up a pad and reaching for a pencil. "I can shop and take the bus home."

"He doesn't like talking when he's sculpting," Henry says.

"Is he sculpting today?" Ava asks.

"I don't know."

"Well. If he doesn't want me there, he can charge me at the car and knock me over."

Henry puts the cooler down and fiddles with his whiskers. "Maybe just a real quick visit to the trailer. How long—"

"I'll be dressed in twenty minutes."

Henry stands there erect, gazing at the yard. Eventually he sighs and says, "Wing'll be excited."

"Wing is staying here."

"He loves it out there!"

"Two sweaty men and a dog is a lot to ask of a woman. I'll entertain Sam. Nan and Joan can entertain Wing."

Nan writes *Nylabone* on the grocery list.

"Fine." Henry sulks. "But you're the one who tells him."

If Ava didn't know better, she might have assumed that he was harboring a woman in the woods, a thought that makes her smile, since he can't hide a Christmas gift without her knowing what it is, where he bought it, and how proud of himself he is for keeping it a secret. She talks little on the drive across town, calmed by the wind swirling up her hair. Henry's quiet, too, and even when she wants to point something out—a double-seat bike, a license plate that reads DR FOOT—she keeps it to herself to see if Henry says it first.

"Why didn't you want me to come?"

"Huh?" Henry says, drifting in the road. "What makes you think that?"

"You said I shouldn't come."

"I didn't mean it that way. I don't want to pressure Sam is all. I can't figure him out," Henry says. "He seems happy one minute, then a black cloud hits him out of the blue. He got talking about suicide the other day."

Ava shuts the window right as Henry says it, and it sounds as if the word's sucked air from the car. A classmate of Ava's killed herself in high school—pills, coma, complications. No one saw it coming till it happened, at which point everybody swore they saw it coming, her death a kind of pale, backward shadow in their memory.

"It's good he's staying busy," Ava says. "He needs to feel alive, even if it hurts."

Her own philosophy of late, dubious at best. They'd planned to share a bath last night, and even though Henry made it home well before dinner, he'd been quick to eat and roughhouse with Wing before asking how her day was, pacing while she talked, and falling asleep before she finished undressing in the bedroom. She filled the bath, deciding she would take one alone, but the stillness of the water made her open up the drain. They had laundry in the washer, dishes in the sink. She put a blanket over Henry, pinched a snore strip onto his nose, and spent the next two hours cleaning house and feeling terribly alive.

"It might take a year for any kind of normalcy," she says.

"If he makes it that long."

"We'll have to make sure."

They come around the block and Ava's bothered by the openness. The only time she saw Arcadia Street was coming here for Henry, when the trucks were in the road and both the houses were engulfed. It's simpler now, and lonelier, and sadder with the trailer.

"Here we are," Henry says, stopping at the curb.

She's sorry to have come today and isn't sure why, and she's about to call it off when Sam appears around the back. He waves and does a double take a hundred feet away and notices it isn't Wingnut sitting next to Henry. He straightens when he walks and moves a hand to his hair, thinks twice, and does a last-second comb with his fingers.

"This is Ava!" Henry yells. "I should have told you she was coming. Ava, this is Sam."

She hasn't even gotten her seat belt off. Sam offers her a hand when she steps from the car. His palm has the texture of a sawed piece of wood, like it needs a good sanding and a warm coat of oil. He looks at her without quite locking on her eyes and says, "It's nice to meet you," in the same polite voice he used on the phone.

"Sorry to spring her on you."

"I made him bring me," Ava tells him. "I can go if it's a problem."

Sam shakes his head, not exactly answering.

"I'm so sorry," Ava says, expecting him to slump, but he watches her impassively and seems to grow taller in the pause. She gives him back his hand, embarrassed to have kept it. The yellow of her dress looks paler in the sun, and when the silence of the moment carries too long, she faces him again and says, "We brought an extra breakfast."

"Isn't she great?" Henry says. "Let's eat in the trailer. After breakfast I can drive—"

"Let's eat in the woods," Ava says. "I mean, if that's okay."

Sam reluctantly agrees by failing to answer either way.

"Maybe you'd like to change before we go?" she thinks to add, giving him a chance to switch shirts and find deodorant.

They walk across the lawn and Ava lags behind. Henry turns to Sam and whispers something private, likely an apology for bringing her along. She gets a peek inside the trailer when Sam opens the door. It's spartan, neatly ordered: scarcely anything at all. Books, tools, a coffeepot. Nothing on the walls. There's a power cord connected to an outdoor receptacle but otherwise he may as well be living in a box.

Sam returns better dressed. He needs a shave, his hair is matted, and even fresh deodorant has limits, but his white shirt highlights the color of his skin and there's a touch of equanimity about him.

"Off we go," he says.

Henry's at his side but Ava pulls him back, pretending that she wants to hold his arm in case she stumbles. But the path is clear of obstacles and relatively level and they walk between the ATV's tire grooves, the Coopers in the back and Sam far ahead. He often vanishes completely when the trail makes a bend. Henry's silent as can be and Ava doesn't press, preferring now to study her surround-

ings more attentively. The air is full of fragrances that fill
her with up with color: mushroom, loam, evergreen, and
violet. Something's in the trees, deeper in the shade, where
she can't quite see and where the trail would be invisible.
She thinks of hiding out there, on a bed of soft fern, with
the jigsaw blue through the overhead leaves. She would
sleep. She would wake and find pollen in her hair and it's
delicious to imagine being free of any care.

She's startled to her senses by a cabin in a clearing. Half
a cabin, rather: four walls without a roof or even windows,
extra logs piled neatly near a smattering of saws. Henry
tenses and his arm feels leaden in her hand, and when she
looks at him he winces with a shrug.

"He made me promise."

"Promise what?" Ava whispers, watching Sam across
the way. "Tell me that you didn't—"

"No, I didn't lift a thing. He didn't want Peg to give
him trouble with inspectors. He said to keep it secret."

"Not from me," Ava says.

"She loves it!" Henry yells, drawing Sam's attention.
They walk toward the cabin in the flickers of the sun. It
blinds them here and there and Ava shields her eyes, sizing
up Sam and the muscles of his arms. He carries a pair of
crosscut stumps one at a time and sets them in the grass,
apparently a good deal stronger than he looks.

"I'm sorry I don't have chairs," he says. "I built a table,
though."

It's standing in the shade: small, jointed oak, immaculately made. He places it between the stumps and Ava puts
the cooler down.

"It's perfect," she says, claiming one of the seats.
"What are you and Henry working on today?"

"Nothing big," Sam says, hesitating slightly. "I need to chop some firewood but Henry—"

"He can do it," Ava says, setting out the food.

"Is that okay?" Henry asks, like it wasn't her idea.

"Go ahead," Ava says. "Just take it easy. We'll be here."

She stares at him and tries to make it clear: let us talk. Henry blanks for a second, then nods conspiratorially, subtle as a whisper in a five-foot room.

"Yeah, take a load off," he says. "Just stay away from those pepper sandwiches she brought."

"I have bagels, too," she says.

"Isn't she great?" Henry mutters, heading for the trees where the chain-sawed limbs are waiting to be split.

The air is smoother in the clearing, like the middle of a lake. Ava settles on a stump and watches Henry start. He looks tremendous, sturdy-shouldered with the ax overhead, and yet he keeps glancing over, mindful of exertion. All at once the sun's above the tree line, shining on the table and her pale, pale arms. Sam dwells on his bagel as a way of keeping quiet but he's equally attuned to Ava's pepper sandwich.

"That's your breakfast?"

Ava smiles through a bite.

"What do you put in that?" he asks.

"Grilled red peppers, jalapeños, pepper jack cheese, and chipotle garlic mayonnaise. Now and then I dice some habanero in for kick."

The heat begins to peak and Ava sips her water. She perspires and her sweat feels vaporous and clean. She dabs her temple and relaxes with her chin toward the sky, radiating up in answer to the sun.

"I've never understood the appeal," Sam says, and even though her eyes are closed, she feels the rapt expression on his face.

"When chefs prepare puffer fish," she says, "they leave just enough poison to make your lips tingle. Danger's part of the experience. You feel entirely alive after dinner."

"Have you ever eaten puffer fish?"

"Not yet," Ava says. "There's another pepper sandwich in the cooler."

"Maybe later," he says. "Where's Wing today?"

"He's home with Nan and Joan."

Then he's silent once again and doesn't ask about the Finns. She gives him time, thinking maybe he's affected by their names, but he sits without a word. They always ask about *him*.

"Henry didn't tell me you were building out here."

"That's surprising," Sam says.

"I can't believe you did it by yourself."

"It's easy with a plan."

"How did you lift the logs?"

He looks at her and takes a sip of coffee from a travel mug, comfortable and smiling very faintly, like a swindler.

"I use a block and tackle with the ATV. You set a pair of logs like ramps against the wall and pull the other log up."

Ava pictures it—a fairly simple thing, after all—and yet she can't imagine Henry standing idle and observing it. She's seen him look at Nan when he's prohibited from helping, even when it's baking or something else he has no business getting involved with. It must have killed him, picking weeds while the cabin came together, and she wonders if he really kept it secret from embarrassment.

"You didn't let him help?"

Sam's smile falls away. He looks at Henry in the distance, mulling what he sees. "He's lucky I let him do anything."

Ava draws away, wounded by his tone. Sam's mood abruptly shifts, just as Henry had described, as if the conversation siphoned off everything he had. His exaggerated sulk feels personal to Ava, a wall of humid air that cushions her away. The forest sags in, somnolent and dense. She has a very strong urge to slap him in the face.

The heat's grown heavy and the gnats are coming out. Ava yawns to get a lift but her chest won't rise. She stands and moves away. Henry notices at once. He runs a hand through his hair, flexing inadvertently, and walks directly over like she wanted, like she hoped.

She hugs him and his body feels succulent and firm.

"He wants to be alone," Ava whispers in his ear. "He doesn't want to talk about it."

"Right," Henry says.

They turn and face Sam, who's slouching on the stump.

"I think we're heading out," Henry says.

Sam nods.

"You need me here tomorrow?"

"Whatever you want."

"Okey-doke," Henry says, turning awkwardly to Ava.

"Thanks for having me," she says.

Sam's determined to ignore her. She hugs him where he sits, one quick pump. He doesn't see it coming and he doesn't see it ending, and she wonders if the gesture was a terrible mistake.

She and Henry say goodbye and leave him there alone, sitting like a prop balanced on the stump. They walk along

the path and feel the closeness of the shade. Even Henry
doesn't speak until the cabin's well behind them. Ava picks
a small red flower and examines it. She twirls it in her fingertips, holding it at the stem, until her body and her
thoughts start to loosen with the petals. Henry's sweat is a
like fresh-cut onion on the breeze, too new to smell rank,
closer to a chive. She wonders if the soil ever steams in the
dark. She wants to feel pine sap melting in her palm, soft
needles on her back and in the arches of her feet.

She wanders off the trail until she's ankle-deep in
maidenhair, soft green leaves swishing at her calves.

"Where you going?" Henry asks.

She throws the flower at his feet. Henry picks it up as if
he's meant to read a clue. Ava bends low to let her neckline
breathe, and then she looks at him and grins and beckons
with her fingers.

"Av, we can't," he says, wanting to but glancing up the
trail.

"Shh."

Ava turns, forcing him go follow.

She finds a chestnut tree, out of sight from the trail, and
leans forward on a low-slung, belly-high branch. Henry
crackles up behind her, unfamiliar in his sounds. She hikes
her dress to her waist so it bunches on the limb, pillowing
the bark so it's softer on her skin. She totters there a moment, heels off the ground, while she uses both thumbs to
roll her panties to her thighs. Henry doesn't move. Ava
stares around the forest, far as she can see, and right as
she's about to pitch forward on the branch, he grabs her by
the hips and pulls her back, nice and hard. She lets herself
drape, hair crowding at her eyes and her breasts falling
upside down around her throat. It's slippery for a change

when he shoves right in and now she couldn't get away even if she tried. She reaches for the soil just beyond her fingers, and a millipede curls and the rot smells clean. With every sudden oomph, Ava gazes more directly, past the trees, and those behind them, and the shadows in the gaps, pressing urgently against him when he pushes her away, leaning forward to escape when he pulls her up tight.

Sam thinks about the hug and the pressure of her hands. He was hugged so often in the days around the funeral that he finally ceased to notice it was happening at all. But for nearly seven weeks he's been limited to handshakes, nothing more intense, let alone from a woman.

The forest closes in and makes it difficult to breathe. It's humid in the sun and windless in the shade. He takes his shirt and jeans off and lounges in his boxer shorts. Stands and walks around. Tries the radio, discovers that the batteries are dead, and leans against the cabin wall, tired in the glare. There's a bird that he's been hearing all week, *Drink your teeeea*, but he doesn't have the will to go and seek it out.

He finds the half-eaten sandwich Ava left behind. He peels the wrapper at the table, examining the peppers: visceral and thick, like slices of a heart. The bread's soggy, cheese and mayonnaise oozing out the sides. He takes a bite, more focused on the texture than the taste, and he's barely started chewing when he spits it on the ground. He's swallowed some; there's plenty more covering his tongue. The flavor shifts color, turning volatile and bright. He pants through his mouth but it rushes up his nose, all acid burn and firelight and Mexican alarm.

He runs around the clearing—*Jog it off, jog it off*—until it peaks and he can't help shouting out loud. The forest comes alive, flickery and fresh. He licks the cheese off his bagel, hoping it'll help, and then he coughs and even laughs when the heat begins to fade, wishing Laura could have seen him at the mercy of a pepper. He collapses on the ground and looks around, wide-awake, and the dirt feels good beneath the bubble of the sky.

A delicate perfume rises in the heat, drifting off his arm and intermingled with his sweat. He pictures Laura in her sleep the morning of the fire, feels the softness of her neck, the ridges of her spine. Down the valley of her back to the dimples at her waist, miniature fingerprints that always made him woozy. Round her iliac crest, down a long pale thigh, to the furrow in her calf with her muscle and her tendon. There's a Band-Aid there; she had a blister from her shoe. The bottom of her heel snuggles in his palm. She notices and rolls, spreading open on her back, and he lies between her legs and all the length of her's alive. When he kisses her, it feels as if she's swallowing his tongue. Their temperatures converge until it's difficult to tell if they're together or apart. He can feel her in his lungs.

14

Billy finishes the drywall and gets a coat of primer on. The panels were a breeze to cut and hang, but the mud had been a mess and when he sanded the joints, he rubbed too hard and frayed a lot of the tape, forcing him to tear the sections clean and start again. There's still a bit of mud splattered on the floor but basically it's done and waiting for the final coat of paint—one or two days and they'll be ready for the furniture again, and then he'll start the bedroom, and look for cheaper siding, and—assuming he can foot the bill—vapor-lock the basement.

He picks the ladder up and turns and knocks a divot in the wall.

"Fuck," Billy says, fingering the spot.

He overcomes an urge to punch it even wider, takes the ladder to the yard, and chucks it near the drywall. They need to get a Dumpster but there's plenty more to come. Sheri scowls at the pile every day. So does Peg.

Billy makes himself spaghetti and watches the television they moved into the kitchen. When Sheri gets home—two hours late—she's mad he ate without her and lets him know by talking about her lousy day, clattering pots, and punctuating her complaints with cutlery and glass. The diner was "slammed" this afternoon, a word she got from one of her girlfriends at work, Mary or Kate, he can't remember which. She has her own private world there, with holidays and seasons, in-jokes and habits Billy doesn't know until they show up at home like second nature. Jake the dishwasher—that's one name Billy has straight—taught her the best way to load a dish rack and now she's militant about it, rearranging Billy's order when he gets it all wrong. And suddenly in recent weeks she's all about the Sox, talking like she hasn't missed a game in twenty years.

"It's big at work," she says.

"With who? That dishwasher guy?"

"Jake? He's an *Orioles* fan. He grew up in Baltimore. You should hear Mary-Kate tease him every day," and Billy can't tell if Jake's being teased about the Orioles, growing up in Baltimore, or something else entirely.

"The living room's done."

"Really?" Sheri says, brightening at last, and he almost has to jog to follow her up the hall. "Oh," she says. "I thought you meant *done*."

"But that was the worst of it."

"You missed a spot," she says, feeling at the divot, like he might have overlooked it if she hadn't pointed it out. But then she says, "The couch'll cover it up," and walks around the middle of the room and even smiles. "This'll look amazing with the color I was showing you. I'm totally impressed."

She smiles right at him.

Billy takes her waist and holds her hand below his chin. They sway a little dance, turning in the room. She lays her head against his shoulder and relaxes with his breathing, balancing her feet on Billy's toes until they're laughing, almost stumbling, and her eyes are full of fun.

"What do you say," Billy asks, giving her the look.

Sheri kisses him and lingers at his mouth. Billy hums.

"I'm tired, though," she says. "I won't be any good. Let me take a nap. I'll be great in half an hour."

After this many weeks, thirty minutes sounds sweet. He drinks another beer while Sheri's showering upstairs and watches *Wheel* and *Jeopardy!*, knowing more of the answers than some of the contestants. All the women in the ads have a summery allure and Billy waits an hour, just to play it safe.

When he goes to wake her up, he finds her sleeping on her stomach in her T-shirt and panties, one foot dangling off the bed. She's sleeping so hard she almost looks drunk. Actually she is—on the table are a few mini bottles of Kah-lúa, the kind you get in airplanes, empty in a row. He didn't know she had them, can't imagine where she got them.

Her calves are faintly orange. She's been using artificial tan and can't get it right, streaking her skin and looking like she ate too many carrots. He's thought about sending her off to a spa, a whole package to surprise her, but it would cost him more than he can justify and honestly, he shouldn't have to try that hard. She looks good to him to-night, though, comfortable and clean. He kisses her and smells her apricot shampoo. He imagines they're together at a tropical resort, and it's thrilling when he's naked with the warm air moving on his back. She rambles in her sleep and curls her fingers into a ball. He pulls her panties down slow and says, "You're beautiful. I love you."

He straddles her and tries a little spit for lubrication, but he hurts her when he starts. Sheri clenches up.

"Shh," Billy says, smoothing down her hair.

"Stop," Sheri slurs.

"Just relax."

"Said get *off*."

She's groggy from the drink but waking up fast. Billy moans at how pliable and velvety she feels.

"Billy . . ."

"Shh."

"Stop . . ."

"I said *relax*," Billy growls.

It's better when she butts and wriggles up against him. Sheri bumps him with her head so Billy grabs her hair, burying her face until it's muffled in the pillow. He tries to think of Ava and he tries to think of Peg, but he ends up imagining he's Jake from the diner, and he pounds even harder, deep as he can go, until it feels like he's pounding right through her to the bed.

He shudders in a sweat, coming to a rest. The slipperiness between them turns clammy in the dark. At some point she must have quit struggling and collapsed; he didn't notice at the time and he's surprised by her now, lying so still, face flat against the pillow.

Billy slumps off and gets a towel from the bathroom. When he comes back out, she hasn't changed position and her underwear's still around her knees. He leaves the towel at her side and takes a shower, soaping up hard in very hot water, but he doesn't feel altogether rinsed until he urinates. He listens at the door and doesn't hear a sound. He turns off the light and hides awhile longer.

When he finally eases out, Sheri isn't there.

He finds her downstairs beneath a blanket on the couch, in the middle of the hall where they had to move the furniture. She's tighter than a pill bug, curled toward the cushions. He can tell that she's awake.

"Sher?" Billy says.

When she doesn't move or speak, he gets a feeling like he killed her. He stares a minute longer and retreats upstairs, knowing it'll stew until they talk and hash it out. The house is so still it's like he's standing underwater. He's exhausted but he's wired. He'll be up all night. He has to do *something* but he can't leave the room, can't eat or watch TV with Sheri on the couch. So he slaps himself repeatedly, hard across the cheek, hoping she can hear how terrible he feels.

Henry, Nan, and Joan share a supermarket cart, and while the sisters choose ingredients for brownies, Henry hums a melody they all recognize but can't identify. They spoke about the tune in aisle three, more than once, and when Henry couldn't name it Nan insisted that he stop. But the melody's persisted in their heads, especially since Henry keeps forgetting not to hum, and it's nostalgically entwined with everything around them, from the muffiny aroma of the bakery to the little blue turkey on the box of Bell's seasoning.

"*Henry,*" Nan says.

"What? Shoot, sorry."

"It's a Christmas song," Joan says.

Henry's swayed for a moment by a passing whiff of cinnamon.

"It's not a Christmas song," Nan says. "We need vanilla."

"It's Bob Carmichael," Joan declares, and the name

assumes a yuletide glow, like Bing Crosby or Johnny Mathis, so familiar that at first Henry's certain she's correct: the song's a Bob Carmichael holiday standard.

Bob says hi and snaps him to attention. He ambles down the aisle with his boys, Danny and Ethan, leaning his weight against the cart even though it's virtually empty: a single loaf of Wonder Bread, half a dozen eggs.

Nan addresses them but doesn't lose her supermarket game face: pleasantries are fine, but let's remember why we're here.

"How are you, Bob?" she asks.

"I'm good, good," he says, the double *good* resonating powerfully with Henry. Bob greets Joan and compliments her sweater; she almost gets teary with appreciative delight. "How's the house hunt going?"

"Peg's doing her best," Nan says.

"She always does," Bob agrees, rather mournfully it seems. *How'd a man like me*, Henry almost hears him thinking, *and a woman like her* . . . he can hear him trailing off.

"You remember Miss Finn and Miss Finn," Bob says to his sons.

"Hi."

"Hi, Miss Finn."

"Hello, Danny," Nan says. "Hello, Ethan."

"You're getting tall," Joan says. "You look like first and second graders now."

"They're going into second and fourth," Bob says.

"*Are* you?" Joan asks, widening her eyes.

The boys shuffle at the cart, stealing glances at the *mailman*.

"You're Henry Cooper," Bob says, growing serious but

not at all cold. He shakes Henry's hand and says, "We ought to clear the air."

"Mr. Carmichael . . ."

"Bob, call me Bob. Listen, Henry, I can't tell you how sorry I am about this"—whispering now in front of the boys—"goddamn lawsuit. I'd have dropped the whole thing the day we cashed the Allstate check. Honestly, the house is even better since the renovations, whatever anybody keeps saying. But 'anybody' says we have to sue, Allstate says we have to sue . . . It's nothing I'm happy about."

"You're suing the postal service, not me directly," Henry says, lowering his head and looking up through his eyebrows. "I hope you know I'd pay you out of pocket if I had it."

Nan hits his ankle with the bumper of the cart. She's warned him not to talk this way, even with a person as innocuous as Bob.

"I never got a chance to apologize to you personally," Henry says.

"Let me stop you right there," Bob tells him, holding up a hand traffic-cop style. "I understand you've already talked to Peg. That's enough for all of us, far as I'm concerned. You're helping Nan and Joan, I understand you're helping Sam Bailey. I'd just as soon call it water over the bridge, or under the dam, or whatever you like."

"Over the bridge," Henry says, and Nan just throws in the towel and starts reading a box of chocolate. "So these are your sons," he adds, standing back to formally size them up.

"This is Danny," Bob says, putting his hand behind the smaller boy's head. "And this is Ethan."

"Nice to meet you," Henry says. "I'm sorry about the fire."

Ethan nods.

"None of our stuff got burned," Danny adds.

"Tell me something now. You guys had a swing set, right?"

Danny bites his lip; Ethan says yeah.

"What about bikes?" Henry asks, widening his stance to more vigorously brainstorm. "You could go wherever you want."

"We already have bikes," Danny says.

"We have to stay on the block."

"On *our* side of the street."

"Peg worries about strangers," Bob explains.

Henry rears up to study all their faces—surely one of them, at very least the youngest, will be giggling. Nan shakes her head in mannerly alarm and yet the fact is too incredible.

"That's crazy," he decides. "I rode clear across town when I was your age."

"We don't have a tree house."

"Ethan," Bob says.

"Done!" Henry shouts. "As long as your Dad says it's okay."

"You really don't—"

"I know I don't, Bob. But I really, really want to."

The aisle has a flutter. There's a bad fluorescent bulb. The music stops—the deli has a call on line two—and then the radio and light are gracefully restored.

"That'd be up in a tree," Bob clarifies, all of them considering the glaring complication.

"There's grass under the tree," Danny says.

"It wouldn't have to be that high," Ethan adds.

"We'll make it strong enough to hold a few adults," Henry tells him.

Bob's rubbing at his neck as if a talon's digging in. "If you truly want to do this—and you don't have to, I mean that—but if you really do," he says, eyes going shifty, "then you maybe want to come unexpected with the lumber. On a Saturday morning. Say around nine."

"Does this Saturday work?" Henry whispers.

Bob turns toward his boys and grips the handle of the cart.

"Sure. Go ahead. This Saturday morning. Just between us for now," he says to Danny and Ethan. "It'll be a nice surprise for Mom when she makes it home for lunch. Assuming she even goes out . . ."

"That reminds me," Nan says. "I found a few more houses worth seeing this weekend."

"You did?" Joan asks.

"Several hours' worth. If you wouldn't mind telling Peg," she says to Bob, "we're available Saturday morning. She'll have to pick us up. Henry has plans."

The men shake hands, the boys and sisters say goodbye, and the groups part ways and carry on with their shopping. At the very end of the aisle, Joan spots a platter and says, "'Smoke Gets in Your Eyes,'" but it's Henry who's arrested by a dawning realization.

He turns so fast, Nan strikes him with the cart again.

"What?" she asks, straightening the groceries that have toppled.

"I don't know the first thing about tree houses."

"Hm," Nan says. "If only you knew an obsessive wood-worker."

15

When the Coopers drive up, Sam goes out to meet them. Wing's got his head jutting out the back, choking on the partly rolled window, and Ava's in the passenger seat with flowers on her dress and her hair blown free around her eyes.

Sam is laundromat clean, newly shaved and showered, and before they're out of the car he double-checks his shirt and tucks it in more precisely, smoothing out the front. Wing bounds up and paws him in the crotch; he leaves a muddy print and runs off, hitting every puddle till he finds a patch of muck and flops down, with a somersault, in animal delight.

"He gotcha." Henry laughs.

Sam attempts a casual removal of the stain. Ava meets him on the grass with a gesture of hello, her smile and her wave partially withheld. She's prettier and plainer than the woman he remembers, and he hesitates, adjusting to her actual appearance. He invited her today, having mentioned it to Henry, but she stands apart, looking at the homes on either side and at the fast-moving scud right above the trees. It's been intermittent showers, intermittent sun, the weather changing hourly but blustery and damp. Thunderstorms are coming. He can smell it on the breeze and in the rills of cooler air that ripple through the heat.

"I ate some of your sandwich last week," Sam says.

Ava turns to him at last.

"I ran around like Wing," he says. "I almost started bawling."

"I warned you," Henry tells him, proud of Sam's gumption.

Ava doesn't speak but has a ruddier complexion, maybe tickled or intrigued, maybe thinking—and it only just occurs to Sam now—about his mouth upon the partly eaten sandwich of a stranger.

He insists on carrying the cooler. Ava leads the way while he and Henry walk behind her on the path toward the clearing. Wing's beside them and around them, everywhere at once, and as they talk about the progress he's been making on the cabin, Sam admires Ava's dress and how it flourishes around her. She's ample in her figure but her stride is full of buoyancy, every swell balancing another as she moves.

"Oh," Henry says, snapping his fingers and doing the worst I-just-remembered-something Sam's ever seen. "I ran into Bob Carmichael at the supermarket. He was shopping with his boys. Really nice kids. I kind of offered to build them a tree house."

"Really," Sam says, eyebrows just about rising off his head. Ava doesn't turn but steps a little harder. "I can't see Peg letting her sons into a Cooper-built structure."

"Neither could Bob," Henry says. "But the boys really want it, and Peg'll be out of the house this Saturday morning. I figure if it's far enough along before she gets home . . ."

Sam shakes his head very slowly, very widely. "She wouldn't let her kids take candy from the *Finns*."

"We're aware of Peg's charms," Ava says, peeking back without stopping. "What Henry needs is someone who can build a tree house."

"For the boys," Henry adds. "I wouldn't ask if I was doing this for me."

Sam remembers Danny and Ethan on their bikes, how they used to jump the curb when Peg wasn't watching. He once caught them peeking at his sculptures through the window. They often helped Laura shovel out her car. He can see them doing plenty with a tree house, stocking it with M&M's, defending it with traps, but the thought of showing up with Henry like a team . . .

"Can I think about it?"

"Yeah. No, forget it," Henry says. "It's basically a box and a ladder. How hard can it be?"

"I'm not saying no. It's just—"

"Say no more," Henry tells him.

They arrive at the clearing sooner than expected. Sam wishes he could get a better look at Ava's face. Instead she wanders off to see the cabin with its newly finished roof, its windowpanes darkened from the lack of inner light. There's something grim and even fearsome in its being here at all, a quality he recognizes now through Ava's eyes and through her standing there, tiny and domestic at the door.

There's a rumble of thunder in the west, not the day's first but more convincing than the others. They had planned to move a heap of rotten limbs that Sam had cut, but with the storm moving in, he suggests they all relax and have an early lunch inside.

"I'll get the branches," Henry says. "You and Ava see the sculptures."

It's part of what he offered when he made the invitation. "We have a little time."

"I'd love to," Ava says.

They both regard the sky, neither of them moving, but the storm, having growled, isn't forcing them to stay. Henry carries branches, nothing heavy or unwieldy—a completely different worker in the presence of his wife. Sam and Ava start hiking through the trees without a word. Her body has a corseted rigidity and poise, and now that they're alone she looks at everything but him. The wind comes and goes. They hear it in the leaves deeper in the woods, swishing closer till it's rushing overhead and passing on. Sam's noticed that the forest feels smaller when it's gloomy—not at night when the dark makes it infinitely vast, but on days like today, in the muted light of clouds, when the trees seem to huddle and the ground feels warm.

They begin with *The Reacher*, the first Sam did and nearest to the cabin. He watches her the last ten seconds of the walk before they come around the thicket, long enough that Ava grows uncomfortable and faces him. She can't imagine what he's staring at her for, and then she turns and understands, gasping at the figure. Sam's been staining all his work to gentle browns and grays, weathering the fresh-cut whiteness of the wood and keeping them in harmony with everything around them. Ava cranes up, mouth quietly ajar, and then she elevates her hand—barely lifting it, he sees—as if to touch it in her mind or make an empathetic gesture. But it's fear as much as wonder in the color of her eyes, a thrill that makes his own dull pulse start to race.

He goes before they're tempted to discuss it and she

follows him, attuned to what's around her and prepared to meet the others. She marvels at *The Strongman* shouldering the tree, how his knees seem to quake beneath the overbearing weight. Sam regrets it, having killed the tree, in all likelihood, by cutting up the trunk, but now he gets to watch Ava put her hand upon the form, pressing on the great round muscle of his heart.

They pass *The Pusher* with the rock and several more that he's completed—disembodied arms and legs breaking from the ground; a man with antlers in the agony of changing to a stag. They come upon *The Prisoner* with the hollow in his chest, and even with the beard she seems to recognize the face.

Sam studies her expressions while she studies all his sculptures. Just the sight of Ava's hair summons memories of Laura. How she used to bite an apple up and down instead of sideways. The smell of her in spring after jogging in the rain. He starts to cry without a sound, feeling nothing in particular, the symptom too familiar to conceal or make a fuss about. It passes just as quickly but it wearies him tremendously. He lets her walk ahead and tries recovering his breath.

Ava leaves him to his thoughts and gets a wave of déjà vu that's difficult to clarify, a memory of having some memory before. She stops before an evergreen toppled by the wind, horizontal but supported at an angle by an oak. There's a woman on her back. She's naked and supine, semi-arched with her stomach and her knees rising up. Her ankles are together, ten toes in a row, and her wrists cross high above her head as if they're bound. She's luxuriant and warm, stretching in her sleep, in the contour of someone in surrender to a dream. A giant wingtip is covering her eyes like a hand. A second wing folds around the middle of her waist, holding her secure and covering her navel. All around her, by the hundreds, lie the shavings of a wood plane, each of them a fine white feather in the leaves.

Ava holds a hand to the bottom of her stomach, breathing through her mouth and following the swell. When the breeze soughs up, it's downy and caressing, softening her hair and moving through her dress. Rain begins to patter on the highest of the leaves; they can hear it, like static, long before it lands. Lightning flickers in the shade and there's a thunderclap, close. She picks a shaving up and keeps it when they start back out.

The woods have darkened imperceptibly and suddenly it's cold. The quicker pace enlivens them, dispelling what they saw. Sam is clearer now, approachable—a sculptor, nothing more. For a while there, he might have been a shadow or a ghost.

"What are you doing out here?" Ava asks, over-bright.

Sam continues on beside her, neither tensing nor exhaling.

"I mean, it's wonderful," she says. "But with the cabin now it's . . ."

"Strange."

She's surprised to hear him speak the very word that she was thinking.

"Henry's worried," Ava says. "So are Nan and Joan."

"And you?" he asks, turning and impossible to gauge.

"I don't know you."

Sam smiles. Ava wonders what it means.

They reach the cabin right before the storm opens up. Wing's in a corner, hiding from the thunder. He's relieved to see them back and greets them with a wag, but his fear's too instinctual to meet them at the door.

"This ought to be interesting," Sam says, looking at the rafters. "There hasn't been a serious rain since I finished the roof."

He lights a kerosene lantern and the room comes alive, shapes overlapping on the firelit walls. The table's in the middle with a set of plastic chairs, but aside from his chest of supplies the place remains unfurnished, comfortable but lacking any quality of home. Another great bolt brightens up the clearing and the rain falls strong, blowing in the door. Ava looks for Henry but he isn't in the clearing so she settles on her heels, reassuring Wing.

"How long were you married?" Ava asks.

"Three years," Sam says. "We were together five. It feels like less."

"Henry and I have been together twenty. It feels like more."

"That's good."

"It depends on which year we're talking about," she says with a smile. "Why do you think it felt shorter with Laura?"

He pauses at the door, looking at the rain, and holds the lantern overhead to reassess the ceiling.

"We were apart a lot of the time," Sam says. "She worked nights. I was sculpting. In the last year, we were probably together, I don't know . . . an hour a day? Even less sometimes. Neither of us liked it. But you form certain habits . . ."

He stops what he's saying when he notices a leak. It's minor but it hisses on the lantern glass. He puts an old paper cup underneath it on the floor, missing five or six drips before aligning it correctly. It's comical, she thinks, because the door is standing open and the floor around the entryway is positively soaked.

Henry appears in the distance, striding through the mud, blurry in the storm with an armload of wood. Thunder cracks, zero Mississippis from the flash, but when Ava calls him in, he doesn't hear and carries on.

Sam joins her at the door to watch him in the clearing and they're misted by the rain, arms pressed together, following his shape until he lumbers out of sight.

"How serious is Henry's heart condition?" he asks.

"Serious enough."

"I lied to you," he says.

"Lied about what?"

"About the cabin. He's been helping all along."

Water gusts in and Ava shuts the door. "Doing what?"

Sam sits but isn't comfortable; he fidgets in the chair.

"Everything," he says, muffled by the rain. "Cutting trees, hauling logs. Lifting them in place."

Ava paces with the table like a barrier between them.

"You knew about his heart?"

"He told me it was nothing. I took him at his word," Sam says. "But when he asked me not to tell you . . ."

She forgets about the cup and kicks it over with a pop, most of what was in it splashing on her shoe. When she bends to pick it up, the cold leak dribbles on her neck. Then she can't reposition it no matter what she tries. Sam observes her—that's the word—as if afraid to intervene, and Ava notices her dress is clinging to her breasts. She tries to fluff it loose but then she really doesn't care, facing Sam and swelling up, daring him to look.

"It's not your fault. You didn't know," she says. "I'm glad you told me."

"Let me get him . . ."

"Let him finish," Ava says.

Henry stumbles to his knee with the last load of wood. The moisture in the air makes him feel as if he's drowning. It's astonishing humidity, a swamp of steamy air. He breathes as deeply as he can but the pressure's overwhelming and he sways, and his vision turns to particles and fuzz. He can't see the cabin and the sky feels low, right above the leaves and smothering him down. Then a breeze lifts up, freshening his skin, and the world comes clear after several hazy minutes. He decides he ought to eat and tromps across the clearing.

The thunderstorm's passed. It's more impressive at a distance, charcoal and guttural and burly through the trees, and only now do the flickers of the lightning make him nervous. He can see Sam and Ava in the cabin setting lunch. Wing wriggles at the door; he isn't sure it's safe yet but can't bear to wait, so he runs full tilt and almost knocks Henry down. They grapple in the mud, man and dog reunited.

"I'm all right," he says to Wing, who can tell something's off.

Henry strides in, showing off the mess, but his smile falls apart when Ava turns around.

"Oh!" she says, deflecting his embrace with a palm. She notices that Wing is muddying her dress, pushes him away, and says, "Look at the *floor*."

"Ah, shit," Henry says. "Sorry, Sam. I'll clean it up."

"It's a cabin." Sam shrugs. "Come inside."

Ava bristles.

"Nan'll get that out," Henry says about her dress.

"*I'll* get it out," she says, handing him a sandwich.

Sam sits and eats potato chips, tipping in his chair. Ava opens all the windows, desperate for the air, and pretty soon they're being bitten by a swarm of fresh mosquitoes.

"What I say about the sculptures?" Henry asks through bologna. "Especially the lady with the wings. That's my favorite. Not exactly my type of woman," he adds, patting Ava's thigh. "I'm more of a meat-and-potatoes man myself."

She puts her sandwich down.

"You ought to use Ava as a model sometime."

Sam eats a chip, leaning farther in his chair, staring at her face as if to honestly consider it. They all go back to eating in silence until Henry finishes up, gives the last bite to Wing, and starts talking nonstop about Nan and Ava's garden, Joan's puzzles, anything that zips through his head. He comes around to Bob Carmichael at the supermarket again, mentioning the boys and the bicycle rule.

"It's different now," Ava says. "Parents worry about abductions."

"I never got abducted."

"Maybe no one wanted you."

"I'll do the tree house," Sam announces.

Henry gets a rush—even Wingnut stands—but it's Ava who's the most transformed by the news. She looks sunlit and full, gazing privately at Sam, seeming prouder of his help than Henry's offer to build the tree house in the first place.

Henry thanks Sam repeatedly and asks about lumber,

screws, table saws, nails—Billy Kane knows tools, maybe he could help them out. Sam reminds him that Billy's real house is structurally questionable and that the Kanes, by and large, are better left avoided. If they need an extra hand, they can always use Bob. They agree to buy supplies tomorrow afternoon and have them ready for construction right away on Saturday morning.

Ava yawns through a stretch and says they ought to go. She took the day off from work to get a handle on the house and here she is, lounging over lunch and listening to tree-house plans. She's vague when Henry asks about her housework, and when he asks a second time, her expression's all the answer that he's willing to pursue.

They say goodbye—Sam and Ava share a look that Henry can't interpret—and after finalizing a time to meet at the lumberyard, they follow Wing's lead along the trail toward the car. Cold water dribbles on their heads from the branches and it's difficult to walk without slipping in the tire grooves. They concentrate and Henry tries supporting Ava's arm. She pushes him away, walking in a puddle and reacting like he put her off balance with his help. He notices her cleavage, made apparent by the rain, and wishes she would brighten up and lead him off the trail again.

"Is everything okay?"

"Yes."

"You sure?"

"Yes."

"I didn't do something wrong?"

She looks at him and stops.

"I know about the cabin."

Henry sinks, really sinks, several inches in the mud. He moves his foot. It makes a slurping sound, futile and revolting. With the lunches and the tree house, the easy conversation, he's been thinking more and more that Sam was like a friend.

"I can't believe he told you . . ."

"He was worried," Ava says, speaking through her teeth.

"He needed help," Henry pleads. "I burned his house down, Av. Then he wants to build another one and I'm supposed to tell him . . ."

"But you should have told me."

"I knew you wouldn't let me! Don't you see . . ."

Yes, she does.

"You could have killed yourself," she says. "Where would that have left Sam? Where would that have left *me*?"

Nan and Joan notice the unnatural silence between Henry and Ava, each of whom makes plenty of noise doing chores and it's precisely those sounds—clinked cups, the rustle of a trash bag—that makes the lack of talk so apparent. Dinnertime's efficient. Henry eats politely, chewing each bite and dabbing with his napkin, and it's Ava eating briskly, finishing her meal and clearing plates and making coffee while the rest of them remain bolted to their chairs. Wing walks around the room, cowering and yawning. Nan rubs him on the head, eliciting a wag, but then he's teary from his yawns and too alert to settle down.

The Finns agree without a word to say good night at seven o'clock. They miss their shows and spend the evening in their room reading magazines, very like the nights following the fire.

Joan's been so preoccupied with puzzles in the living room, she's scarcely given thought to her beloved figurines.

She got her first when she was eight, an ivory turtle from her mother, and collected them religiously for seventy-two years. Animals and trees, Virgin Marys and the saints—they were a constant in her life, from her childhood home to various apartments in adulthood, throughout her long career at the paper factory, her double hip replacement and recovery, retirement and spinsterhood, the last ten years of living with her sister. None of them survived, not a single figurine. Henry got her three from a vendor at the mall: a sphinx, a tree, a Cupid he had told her was an angel. Now she holds the little tree and tries remembering the others, staring at the drab medallion pattern on the wall. Her eyes begin to well. The medallions start to blur. She hides behind her magazine and waits for it to pass and then she eases into bed and says her prayers next to Nan. The words are older than her life but still surprising, still a riddle. It's the mysteries themselves she finds reliable and soothing.

Nan stays awake until her sister falls asleep. She expected Joan to cry and wonders why she didn't—what it means and what to do with all her unspent care. The room is stifling but she shivers, feeling feverishly chilled. She pulls the bedspread up, hands beneath her chin, remembering the homemade quilt she used to have, each square its own design from cornucopias to wrens. She thinks of one particular square, an evergreen she sewed the day after Christmas, 1985, the year their father died of cancer. She cries a little while, softly as she can, covering her face so she doesn't wake Joan.

In the morning after Ava leaves for work and Henry's out with Sam, Nan leads Wingnut into the living room where Joan is at the table, humpbacked and focused, working on her latest thousand-piece puzzle. It's the ceiling of the Sistine Chapel prior to restoration, murky brown and difficult to see, with none of the vibrant color Michelangelo intended. Joan prefers it this way, the sameness of the tones more a master-class challenge. She has the border and a number of the lesser-known figures: Amon and Manasseh, Judith carrying a head.

"We never got to Rome," Nan says, sitting down. They had talked about it often, visiting the Vatican, touring through the ruins and museums and cathedrals.

"Mmm," Joan says.

"Centuries of candle soot," Nan continues, fingering a piece: a little tan elbow, maybe one of God's. "Remember when they cleaned it? People were afraid it wouldn't be the same."

"I'm looking for a baby leg."

"It's time for us to go."

Joan takes a long, broad survey of the table, then emerges after hours in her own private chapel.

"Where are we going?"

"We need a place to live."

"Did Ava say something?"

"No."

"Henry . . ."

"It's been two months," Nan says. "We've looked at seventeen houses."

"None of them were right."

"None of them were home. You're doing puzzles every day in someone else's living room. I'm gardening in someone else's yard," Nan says.

Joan's body doesn't move but the table has a quiver. Nan steadies it and says:

"They need their house back. They're too young to have a pair of old ladies underfoot."

"Where do we go?" Joan asks, teary in alarm. "Should we go to the Days Inn? Do we have to leave today?"

Nan holds her hand and smoothes the wrinkles of her knuckles, softening her posture and the color of her voice. "Take a breath," she almost whispers. "We're doing this together."

Joan dutifully inhales, growing dizzy from the air.

"All I'm saying"—Nan sighs—"is that we have to take it seriously. It's time to put our life back together, even if it's different."

She kisses her and leaves her on her own to think it through.

Wingnut settles on the tips of Joan's feet. She wouldn't dream of getting up or moving him away. She looks around the room at all her finished puzzles. Henry's framed every one and hung them on the walls, and with her table, and her tea, and her music on the radio, the room belongs to her and no one ever claims it. She's caught herself imagining a different shade of paint, brighter eggshell, closer to her living room at home.

She connects a bare foot—the foot of the Delphic sibyl—and sifts around the table for the body and the robe. The sibyl looks familiar when she's finally put together. It's Ava, Joan thinks, beautiful and strong, healthy in her youth, with a luminous expression. Lips parted with a breath, all the rest of her in motion. She hasn't seen Ava this summer in weeks.

She holds another piece, airy as a wafer. When it clicks into place she feels a flutter of delight, still surprised when a pair of odd shapes interlink. She thinks of challenges ahead: Easter Island, Norman Rockwell, never-ending beaches, and the surface of the moon. She finds herself envisioning a brand-new room, permanently hers, any color she decides. They could host Thanksgiving with the Coopers, maybe Sam. She could decorate every last wall with a puzzle.

16

Sam and Henry arrive in a rental truck at 8:57 a.m. and Bob, Danny, and Ethan meet them at the curb, the boys light of foot, their father antsy but at least superficially enthused. They've been parked around the corner for the last half hour, waiting for Peg to drive away and clear the coast, and all five conspirators are mindful of the challenges ahead, especially once they start unloading the truck and all the lumber starts mounting in the grass.

The yard is long and narrow, chain-link-fenced, meticulously mowed and thoroughly boring, with a couple of lilac shrubs and a flower bed of wilted marigolds. There's a bare patch of dirt where the swing set had been and a Japanese beetle trap every twenty feet. Henry sets the table saw under the tree, an egg-shaped maple with a straight, thick trunk, and after running an extension cord across the lawn, he stands back, admiring the two-by-sixes, two-by-fours, plywood, decking, nails, screws, hammers, saws, and drills they've strewn around the whole back section of the yard.

"This is a tree house, right?" Bob says, finally grasping that even with Sam and Henry working full bore, construction's liable to take longer than the weekend. "How can I help?" he asks, and though the boys are of a similar mind, eager to grab a board and start hammering, Henry won't allow it.

"This is my gift to you. *Our* gift," he hastens to correct, looking around for Sam. "I don't want any Carmichaels getting so much as a splinter until it's done. Pull up a chair and watch us work."

Sam disagrees—it'd be good for Danny and Ethan—but he keeps it to himself and maybe Henry's right. If there was a little injury, even just a splinter, they'd be equally responsible explaining it to Peg. It's bad enough already, simply being here to help. Sam regretted volunteering from the moment he committed. He was quiet when they drove to rent the tools and buy the lumber, waiting to explain—as if he could—the reason he had broken Henry's trust about the cabin. Only Henry didn't ask; he was upbeat as ever. Either Ava had forgiven him or what? Who could say.

Sam lingers out front, having gone to get the last box of tools and finding, after the hubbub of showing up and leaping into action, his first real chance to soak it all in. He had met Bob's eye and taken his condolences, and yet before the handshake had gotten too warm, before Danny and Ethan were required to say something nice, he found a practical excuse and walked toward the truck.

Now he turns and sees the compost pile in the distance, right beside the trailer where he's learned to overlook it. He remembers how it was—leaves that he and Laura had piled over watermelon rinds, coffee grounds peppering banana peels and eggshells. Apple cores. Sawdust. Jack-o'-lantern. Grass. There were parts of every meal they had eaten last summer and the mound had been enormous, colorful and loose. It had all turned to rich black soil in the spring, smaller than a tenth of its original material. Laura would have spread it in the garden with her hands.

"How do you start the saw?" Henry hollers from the yard. "Whup, there it is! Never mind . . . never mind!"

Sam listens to the sounds—power saw whizzing in the open air, a tinny radio. He thinks of dropping everything and walking to the cabin. Then he hears Danny's voice calling out his name.

They start by measuring, cutting, and organizing platform beams while Bob and the boys play Wiffle ball. Ethan hits a line drive off the top of Henry's head and everybody laughs, most of all Henry. They build the platform six feet off the ground using ladders, safety ropes, and hex screws, a crosshatch of planks fastened to the trunk. They cut support beams and fasten them securely at the corners, and the Carmichaels watch when Henry stomps around the edges, testing every inch with absolute faith in Sam's abilities. It's late morning by the time they've decked the floor and gotten Danny and Ethan up to have a look—no walls or roof yet, but a platform with a view—and they're up there still when Peg explodes out the back screen door.

"What the hell is this?!"

She's wearing heels and hasn't put her portfolio down, having walked through the house, seen Henry in the yard, and marched straight out in one brisk motion from the car. She doesn't stop until she's right in front of Henry, who stumbles backward over the two-by-fours, landing on the wood with his sneakers off the ground.

She sees the lumber, the platform, her sons overhead, Bob with a Wiffle bat and Sam with a drill, unable to parse it all and focusing on Henry.

"I'm calling the police. This is trespassing. This is

harassment. Get down," she says to Danny and Ethan. "Did he touch you? Did he touch you?"

"I said it was okay," Bob says, barely audible but shocking her anew, and then she goes to work on him, gesticulating so wildly that most of her portfolio scatters on the ground. Bob holds the bat feebly in defense.

Henry's on his back, dark red, almost crying—is he crying? No, but terribly familiar in his fear. Peg snaps her papers up, squatting in the grass with her slacks stretched tight along the furrow of her buttocks.

"Get down!" she tells the boys, angry they've defied her.

"No one's steadying the ladder," Ethan says.

"I don't *care*."

Bob holds the ladder till the boys reach the ground.

Sam breathes through his nose, helps Henry off the wood, and picks a paper off the ground, handing it to Peg.

His being there confuses her and forces her to focus.

"Sam," she says, almost like an answer to a question.

"This was my idea," he says.

"What idea? What?"

She blows away her bangs except they tumble round her eyes again.

"The tree house," he tells her. "I wanted to do something nice for Danny and Ethan."

She watches him but never stops grasping at the ground. He'd like to chuck the folder like a Frisbee at the tree. Instead he helps her finish and says, "Come on, let's talk a little closer to the house," guiding her over by the elbow and trying not to squeeze.

"I'm sorry," Sam says. "I should have let you know."

"You're goddamn right." She struggles for composure.

He can see it's quite a battle by the sharpness of her pupils
and the count, one to five, she takes to calm herself down.
"I don't understand."

"It was an impulse," he says. "I've been thinking about
your boys. How the fire must have scared them."

Yes, you're right. Peg nods. "I had to make a rule: no
more talk about the fire. It isn't healthy, dwelling on something negative for weeks on end. My college roommate's a
psychologist now, she told me the same thing. We've been
trying to redirect them."

"Exactly," Sam says. "Give them something fun, something built instead of burned. I'm pretty good with wood
and thought, What about a tree house?"

"I appreciate the concern, I really do . . ."

"Peg," he says, lowering his voice. "I want to be honest
here."

"Okay?"

"I meant what I said, about doing this for them. But I'm
also doing this for me. I haven't been myself. The fire's all I
think about. I thought if I could build this tree house, if I
could force myself to be around people for a change . . ."

He clenches both eyes until it looks like tears.

"Sam . . ."

"You've been so good to Nan and Joan, helping them
find a new place. We've all pulled together," he says. "Now
it's my turn. We were a neighborhood. A real community.
I know you can appreciate that."

"I'll be honest, too," Peg says, drawing herself together
like a proper truth-teller. "I don't think it's safe."

"Oh," he says dismissively. "This is what I do. They'll
be safer up there than in your actual house."

Peg blanks a few seconds, wobbly in the grass, until her heel sinks deeper in the lawn like a stake.

"Not with him," she insists.

"It has to be him," Sam whispers, sounding both weary and mysteriously wise. "Like it or not, Henry's part of this. Why do you think the Finns are letting him help? Listen, Peg," he says, moving in close. "I'm not saying you have to forgive him, but you see the way he is, how he's always showing up. If we let him do this, for you and me, for Danny and Ethan . . . this is everybody's chance to move forward. One tree house and we can all get on with our lives."

She gazes at him, sweating at the corners of her eyes. A heat bug's drone seems to issue from her head.

"How long?" she asks.

"Three days."

"That's what the siding people said."

"Trust me," Sam says.

"He doesn't speak to me. He doesn't come inside, not even for the bathroom. *Especially* not for the bathroom."

"He'll use the trailer. I appreciate this, Peg. If there's anything else that I can do . . ."

"No, you're doing enough," she says, sounding like she's giving him a break from obligation. "Danny, Ethan. I want you out of the yard. *Now.*"

Henry and Bob, unsure of where things stand, huddle arm to arm when no one gives them orders.

"You can stay," Peg announces to them both, sanctioning Henry and banishing Bob with one all-encompassing decree.

Sam smiles at the boys. They discreetly smile back.

As soon as Peg takes them in and shuts the door, Sam

says, "We're back in business," clapping his hands Henry-
style and grinning at the two men's amazement.

"What did you say to her?" Bob asks, looking at Sam
as if he's some kind of mystic.

"I appealed to her decency," he says, raising far more
questions than he answers, and it's only then, having tried
whatever he could to win her over, that he finds himself
believing everything he said.

hey hot stuf. tnx 4 lst nt. Sx pty sun.

Billy reads the text on Sheri's phone several times. All
he did was hear a chime and pick it off the table. Now he's
trembling in the heat, breathing shallower and shallower,
caught between a double urge to sit and walk around.

He sees her out the window, lying on her stomach in a
candy-red bikini with her top pulled off. *Hey hot stuf.* She
was late last night—ninety minutes, unexplained—and
she didn't say good morning when she shuffled to the yard.

"*Sx pty sun*"—*what the fuck*, Billy thinks, positioning
the phone exactly as he found it. He simply can't imagine
any safe interpretation, and the sender's name, South-
sider2005, is maddeningly definite and vague all at once.
The stubble of a stranger in a real backseat. Sheri's hand
on the zipper of a real pair of jeans.

He's been trying so hard since the night she got drunk.
He finished up the living room and rearranged the furniture, paid to get a Dumpster right away like she wanted.
He's been doing all the garbage, all the dishes, all the laundry, and he's never once expected her to thank him or acknowledge it. He calls her at the diner just to say hello. Buys
her wine. Buys her cookies. Gives her anything she wants.

He's been trying even harder than the year when they were dating and he can't just tell her he's been reading through her texts.

He takes her out a beer and pops it at her side.

She didn't hear him coming. "*Jesus*," Sheri says.

She peels her body off the lounge chair, cross-hatched pink, not the least bit rushed to grab her top and cover up.

"I brought you a beer," Billy says.

She flops back down and says, "Put it on the grass."

"Your phone made a noise."

"It's probably work."

"I think it was a text."

"I'll check it later," Sheri says.

They're interrupted by a power saw. He's heard it on and off today without a second thought, assuming it's the Carmichaels' latest renovations. Billy sees a man cutting lumber on a table. Before he registers the tree house or either of the kids, he tips the bottle with his knee and says: "Sam . . . what the hell?"

The saw quiets down just as Billy says it, and the one word—*hell*—carries on the air. Sam looks around, sees him crouching there, and nods, and then he's picking up a two-by-four, apparently too busy to walk across the lots and say hello. Another man waves more broadly from the tree.

"Holy shit. Is that—"

"Henry Cooper," Sheri says, muffled through a towel. "They've been there all morning."

"They're building a tree house? Peg's gonna flip."

"She already did. Sam calmed her down."

He tries to get his head around it—Cooper there at Peg's—and feels as if his skull is physically contracting.

Billy presses on the lounge until it buckles at the joint. Sheri lifts her head, squinty in the light.

"Honestly," he says. "This is totally insane."

"Right." She yawns. "What kind of monster does a nice thing for kids?"

"Gimme a break," Billy says. "*I* could have built those kids a tree house."

"But you didn't."

Billy looks at her and frowns, kneeling in the beer. He picks the bottle up. An ant waves faintly from the rim.

"I'll get you another one," he says.

"Why don't you bring *them* a couple beers while you're at it."

Every bone in Sheri's back disappears when she relaxes, like her body isn't real—like she's made of soft rubber. Billy holds the bottle, staring at her spine.

"Do you have to do this today?"

"What?"

"At least put your top on. They're right there. *He's* right there."

"Let him look," Sheri says. "You're standing in my sun."

He isn't but he steps back anyway, conscious of his shadow and distracted by its shape, how the edges seem bristly and distorted in the grass.

Billy goes inside, opens a beer of his own, and watches Henry Cooper out the upstairs window. He drinks until the power saw's buzzing in his ears, and when he finally hears Sheri clattering the screen, he slumps downstairs and meets her in the kitchen. She's standing at the table, closing up her phone.

"Who was it?"

"Mary-Kate."

She opens the fridge and pours herself a lemonade.

"What are we doing tomorrow?" Billy asks.

"Nothing. Why?"

"I thought you said we might be doing something."

"What?"

Billy shrugs. He glances at her phone, longer than he should, and yet he's stunned when Sheri notices and guesses what it means.

"You read my text?"

"What? No," he says, nasally and odd. "It was laying right there and made a noise. I couldn't help it."

"It's a flip phone, Billy."

"So?"

"You have to *flip it open*."

Sheri cocks a hip, waiting for an answer.

"I didn't know it was such a big deal. You're the one who's acting all sneaky."

"It was *Mary-Kate*," Sheri says. "I covered the end of her shift last night. She had a date."

"What's the party, then?"

Sheri folds her arms, still in her bikini, with her long bare feet planted on the floor.

"It's a Sox doubleheader. Mary-Kate's brother's having us over."

"I'm not watching baseball with a bunch of your work friends."

"'Us' is me and Mary-Kate."

"Is Jake going?" Billy asks.

Sheri skips a beat, honestly perplexed. "What do you care?"

"Think about that."

"What." Sheri coughs. "You're jealous of *Jake*?"

"You talk about him enough."

She holds a palm against the table, going squiggly at the knees, with her face so clenched it's like she's hurt instead of laughing.

"He's a sixty-year-old vet," Sheri says. "He hasn't cut his beard all year . . . he's like a pirate!"

Billy staggers there and snorts. "How was I supposed to know? You throw yourself at everyone except around here."

Sheri reddens and her face looks greasy from the sun. The temperature and beer start fizzing in his head.

"What is *that* supposed to mean?"

"Like the yard," Billy says. "Laying outside with Cooper leering over."

"Leering," Sheri says.

"I saw him out the window."

"Who cares?"

"Who cares?" Billy asks. "This place sucks because of him."

"What do you want from the guy?" Sheri yells. "He offered to help us out, you said no. Now it's bad he's helping other people?"

"You want him helping over here? I'll ask him right now."

She rolls her eyes until her head begins to swivel.

"Fine," he says. "Sprawl around naked all day."

"Well I didn't think he'd *rape* me."

Billy lunges at her chest. She bumps her head against the wall, limbs helter-skelter and her hair thrown messy at the edges of her face. She's slippery from the tanning oil, hard to get a handle on. Billy grabs a wrist, her other hand scratching at his arm until he catches that, too, and holds tight, pressed between her drawn-up legs when she squats. He tastes blood—he must have bitten his lip—and Sheri fights back, smelling dangerous and hot.

"You think he's so great," Billy says. "You think he's so great. Say it, why don't you say it?"

"Get the fuck off me. Asshole!"

"Say it."

Sheri grunts.

"Say it," Billy says. "You think he's so great."

"Stop . . ."

"I dare you to. I *dare* you to. You think I'm shit and he's so great, go on. Go on and say it. *Say it.*"

Sheri shakes her head with more defiance than he wants, so he bumps her own hands into her forehead and lets go, sitting on the floor and breathing through his mouth. The second Sheri's free, she covers him with slaps, a crazy burst he can't fend away until she scrambles over his shoulder, trying to escape. Billy hooks her foot and Sheri falls behind him, but after a few blind kicks to his ribs, he lets her go again and curls into a ball, grinding his knuckles into his eyes until the colors start swirling in the dark.

Sheri runs upstairs and slams the bedroom door. It's quiet outside: not a tool, not a bird. Billy sits with his heartbeat thrumming in his ears, thinking how her sunburn whitened when he grabbed her. He doesn't notice when she comes downstairs, doesn't even know she's left the bedroom until the front door clicks and Billy hears the car out front, peeling off and revving up the street.

•

Henry and Sam spend the better part of three days working in the Carmichaels' yard and finally, on Monday afternoon, Sam drives the last roofing nail and Henry helps
him out of the safety rope and into the finished tree house.
They sit knee to knee, sweating in the shade, in a room
with a maple tree rising up the center. It's true at every
joint, big enough for two boys and a chest full of weapons,
soda cans, and books, with plenty of space to lie about
and share an hour's worth of solitude.

Sam takes an overhead look at Laura's garden, where a
pumpkin vine has grown twenty feet unassisted. Her tomato plants have withered but her flowers have exploded—
foamflower, coral bell, peonies, and hostas. She brought
them home in April, trayfuls of pots with little tabs, and
when he helped her from the car, jogging back and forth,
they laid them in a pattern on the long kitchen table.
They'd been living in the house for almost a year, but it
was that particular morning something clicked and he
imagined they would live there forever, sharing holidays
and meals, airing out the rooms, pausing every spring with
a garden on the table.

Sam and Henry pass the only remaining Coke back and
forth, breathing in the fresh-cut fragrance of the lumber.
Before they get the boys, they take a minute to themselves
and for a second, just a second, Sam's perfectly content.

"I'm sorry I knocked you down," he says.

Henry stiffens up.

"When you first came around," Sam says, "I thought
you were trying to get yourself off the hook. Do some
work, make yourself feel better. It pissed me off. And then
you came back and I wanted to hurt you. I really did. But
not for the fire. I wanted to hurt you for apologizing."

Henry looks down. "I shouldn't have apologized?"

"I'm out there trying to make sense of what happened. Blaming fate, blaming the fire. Then you come along saying, 'Sorry, it was me.' You must have known what would happen. But you kept showing up."

Henry gazes at a cloud, so white it's faintly haloed. The soda can ticks and fizzes on the floor. "Can I ask you a personal question?"

"Sure," Sam says.

"How you holding up?"

Sam lays his hammer down without letting go. He leans against the wall, stretching out his legs, seemingly at ease but rigid as a plank. There's a tiny thread of sunlight coming from the wallboards, running like a crack down the middle of his face.

"I don't know," Sam says. "It's like an aftershock of aftershock. It's scary looking back and worse looking forward. Fifty more years of ordinary days."

Henry gazes at the grass through the open trapdoor, trying hard to empathize and feel it for a moment. Last night around three, he'd woken up and turned to Ava. She was sleeping on her side, face toward him on the pillow, and her head looked perfectly cocooned by her hair. He wasn't accustomed to the silence of the middle of the night, how his thoughts, made clear, had the quality of whispers. The crickets outside seemed near enough to touch but there was something in the lulls that went beyond the room, past the neighborhood and town and everything he knew, spreading like a great broad emptiness around him.

"You religious?" Henry asks.

"No," Sam says. "I don't know. How do you mean?"

"You think Laura's in heaven?"

"As opposed to where?"

"I didn't mean . . . of course she is," Henry says. "I just wanted to know . . . you know."

"If I believe it." Sam sighs, pulling into a crouch. "Even if that were real—whatever that'd be, heaven or souls and all that—I can't feel her anymore. It doesn't help me. The sculptures do," he adds. "All the work along the way. I get a lot more meaning out of doing it than finishing."

"I felt the same way about my route," Henry says. "It was good most days just shouldering the bag." He feels a subtle wave of vertigo, enough to shut his eyes, and an uncanny sense that the tree's started moving.

Sam drops the hammer through the door and takes the ladder. Henry follows him and doesn't feel secure until he's down.

The Carmichael boys hurry outside, bang-*bang* out the back screen door.

"Is it done?" Danny asks.

"Done!" Henry shouts.

Sam laughs at their expressions—saucer-eyed, panting, almost like Wingnut's face around food. They sprint away and scramble up the ladder, Ethan jumping onto the rungs and Danny climbing at his heels. Sam begins to wonder if they should have built it lower. But they make it up fine and shut the trapdoor, yelling and stomping around with more barbarian joy than Sam's ever seen from either one of them.

"Success," he declares.

He feels relieved and full of summer, clean sweat

prickling in his shirt, the smell of sunlight rising like a warm bloody nose. He thinks of bike-tire rubber, waffle-cone drips, the fragrance of a small backyard after dinner.

Bob saunters out and meets them on the lawn. He grins and shakes his head, enchanted by his sons, who spot him on the lawn and wave before ducking back down, keepers of the tree, perfectly at home.

"I always wanted one of those."

"It's strong enough to hold you, too," Sam says.

"That's good to know," Bob murmurs, nodding at the thought. "You guys ought to go into business. That thing's a work of art."

"You ought to see the cabin," Henry says. Then he pales.

"What cabin?" Bob asks, eyes widening and darting. "You don't mean . . ."

Sam sighs. "I've been keeping it a secret."

"Wait till Peg finds . . . *ah*. Well, she doesn't need to know." Bob straightens out his shirt and offers Sam a hand. "Thanks for this."

"You're welcome," Sam says.

Bob turns to Henry, who refuses to be thanked.

"Not a word!" he says to Bob. "It's the least that I could do."

"Did the boys says thanks?"

The three of them pause to look at the tree, where the unspoken gratitude is wonderfully apparent.

"Listen, Henry," Bob says. "The way Peg's been acting— don't take it personally. There's sides of her I married, sides of her I'm married to. She has her own moral compass and it doesn't . . ." Here he pauses, taking time as if to see the tiny compass in his mind. "She's a good woman," he says. "Good people make mistakes."

He and Sam look at Henry, who accepts it with a nod.
Bob remembers something else and perks back up.
"Peg just called. Nan and Joan pulled the trigger."
"Holy smoke," Henry says.
Sam stares across the lots.

17

Ava moves the Finns' new table again, just a few more inches to the left with her hip, before deciding it was better as it was. She has a bag full of spice—cinnamon, oregano, rosemary, ginger—and readjusts her grip so she can pull the table back. It was Henry who had pointed out the humor of it all, Ava's fussiness in rearranging someone else's home. He's said it more than once, right in front of Nan, and she's been conscious and embarrassed of the fact ever since.

Nan carries a tray of silverware into the kitchen, with its bleached sink, avocado fridge, bare countertop, and this—the table Sam built them as a housewarming gift, complete with two straight-back chairs that fit the Finns' posture to a T. Joan cried when Sam and Henry unexpectedly revealed them, and even Nan grew tearful after weeks of practicalities and paperwork and *paperwork*. They can make a new home from a table like this, organize the kitchen in relation to its placement and from there . . . well, from there, the whole house will come together.

Wing hurries through the kitchen, clattering his nails.

"Slow it down!" Ava scolds, speeding him along.

He's come from out front, weaving through a maze of

cardboard boxes and dashing into the yard, one of many
paths of action he's been trying all day. He's sniffed his
way around the bedroom, bathroom, living room, and
dining room, thrilled by the newness of the house and by
the constant activity of Henry, Ava, Nan, Joan, and Sam
moving furniture and boxes from the truck—a truck with
a *ramp* that he can scamper up and down. He looks around
the yard and trots back in as if the thrill of going out were
all he really wanted.

Nan fills a water dish, inordinately pleased with the
pressure of the stream. She turns the spigot once more,
just to hear the hiss.

"Oh . . . ," Ava says—she wants to say *shit*. "I forgot the
nutmeg."

"I'll put it on the list," Nan says.

"I *had* it on the list. I should run back out."

"I can see the story now. *Two elderly sisters were abandoned this weekend without nutmeg.*"

Ava grabs her in a hug, too impulsively for Nan to see it
coming, but it's Ava who's surprised and off-balance when
they separate.

"I'll help you with your garden next spring."

"I mapped it out last night," Nan says. "I'm growing
red bell peppers just for you."

"I hate that we gardened all summer and now you're
here with an empty yard."

"Tabula rasa."

"Terra firma," Sam says, easing in behind them.

He lays a box on the table, squaring up the corner like
it's staying there for good, and easy as that, the table itself
looks faultlessly arranged. Ava smiles at him, standing with
his handmade gift. He's done the lion's share of lifting for

the sake of Henry's heart but looks as ready to assist as if he's only just arrived.

Ava worries what'll happen when he learns the secret news—such a coincidence, in the very week the Finns are moving out, that she can't stop trying to interpret it as fate.

"Coming through!" Henry yells.

He bumps a box through the door and shoves it on the counter, knocking all the spice jars askew. A bottle of vanilla extract shatters on the floor.

"Whoops, what I hit?" he says, stricken by the sound. He sees the wreckage underfoot and says, "My mistake, I'll get it. Give me the paper towels."

Sam tosses him a roll and Henry squats, bumping Ava with his head and smearing extract with no apparent notice of the glass.

"At least it smells good!" he says, tossing a dark wad of towels into the pure-white sink. "Hey, I'm bleeding."

Henry rinses at the faucet, sure he's cleaned it up. Ava grips the towel roll and kneels to do it right.

"Watch your fingers," Sam says, right beside her ear.

He's holding out a dustpan, breathing at her cheek. She sees him indistinctly through the curtain of her hair. Before she has a chance to say thanks, Sam spots Wing coming from the yard and heads him off before he runs through the spill, catching his collar and standing there backlit and tall inside the door.

"I'm okay," Henry says, almost trampling on her hand and squeezing a towel—an actual towel they bought for the house—onto his cut.

"I'll go around front and check on Joan," Sam says.

Ava sweeps glass into the pan, the odor of vanilla cloying in her nose, and when she turns to look at Sam he's already gone, the door is full of sky, and Henry scrapes the table right against the wall.

Joan lingers on the sidewalk, persuaded by a whisper. She's heard it before, often at night and right before sleep: a still small voice, more a cipher than a word—a reminder that a person or a thing needs attention. The neighborhood's quiet, an avenue of bungalows and tall silver maples, and it's not until Sam and Wingnut come around front that she remembers when the Baileys, just last year, moved into their own new house and stood outside admiring the leaves.

"You missed the christening," Sam says. "Henry broke a bottle of vanilla."

"I've been thinking it's a miracle how much is still intact."

"So here you are, home at last. How do you feel?"

"Ready," Joan says, the firmness of her voice drawing his attention. "What about you?"

"I'm beat," Sam says, stretching out his arms. "You have a lot of heavy stuff for people who lost everything."

"Will you teach again?" she asks.

He holds his wrist behind his back and stretches out his shoulders. His vertebrae crackle when he pulls himself taut and then he seems to loosen up and looks around the block.

"I'm taking the school year off. All I need are groceries. I don't even have a water bill. But listen," he says, giving her a Peg Carmichael smile. "This is *your* big day."

Joan stands in admiration of her new front porch.

Three doors down, a family named the Mitchells files into their car. They introduced themselves today, a portly couple in their thirties with a pair of skinny daughters that remind her of them—Nan and Joan—when they were girls. They wave to her again and Joan waves back, having missed the sight of children in the last few months.

"There was one afternoon," she says to Sam, turning back. "Nan sat down and said we had to go. We were comfortable. We could have kept looking all year. But we had to get a house, and it wasn't just for us. We were burdening the Coopers and they wouldn't dream of telling us."

"You shouldn't think that," he says. "They were happy to help."

Wing stands beside her and she bends to pet his ear, grinding at her hip and causing it to pop.

"The worst of it," she says, "is that I hadn't even noticed."

Joan looks at him and pauses, drawing out the thought.

"Eventually," she says, "you have to give them back their lives."

Sam's scalp ripples up, broadening his forehead. He squints as if the sun were glaring in his eyes.

"You think I'm burdening Henry and Ava?" he asks. "That's the opposite of what I'm doing out there. I even helped *him* when he had to build the tree house. I'm helping them today, lifting all the heavy boxes."

Joan frowns, standing up. Wing presses on her leg.

"I haven't asked for help since he offered," Sam insists. "I never ask for anything."

"Neither did we," Joan says, "once we all got used to the routine."

Now that no one's petting Wing, he moves to Sam for

more attention, where he wags unregarded and eventually sits, content to occupy the dead space between them. The earlier constriction has returned to Sam's shoulders and he stands with a hunch, refusing to respond. Joan's tired on her feet and eager, truth be told, to see them all away and share the kitchen with her sister.

"Thank you for today," she says. "It's always good to see you, Sam. We'll have you here for dinner once we're settled in."

"Mm," Sam says, staring down the street.

"I'd love to see your sculptures sometime."

She rubs him on the arm and leaves him on the grass. Wingnut's torn between staying outside and following Joan up the stairs, but he's spared the choice when Henry trots out and gives both Sam and Wing a hearty thump on the back. He's wearing sweatpants with the legs tucked into his socks and makes it work, by God. He really makes it work.

Henry breathes deep and exhales large, turning sober as the day Sam met him with the ax.

"We gotta talk about something."

"Please don't tell me that I ought to buy a house."

"No, it isn't that," Henry says. "Though you gotta admit, this is one sweet place they have here."

Sam pictures it enwreathed, swirling up flame.

"I got my route back," Henry says. "I start a week from Monday."

Sam expected something worse, at the very least surprising, but his stomach goes fluid and the curbside moves.

"That's great," he says. "Congratulations. Henry, that's . . . I'm glad, I really am. You deserve it."

"Yeah." Henry frowns. "I can still come out certain

nights after work, but it's gonna be more of a weekend deal from now on." He shakes his head, sighing at the trees. "I'm going to miss being out there every day. You and me," Henry mumbles. "Sam, listen . . ."

"So this is why everyone's inviting me to dinner."

"It isn't pity. That's the last thing it is. I know it's crazy but the last few months, working in the woods . . ." Henry stands up firm, trembling at the eyes. "You're a good friend. One of the best I ever had," he says. "I know it isn't mutual, but really, that's the truth of it."

Sam takes it in, scared to move a muscle, any possible reply rushing from his head. They wait until the words have a temporary glow. Finally Henry moves to circulate his arms, looking like he physically intends to clear the air.

"But like I said, I'll be seeing you a lot," Henry says. "We've got to prep the cabin if you want to spend the winter. Plus Wingnut'll miss you. He still hasn't forgiven us for building that tree house without him. And I'll tell you something else. Ava cares about you, too, so that's another shoulder you can call on. The important thing is staying positive. You're not alone, even when you are."

Sam can tell he wants to hug him, that's he actively resisting it. He wanders off the sidewalk and totters on the curb. The moving truck is cavernous and dark, and Sam realizes that the Finns have gone inside for good, where all that's left to do is cleaning and arranging.

There were boxes in the basement Laura never unpacked—things that they forgot about. He wonders what was in them. She's been with him all day, ghostly and alive. He recognized her writing on a box marked PLATES. From the bathroom he had sworn he heard her speaking outside, and when he walked out front to shake it from his mind, Ava smiled like he only just missed her by a second. They've behaved that way on and off throughout the day, as if an ongoing secret were unfolding all around him. *This is it*, Sam thinks. Pretty soon they'll say goodbye and even Laura's fleeting presence won't accompany him home.

18

The last Billy heard from Sheri, she was staying with Mary-Kate. She called once to see if he was home and hung up as soon as Billy answered; Mary-Kate's name was on the caller ID and when he tried calling back, the phone just rang. He figured she'd eventually settle down and listen to reason, and he wasn't prepared to return from work one afternoon and find the place emptied out.

She'd taken too many things to fit in her backseat and must have had help, someone with a truck or at least a second car. She didn't call after that, and when he went to Mary-Kate's apartment and the diner—painfully polite, only asking where she was—the owner of the diner told Billy to leave and Mary-Kate's brother met him at the door and threatened to kick his ass. He wondered if Sheri might be staying with the *brother*—countless men had crossed his mind over the weeks—but in the end, all he learned was that she'd quit her job and disappeared. He missed so many days of work looking around town he almost got fired from his own job, and when he comes home tonight, it's no surprise that the answering machine's 00 and the phone ID shows that nobody called.

Everything's exactly as he left it: takeout bags, empty

cans, Showtime on the television. There's a heap of Sheri's clothes on the living room floor, all of which he searched, some of which he tried on, drunk the night before, during a movie called *Penitentiary II*. He keeps discovering things she made off with. They had a single hairbrush: gone. She took the hangers that her clothes were on, a pillow off the bed, the silverware, the coffeemaker, every picture on the walls except the ones that feature Billy. She took a table lamp and now the bedroom has a dim, eerie corner after dark.

He's taken to sleeping on the couch, where the television flickers with a reassuring light. It crinkles when he sits on it now; there must be a can underneath the cushion. He opens a beer, flips around the channels, and finds Charlton Heston, dirty and enslaved, but he's disappointed when it's *Ben-Hur* and not *Planet of the Apes*. He leaves it on and has another beer, telling himself he'll clean the house after one more scene, but he ends up watching it for hours, and by the time they reach the Valley of the Lepers, he's drunk enough to take the story personally.

He falls asleep and wakes up foggy in the dark. He doesn't remembering turning the television off. When he clicks it back on, the empty doorways are sinister and black. He ties his shoes, grabs his keys, and drives around town. He thinks of going to the mall, but eventually and only partly on purpose, he finds himself at the Coopers' house and parks across the street.

The light inside is warmer than it ought to be, almost like they're using better lightbulbs. Much of the effect is one of neatness and simplicity, every window perfect as a picture frame, the creamy colors in the rooms accentuated by the houseplants, hardwood furniture, and drapes.

Especially the drapes, how they soften up the angles, cozier than blinds or ordinary shades. There's movement upstairs, a shadow in the glow, too quick for him to tell if it is Henry or his wife. He remembers Ava standing in her dress that day, satiny and clean, beautifully at ease. He opens the car and walks across the road. There's no one on the street, not a sound aside from crickets in the yards. He creeps around a hedge to an unlit window on the side and has a look.

It's a guest room with a double bed and a dresser. It must be where the Finns stayed—he heard they bought a house. He likes the dresser. Likes the wallpaper, too. He wonders how the carpet and the bedspread feel. The hall-way's lit and Billy has a view of the downstairs bathroom with a mirror less than twenty feet away. When he stands up straight, he sees the window in the mirror and the glass looks black as if he isn't really there.

Henry tells himself it's okay to wear boxers in the kitchen, okay to move the table out of the living room. It's fine that the Finns are way across town and fine—of course it is—that Sam's entirely alone out there. Same as last night, really, and the night before that, but when Henry's in the yard watching Wingnut pee, he can smell a hint of autumn and he really does wish Sam would get himself a house.

He's up for doing chores but Ava's always drifting into some new room, one minute upstairs, another in the base-ment, whipping up dust, brisk and unapproachable. He used to make her laugh without trying, mispronounc-ing words and giving his opinions, but tonight, when he rubber-bands a pair of her underwear, she snaps them off the floor and says he's killing the elastic.

He used to give her spanks—little pats, just for fun—but he hasn't had the gumption in a very long time.

I'm out of practice, Henry thinks, warming up his palms, and when she lumbers from the basement with the laundry in her arms, he stands aside, lets her pass, and spanks her in the doorway. It's more of a hip shot than he intends—his aim's rusty, too—and Ava jerks around.

"What was *that* for?"

He smiles and recoils. "Just kidding around."

She rolls her eyes right out of the kitchen, and she's already halfway up to the bedroom when he offers to carry the basket.

"I've got it," Ava says, militantly crisp, her derrière wondrous from the bottom of the stairs.

He follows her up, Wingnut shadowing his heels.

For one exhilarating day, Wing had had them all together. Then they just left and now the Finns aren't here. He doesn't remember eating but he's far too tired to complain, weary of foot and limp of tail and yawning with a whine. He'd like to sleep but can't relax, kept alert by Ava's busyness and Henry's aimless circuits through the house, and he's already forgotten that he heard an unfamiliar car outside, an engine and a door that electrified his fur.

Henry watches Ava pick through the laundry. She pats it back down, shakes her head, and steps away as if deciding what to fold is more than she can handle. Henry creeps up and starts to rub her neck. Ava jumps away, startling them both.

"Geez," he says, and laughs. "I'm not the Strangler."

Ava looks at him and frowns.

"What am I doing wrong?" he asks.

"Nothing." Ava sighs. "I'm just trying to get this done. We haven't changed the sheets in two weeks, I haven't showered. Just give me room," she says. "Down!"

Wing, so distracted by the long day's events, has violated protocol and jumped onto the bed. He leaps back down, belly to the floor, more startled by his gaffe than by the sharpness of the reprimand.

"Take your shower," Henry says. "I'll get out of your hair."

He and Wingnut retreat without looking back.

Down in the kitchen, they share a meatball hero and mull the atmosphere—a fall-fresh night in late summer, someone's chiminea up the block giving off a scent of wood smoke that makes them want to go outside, makes them want to snuggle up in bed.

"She needs a vacation," Henry says to Wing, who answers with a wag and earns another meatball.

Except she'll never agree to take one, Henry thinks, and even if she does, she'll spend the whole time cleaning. The next bite of food reminds him of the woods and all the days he and Sam had their lunches in the open.

"I'm a genius," he declares, drumming on the table.

Wing licks his chops and thoroughly agrees.

Ava's haggard and sore and nearly falls asleep standing in the shower. After the spic-and-span newness of the Finns' empty house, her own little realm feels woefully neglected. Gritty carpets, scuff marks, cobwebs swaying in the corners of the ceilings. But now that she's gotten the emergency vacuuming and laundry out of the way, she resigns herself to finishing tomorrow and surrenders to the water.

The summer's been a blood vessel swelling in her head. She takes her first rejuvenating sigh of the night and segues into a yawn. With the inrush of air, she can finally think clearly. Bed tonight, quiet morning, breakfast at the diner . . . then *nothing*. The weather's supposed to be sunny and warm. No one in the house, nowhere else to go. Sam, unprompted, asked Henry not to visit.

She towels off and rubs lotion on her knees, between her toes, and up her arms, smoothing out her skin. She has color in her face and the air has that miraculous warmth that feels soft, giving her body a lightness and a gracefulness she feels only once or twice a year, usually in spring when the cold slips off.

Henry's humming through the door, back from having eaten. They haven't made love in over a month, and even though the Finns hadn't strictly been a damper, she feels like they're alone without a parent in the house. He made an overture before—right there on the proverbial kitchen floor—and yet it's now, only now, she feels the tingle of the spank. She puts her nightgown on; it's billowy and long, enough to hide her shape and give her confidence to face him.

He's lying on the mattress, staring at the ceiling. Ava stands with her hip cocked against the doorway, one hand high along the frame, and when he sees her there in such an accidentally fetching pose, she's instantly aflutter from his absolute attention.

He rolls onto his elbow and says, "I have an idea."

She meets him on the bed and studies his expression.

"Why don't you take a vacation?" he asks. "God knows

you deserve it, looking after the Finns and putting up with
me. Grab a week and unwind before the summer's really
over."

Ava smooths her gown, showing off her legs.

"I can't just call in tomorrow," she says. "And then you're
back to work the following Monday."

"Take it then."

"Without you?"

"It isn't like I haven't been around all season. Get out
of the house and clear your head."

"Where would I go?" Ava laughs.

"I've been thinking about that," he says, sitting up. "Why
don't you spend the week at Sam's? He'll need the company
without me, and the two of you always find something to
talk about. Fill a cooler, sit in the sun. There's even a pond
out there."

She feels her feet against the carpet, heavy and immo-
bile. Henry watches her and lets her mull it over for a while.
By now she's gotten used to this and should have seen it
coming, but all his talk about enjoying herself, deserving a
week in the sun . . .

"Fine," she says.

"I just thought . . ."

"But not with Sam. He's not a little child. You can see
him all you want, but I'm about finished doing penance for
the fire."

Henry shies away, wary of her tone.

"You can shower," Ava says, standing up and walking
to the door. "I'll dry my hair downstairs."

"I don't mind waiting."

"We have two bathrooms again. We may as well use
them."

She leaves him there and finds the house sadly uninhab-
ited, amazed at how much life a pair of old women took
away. She wonders how they're doing, together in the clean
little house across town, Joan with a puzzle, Nan watching
television with a mug of mint tea. Then her thoughts turn
to Sam and the cabin and the trees. She imagines how it
looks with the lanterns all aglow—maybe, if he's brave,
with a fire in the clearing. Would he sit there alone, surrounded by the dark, and think of Laura and the Finns?
Does he ever think of her?

She sees the window of the guest room reflected in the
mirror. Even here, after dark, night presses in. The woods
are different in the daylight, though, with the warm smell
of pine and the sparkles in the water trickling from the
rock. There are chickadees and squirrels and the quiet
has depth. She moves the dryer in a swirl, pretending it's
the wind, and shuts her eyes when the air makes ripples in
her gown.

19

Ava surprises Sam when she arrives unannounced, carrying a cooler and a folding chair, and finds him in the middle of a thousand feet of grapevine. The vines are cut and tied and spread around the ground, like a complicated net, inside a clearing in the pines. There's a fresh-cut trunk inverted in the center and it's this he means to carve. She's interrupting everything.

He reaches for his shirt as if she's caught him in the bedroom, flustered by the sight of her and frowning at the vines. She hasn't seen him since the moving day, and even when he's calmer and she hastens to explain herself, he's hesitant to answer, like he's talking to a stranger.

"I can go," she says. "I should have let you know."

He steps around his work and says it's fine, not a problem. Ava can't decide if it's sincerity or manners, but she can't second-guess him now that he's accepted her. She situates her chair precisely where he tells her, in a corner in the sun where she won't be in the way. He doesn't mind the company but says he has to concentrate.

"I promise," Ava says. "I'll be quiet as a leaf."

She watches him in silence, looking down when her staring feels apparent, reading magazines and trying not to

fidget in her chair. An hour in, she shuts her eyes and relishes the sun. The pinkness through her lids feels enveloping
and womb-like. She listens to him hammering a chisel at the
trunk, but the mallet's made of rubber, not at all harsh, and
the softness of the blows complements her mood.

She moves her chair now and then, following the sun,
an inconvenience she enjoys because it keeps her half-
drowsy, half-alert, a perfect balance for a day she wants to
savor. A week like this could be a miniature summer and
she's happy to have come, happy to be with him.

"There's a big pool of sun over here," Sam says, pointing to a heavenly expanse near the sculpture.

The overturned trunk is five feet tall. Its roots splay wild
in profusion out the back, higher than the rest, dirty and
bizarre. What it looks like, really, is a full-sized tree that
someone's flipped so the bulk of it is buried in the ground.
Sam's cleared away the bark and started roughing out the
figure but it's early yet, genderless and mostly undefined.

Ava puts her chair just beyond the chippings, drinking
seltzer from a can and smiling at the fizz. She likes to see
him work and tries predicting what he'll cut, what exactly
he'll remove with each little tap. His boots are worn, his
T-shirt's ripped, and his jeans are like the sanding cloth he
uses on the curves. He needs a haircut, too—he hasn't gotten one since Laura was alive—and how would he react if
she suggested more deodorant?

He asks about Henry going back to work.

Ava saw him off earlier this morning—straightened his
shirt, fixed his hair, did her best to reassure him when his
nerves went awry. "I know it seems new," she told him at
the door, "but it's still the same job. *You're* the thing that's
changed. But you're ready. You're okay." And then she

walked him to his car and saw him on his way and she's been anxious ever since, despite her efforts to forget him.

She didn't tell Henry she was coming here today. She hadn't planned it. She'd intended to remain around the house, but the minute he was gone, she'd packed a bag and started off.

"I feel like a worried mom," she says. "I keep telling myself he needs to do it alone, but sending him off like that, looking so small after such a long summer . . . I can almost sympathize with Peg. I wouldn't let a child out of my sight."

Sam steps down and hones a chisel on a stone. "I'm surprised you don't have kids."

"We couldn't," Ava says. "It broke Henry's heart."

"Amazing. That's the last thing I would have expected of Henry."

"He had the highest sperm count the doctor ever saw," Ava tells him. "It was me."

She's been facing into the sun and when she looks at Sam he's pausing with the chisel, hard to see and more of an impression at her feet. He reminds her of a teenager, hesitant to speak. He is in fact younger—quite a lot, she remembers, possibly enough to view her as an aunt.

"I never would have guessed," he says. "You seem so fertile."

"I have breeding hips."

He laughs and says, "That isn't what I meant."

She puts a hand to her stomach, following a breath, picturing her body full of daffodils and fruit. He's sharpening the blade again. There's oil on the stone. He sweeps the chisel up and down with a swift, silky motion and it's slippery in his fingers, wonderfully controlled.

"Did you ever think of adopting?"

"We tried it with a pair of old sisters," Ava says. "What about you? Did you and Laura want a family?"

"Eventually," he says. "We were wait—"

He's cut his finger with the blade.

"Let me see," Ava says, coming off the chair. She kneels and takes his hand and says, "It isn't too bad."

"It's a little bad," he says, immediately faint.

"Tense your muscles. It'll raise your blood pressure."

"Really?"

"I'm a lab tech," she says. "I see it all the time. Here, keep squeezing it. I brought a first-aid kit."

He laughs at her preparedness but wobbles on his heels. Ava digs through her bag and finds the plastic box under the sunscreen. She takes a water bottle out of the cooler and pours it over the cut. Sam gets his first clear look at it and groans.

"You aren't tensing," Ava says.

The cut is relatively deep but the slit looks clean.

"Distract yourself," she tells him.

"How?"

"Talk about winter." Ava dries his finger with her shirt, holds tight, and says, "How are you preparing?"

"I don't know," Sam says.

He has an outhouse. She knows he has a mattress now, too, and a tank to run a sink . . .

"What about heat?"

"I'm ordering a woodstove."

"What about a cell phone?"

"Who would I call?"

"Us," Ava says.

She lets his finger go and dabs a little ointment on the

bandage, doing it by feel so she can keep Sam focused on her face. The dullness in his eyes interrupts her concentration. Ava drops the bandage; now she has to start again.

"What if there's a bear?"

"I can wrestle it," he whispers.

"What if skunks have a litter underneath your floor?"

His head begins to loll. Both her hands are occupied.

"*Sam*," Ava says, inches from his face. "What if you look in the mirror one day and you're a scraggy old hermit with a long dirty beard."

"Like Rip," he says.

"That's right. You're Rip Van Winkle waking from his nap. You'll stagger out one day and there'll be flying cars and microchips in everybody's head. You'll try to get a job and nobody will hire you. You'll walk around town and all the children will be scared of you. Everything that used to be familiar will have changed, and your only real choice, the only way to go, will be coming back here to live with all your statues."

She finishes the bandage and there's color in his face again. She gives him back his hand. He accepts it like a present.

"Have a drink," Ava says, handing him the water.

He finishes it down and dribbles on his chin.

"Thanks," Sam says.

"You're welcome." Ava smiles.

"I'm never good with blood."

"It's a specialty of mine."

He reaches for her shirt with awful fascination. Ava lets him pull it very gently from her skin. She watches him and wonders if she'll have to throw it out. Even Nan would have trouble cleaning this kind of stain.

•

In the late afternoon, Sam walks her out and carries her shoes; she likes going barefoot and doesn't want her soles dirtying her bag. Arcadia Street's abandoned when they exit the woods. Ava's timed it to the last half hour of the workday, the longest she can wait before the neighbors make it home. It's also one or two hours after Henry would have passed and they can see the day's mail at several of the houses.

Sam walks her to the curb and stands behind her at the car. Her hair is sweat-dried and loose, she's wearing one of his clean shirts, and when she leans in to situate the cooler on the seat, the bottoms of her feet are dirty as a kid's. Her face and arms look nourished by the sun but he can see the whiter skin just within her sleeve and smiles at her modesty, the way she sunbathed for hours fully dressed and now, going home, has a farmer's tan exactly like her husband.

"Tell Henry I'm thinking about him."

"I will," she says.

Ava starts the car and Sam shuts her door. She rolls the window down, bathing him with air-conditioned air.

"You can swim here, you know. There's a pond farther back."

"Henry mentioned that," she says. "Is it clean?"

"Clean enough. There's a lot of fresh water from the brook."

"I'll bring a bathing suit."

"Bring a few of those pepper sandwiches, too," he says. "I'm feeling dangerous."

"All right." She laughs. "Don't forget to change that bandage. And when you do, *look away*."

He watches her go until he can't hear the car and takes his time walking back, enjoying the solitude and the prospect of sausages over a fire. Evening birds appear—finches, jays, titmice, and woodpeckers—and back in the clearing, where the sunlight's long and marmalade warm, he notices a bright patch of leaves, high in the uppermost branches of a maple, that have already begun to redden with the season. He starts a fire first try, sips a beer, and plays the radio. Chipmunks skitter over leaves beneath the trees. He feels unusually at ease, no chatter in his head, and his muscles have the smooth, prickling warmth he's used to feeling after working with a chain saw. The woods sound the same way, sumptuous and peaceful, and his thoughts turn fluid in the calm, in the soft light glowing on the pines and in the music, very small, coming from his radio. It's a station Nan and Joan enjoy. He wonders if they're listening together in their kitchen. Ava must be home by now, washing her feet and opening the windows, and Henry's finished with his first day of work, undoubtedly relieved and probably boisterous, letting off a summer's worth of steam and clowning around with Wing.

Sam pictures them together, talking through their days, taking pleasure in the old predictability of dinner. He imagines it's the same kind of light around their yard, the very same birdsong filling up the rooms. He glances at his finger and the blood through the bandage. When he presses it, it stings. He presses it again.

He sees a rusty nail and thinks of Halloween, God knows why, and just as strangely it reminds of him of a sea-green bikini. Why a nail? Why this? It's always the same, the evening calm giving way to memories he won't be able to shake, a stupor that'll deepen till he wakes the following morning.

He throws his bottle at a tree, hoping it'll break, but it ricochets and lands unbroken at the roots. He wishes Ava hadn't made her joke about the skunks because he honestly considers it—he wouldn't know what to do. Fall's arriving any day. He can smell it right now. He hasn't prepped the cabin, hasn't gotten his supplies. Summer's curled away and he's afraid of what's to come.

Instead of slipping into a funk, he runs a couple laps around the clearing. Once his blood freshens up, he opens another beer and finds some country on the radio—newer stuff, poppier and brighter in its sound, not his usual thing but just the ticket right now. For the first time in months, he's looking forward to tomorrow. He can worry later on about the winter and the snow.

Wing goes berserk when Henry makes it home, yelping like a pup and nipping his hand after eight unexplained hours of abandonment. He's been staring out the window all afternoon and couldn't even tell you how many squirrels he saw, and now he trots ahead of Henry into the kitchen, eager to run outside, eager to eat, proud of his work on the business page and doubling back, breathless, to give his Dad another welcome-home pounce.

"All right, all right, I'm here," Henry says. "Atta boy, you're okay. You're okay," mussing Wing's head but troubled, once again, that Ava isn't home.

He left her here this morning in her bathrobe and slippers. They were almost out of coffee but she said to him specifically she wasn't going out—would he please pick some up? Which he did, along with aspirin and another tube of sunscreen, assuming she'd be resting in the yard all day.

And what a day, Henry thinks, moaning through a yawn. So many good, familiar faces on the route, people he hasn't seen in three or four months. The widow Mrs. Lansing, who colored her hair jet-black in the interim and looked pleased when Henry didn't recognize her. Old Ray and his cataract glasses, sitting in a lawn chair exactly as he'd been the day of the fire, greeting Henry with a wave as if they'd seen each other yesterday. Here and there, however, there'd been icier receptions. Becky the crossing guard, with whom he'd always shared early-morning comments on the weather, had given him a look as if he might be a danger to the children, and the Dobermans on Sycamore had barked more ferociously than usual.

In general, though, people had greeted him warmly, and Mr. Cousins had given him a free turkey sandwich at the deli, saying, "Good to have you back. We haven't had the mail before noon since you left." The job itself—sorting, driving the truck, remembering the idiosyncrasies of houses—returned to him at once, but it was all so habitual he kept having doubts, thinking he had skipped a block or mixed up letters.

During lunch, out of nowhere, he wanted a cigar; he threw his sandwich out and left as if the turkey were tobacco. When he finally reached Arcadia Street and started up the block, his chest became a brick and he was forced to take a breather. That was when he noticed Ava's car in front of Sam's. What a thrill to read the license plate and recognize the numbers—he assumed she'd come to bolster him and be a friendly face. Except she wasn't in the car and wasn't near the trailer and he stood awhile, hoping she and Sam would come and wave. But he couldn't cross the lot and certainly couldn't venture up the trail, and after finishing the block and waiting as long as he could, he left Arcadia a good deal lonelier and lower.

He takes his shoes off now and feels the cool white linoleum. Once Wing is done with the yard, Henry opens a can of Alpo, cleans the newspaper off the floor, and roams around the house, unsure of what to do. He hangs his uniform and wonders what they ought to have for dinner. Chicken cutlets in the fridge, asparagus and corn. Cooking's out of the question, much as he'd be willing. He could barbecue the chicken but he doesn't know a thing about seasoning, and while he's pretty sure asparagus and corn are both boiled, he doesn't want to risk doing something wrong. He spreads the food across the counter, along with a stick of butter, salt and pepper, and utensils. He shucks the corn and finds the little corn-shaped holders, rinses the asparagus, and preheats the grill. When he starts through the house to wait up front, Ava walks in before he's gotten to the door.

"You're home!" he shouts, and Wingnut's ballistic all over again, pressing up close and jumping on her legs. "I saw your car," Henry says. "I thought you said . . ."

"I changed my mind."

She has a cooler in one hand and a bag in the other, and she's clammy and disheveled and younger than he's seen her all season.

"Let me take that," he says, grabbing the cooler before she lets go and almost pulling her over. "You look great, look at that sunburn. Hey, you're wearing Sam's shirt," he says, noticing a small familiar rip along the shoulder.

She blows her bangs and Henry feels it.

"Mine was bloody," Ava says. "Sam cut his finger."

"How? What happened?"

"He's fine."

"Is it bad?"

"I handled it," she says.

Henry takes her bag and smacks her on the lips. She tastes like Spear-O-Mint and sun, Banana Boat and sweat.

"It went all right today?" she asks.

"Yeah, I gotta say, all things considered. It was weird to see your car! Wing pooped on the papers, he's been jumping out of his skin wondering where you were. You should have taken him along, he would have loved it."

He dumps her items on the couch. Ava's bag topples open. Wing tinkles on the rug, too excited to contain himself, and Ava doesn't notice till she's kneeling on the spot.

"Dinner's ready if you're hungry."

"Really?" Ava asks.

"Yeah, I laid it all out! The barbecue's on, everything's set to go," and when he shows her in the kitchen, proud of his array—what a breeze it'll be to whip it all together—he doesn't understand why she looks so deflated. Are you supposed to shuck the corn *after* it's been boiled?

Ava says, "You'll have to wait. I want to shower. I'm disgusting."

"No, you look great. But sure, go ahead. I don't mean to rush you. You want me to start boiling the water?"

"Leave it," Ava says. "Can you towel up the pee?"

"Wing peed? Where?"

"Never mind," she says, reaching for the cleaner under

the sink. "Why don't you watch the grill. I'll be down in fifteen minutes."

"Take your time," Henry says, frowning at the food, struggling to identify the part he got wrong.

She sprinkles powder on the rug and goes upstairs, where she shuts and locks the door in case Henry and Wing decide to follow her up and loiter. But she really is relieved he had a good day back. She should have left a note and hurried back to greet him, but he's obviously fine, even happy that she went.

She strips out of her clothes and sets the T-shirt aside so it doesn't get lost amid the other dirty laundry. Then she showers and a day's worth of forest rinses clean, drawing out the color in her face and arms and making her hair feel womanly again. She towels off and gets her bag, looking for the brush, and there's a folded piece of paper hidden in the bottom.

It's a handwritten note ("Sorry. Thanks. —S") wrapped around a pair of twenty-dollar bills: money for the shirt she ruined with his blood. She folds it back up and slips it into her purse, and then she roots around the corners of her underwear drawer, digging out the bathing suit she hasn't worn since the previous summer. It's wrinkly and a horrid shade of red, almost fuchsia, but she tries it on in front of the door-length mirror, smoothing at her tummy, tugging at the straps to elevate her boobs and twisting round to see . . . no, absolutely *not*. She takes it off and puts it away. She'll have to buy another. This time of year there's a good chance of clearance and the Walmart is open well before nine. She can stop along the way, hurry in, and try one on. Something cute, maybe blue. She even has the money.

20

Billy hears a car pull up, rare for this hour on a dead-end street, and goes to the window thinking it might be Sheri. He's in his boxers when he looks outside and sees a woman—Ava Cooper—walking from the street like she's heading for the beach. She's wearing sandals and a cover-up, semitransparent, over a powder-blue bathing suit and shorts. But there's style to her hair, enough to show some effort, and she doesn't look around like a stranger dropping in. Henry's back at work—Peg told him all about it—so she must be here alone. She must have been invited.

Billy presses on the screen, memorizing everything, especially when she passes and he sees her from behind. She walks around the trailer and continues into the trees and then she's gone, swallowed up by the darkness of the leaves. Maybe Sam's getting even. Maybe Ava got bored. He draws the blinds and takes his boxers off, actually in pain until he stretches on the bed and works it out. It's not enough.

He showers for the first time in two or three days. He combs his hair and splashes aftershave in several different places, anywhere his heat will activate the scent. The laundry isn't done but one of his polo shirts smells clean enough to wear, so he puts it on with jeans, adds a belt, and laces up his work boots.

He walks out back and heads toward the trail, cringing from the sun until he's made it to the cover of the trees. All he means to do is ramble out and say hello, and how can Sam resent it when he's talked to everyone else—everyone but him, who's tried to let him be. Ava will appreciate his neighborly concern. She'll offer him a soda and encourage him to stay. And if he comes upon the two of them together like he thinks, he can't be held responsible for anything he sees.

He steps as carefully as possible to minimize the noise. They might have wandered off at any point along the way; the trail could lead to nothing but the ATV. Whenever there's a gap, Billy listens more attentively, studying the ground and peering into the trees. Once he hears a bird that might have been her laugh, and when he stops to look around, turning three or four times, he can't remember which direction he was going when he stopped. He feels ridiculous and stupid getting lost on the trail, but then he seems to get his bearings and continues on his way. He's preoccupied with checking to the right and to the left, and he's amazed to look ahead and see a cabin in the sun.

How could nobody have known? Maybe everybody did know. Maybe *he's* the only person no one bothered telling. He's astonished by the thought that Henry helped him build it.

After waiting half a minute and deciding he's alone, he crosses to the door, knocks gently just in case, and opens it enough to have a reasonable peek. There's a chest and a table and a set of plastic chairs. He steps inside and finds a bookcase, partly full of books but also bottles, cans, and packages of nonperishable food. Lot of beans, lot of soup. Beer and jugs of water. There's a kerosene lantern hanging from a rafter, and a mattress and a pillow in a loft above the door.

He notices a small plastic bag behind a chair. He picks it up—it's from a drugstore—and studies the receipt. Hairclip, chewing gum, vitamins, conditioner. The hairclip's missing but the rest of it is here. He opens the conditioner and blots it on his hand, giving it a sniff before he rubs it into his skin. The chewing gum's open, several pieces gone. He peels the foil back, picks one out, and puts the rest of it away exactly as he found it.

After checking the windows and deciding that it's safe, he leaves the cabin, shuts the door, and wonders where to go. He chews the piece of gum and puts the wrapper in his pocket, wishing he had read the flavor on the package. Some kind of berry, probably a mix, so delicious that he swallows it and wishes there were more.

Ava made the mistake of bossing Sam around the second day, saying "Careful with the bag" after he had volunteered to carry it, along with the cooler, all the way back to her chair. He's been calling her the goddess ever since and Ava's taken to the name, accepting compliments and favors and behaving like a muse. Yesterday he struggled with the newest sculpture's leg—it was forced, too unnatural and crude above the ankle—and he finally had to ask her if she'd model for a minute. Ava held the pose, tilting forward on the chair, while he scrutinized her leg and told her how to flex. She's been glancing at her calf on and off ever since.

The sculpture is a maiden weaving on a loom. She's sitting on a block, leaning forward in a dress, delicately balanced on her fine white toes. Her body's spindly, not a bit like Ava's aside from the calf (and possibly the mouth; Ava's studied it and wondered), and her face wears a look of desperate concentration, focused on a loom Sam fashioned out of sticks.

The roots spreading open from the overturned trunk are growing from her back, right between the shoulders—four crooked limbs, spidery and wide. They're hideously jointed and appear to be in motion, and he's hung the web of grapevine everywhere behind her. It's an intricate design, interwoven from the trees, doubled by the great skein of shadow on the ground.

Ava stretches in the sun, admiring his work. She's enjoyed watching details emerge throughout the week, how the swells became the shoulders and the angles turned to elbows, and even though the roots have made it hideous and strange, it's gorgeous in its way and easily her favorite.

Sam fiddles with the web and stabilizes knots while Ava tells the anecdote, lovingly embroidered, of the day she met Henry in the middle of a china shop.

"An actual china shop?"

"More of a dinnerware store," Ava says. "I needed plates."

He was the youngest mailman she'd ever seen, without a mustache in those days and skinnier by twenty-five pounds. She paid him little mind when he walked into the store with a handful of letters, but he claims to have noticed Ava right away and lingered at the counter while he chatted up the owner. His laugh annoyed her first—she had thought the word *guffaw*—and when she turned and caught him staring, Henry waved instead of hiding. Ava, being gracious, felt compelled to wave back, and that was all it took for Henry to approach her.

He'd been a shortstop in high school and still had the walk—the bowlegged saunter of a player with a cup. Ava held a plate, pretending not to see him. He was handsome, she admitted, but his brashness put her off. In a moment of distraction, just before he spoke, she fumbled with her hands and bobbled the plate. Henry lunged to catch it and collided with her breast. She'd later accuse him of copping a feel—he never did deny it—but the grope was hardly noticed in the thousand-dollar crash. Henry's mailbag snagged along the corner of a table and a pyramid of china—yes, literally china—had collapsed upon itself and shattered into bits.

But he had caught the plate. He gave it back to her intact and his expression seemed to indicate that *she* had been to blame. He made her wait ten minutes while he settled with the owner, who liked Henry enough to let him pay the damages in interest-free installments. She was mortified, prepared to make the finest of apologies, but then he grinned at her and said, "I hope our second date's cheaper."

"And you dated after that?"

"No, of course not," Ava says. "He saw me one day a couple of weeks later and followed me home. Once he knew where I lived, he got my name out of the postal directory. He didn't call me but he followed me around, especially on the weekends. I'd see him at the movies and the market . . . he'd come to my favorite diner on Saturday morning. But he didn't try to hide it. Every time he saw me, he would wave and yell hello. Eventually I just got used to seeing him around. One day at the diner, I said we might as well share a booth if he planned to stare at me the whole time. He bought me breakfast. That was our first date."

She eats an ice-cream sandwich, nearly melted in the cooler. By the last few bites the cookie's soggy in her fingers. The trees look luxuriant, heavy with humidity and late-summer green, and there isn't a breeze so much as a lazy flow of air, syrupy and spreading in a sweet, amber glow.

"How did you and Laura meet?"

"She was working at the drugstore in town," Sam says, tightening another loose section of the vines. "Not in the pharmacy yet, only checkout. She was finishing her degree and I was still working toward my MFA."

"You were kids," Ava says.

"Yeah, we were," Sam agrees. "So I was standing in line behind an old woman with a folder full of soda coupons."

"I know that lady. There must be a thousand of her."

"Laura was at the register trying to explain why certain coupons didn't work with other discounts, and I found myself staring at her throat. There was something about it, maybe the collar of her shirt, maybe the little gold pendant she was wearing. It was summer, I don't know—she looked really good.

"And I kind of spaced out and suddenly the coupon lady wasn't there, and here's this girl at the register giving me a frown because I'm obviously ogling her and two or three people are behind me in the line. I said, 'I'm sorry, I'm a sculptor. I was studying your neck.' One of the customers groaned but Laura said, 'That's okay. I'm a model. I'm only working here to make sure they carry all my magazine covers.'

"So I hopped out of line and got a three-pack of soap. I paid at another register, went in the parking lot, and carved one of the bars into a rabbit like the pendant she was wearing. I wrote my name and number on the back of the receipt, wrapped it up with the rabbit in my shopping bag, and gave it to her at the register. I left before she opened it. She called me that night and asked me out. We had dinner a few nights later and I asked her what she thought about the soap. She said it dried her skin too much and that I ought to switch brands. I couldn't believe she'd *used* it. I thought she might have done it just to mess with me a bit. But later on it seemed sexy . . . really intimate, you know? She was playful like that, at least in the beginning. Everything was thrilling. Just a shower. Just dinner."

He leans along a vine until it tightens from his weight. She hears the creaking of the fibers, half believing it'll snap. He's a hundred miles off in the center of the web, distant in a way that makes her feel alone. She waits until he's sharp enough to tie another knot, and then she notices him wince and says, "How's your cut?"

"Little sore."

"Let me see."

"I'm right in the middle—"

"Stay," she says. "I'll come to you."

She peels her body off the chair, taking her first-aid kit out of her bag and ducking, stepping over, and limboing deftly through the vines.

"You didn't change your bandage last night."

"I forgot."

She takes an antiseptic wipe and a fresh Band-Aid out of the kit, and then she strips the old bandage off and tucks it into his pocket. The cut's healing nicely and it's more or less clean. She dabs it off, blows it dry, and wraps the finger up new, suddenly surprised by his nearness and his height. It's only when he's close that Ava feels petite, especially barefoot, with Sam fully dressed and taller in his boots. She's worn her bathing suit for much of the week, a modest one-piece, unrevealing as can be, but it's moments like these that she's aware of how exposed she is and equally aware of how natural it feels.

"How did *you* get covered in sawdust?" he asks, wiping off her shoulder.

"God, I *am* covered in sawdust. I'm going for a swim." She steps away and backs against a vine, and when she turns she meets another vine, straight across her thighs. When she's finally free and clear, she turns to him and says, "You should come, too. You have your own pond and never use it."

"No, go on."

"I won't be here tomorrow."

"I know," he says, frowning. "But tomorrow I have to haul the woodstove in. I've got to finish this today."

"All right," she says, rolling up her towel with a sigh. "If I'm not back by two, come and fish me out."

"I'll put a pepper on a line."

She slips her sandals on, hikes a hundred yards back, and follows the brook, the simplest way to the pond without getting lost. The footpath, tamer than a week ago, gives her an easy walk through the bushes and the trees, and she meanders with the trickle of the water at her side.

She's spotted three different birds she didn't recognize today, one with a flash of *lime*, early migrants, she assumes, on their way to southern islands. There's a deer in a coppice, flickering its tail. When she moves it merely watches her, curious and calm. Then it turns without a sound and swishes through the ferns. She has her own sense of vanishing—the sculptures, Sam, her job and home, so distant they could almost be another woman's life—and she's as glad to be alone as she's afraid of getting lost.

She comes upon the pond, where a second, fuller stream tumbles in across the way. The double inflow keeps the water moving, not exactly crystalline but fresh enough to swim. When she came the other morning it was blanketed with mist, and here in the heat it radiates a coolness, giving her the first clean breath in several hours. She walks to a bank lipped with mud and soggy moss. It's shady here but twenty feet out, just beyond the overhang of branches, the surface of the water is a brilliant, rippling gold. She takes her sandals off and wades very slowly to her knees, feeling like she hasn't quite felt in thirty years.

She could do without a suit—it's a perfect opportunity—and swim to the sunnier bank to even out her tan. She pulls a shoulder strap down and looks back along the path. Live it up, she decides. It's the very end of summer.

She's been swimming all week but not like this—what a difference just a little polyester really made. She hadn't thought of leeches but she thinks about them now. The mud between her toes seems muddier somehow, and when her feet leave the bottom partway across, she considers going back before committing all the way. Then she flutters in the sunlight and swims right through, blooming in the water and forgetting any fear. She climbs onto the opposite bank and sees her bathing suit behind her in the shade, so unreachable she's free of it and free to be at ease.

She reclines on her back with her hands behind her head, one ankle in the water, one knee toward the sun. Her body feels longer, more elastic on the slope. The grass feels spongy up and down her spine.

It's hot enough to burn but there are days like these, right before the fall, when the light seems sensuous and literally vital. Ava dozes in the warmth, passing in and out of sleep. She thinks of Laura with the soap and wonders how it felt, knowing he had shaped it, knowing she would tell him.

The birds, the rustling trees, the plash of water at her feet, are so harmoniously varied they're essentially inaudible, cushioning her mind and softening her limbs. But she's attuned to what's around her, sensing every little pulse, and she can feel him on the bank as soon as he arrives.

He's a ripple in a daydream, airy as a wish. When she finally clears her eyes and sits to meet his gaze, he's standing with her bathing suit, there across the pond, quiet in the shade and difficult to see.

Sounds sharpen up—chickadees, cicadas—but she doesn't try to hide by jumping underwater. He's a vague silhouette. The water undulates around him, moving out in circles when he steps, very gently, from the safety of the bank. Ava hugs her legs, all curves, like a G clef. Her knees are at her breast, pulsing with her heart.

He watches her and waits, still faceless in the shade, leaning forward like he's one small push from swimming over. Ava almost stands, almost speaks, almost laughs. Then he turns and leaves her suit like a lily pad behind him.

She's alone, so alone she almost doubts that he was there. Her body's goose-fleshed, paler in the midday sun. She'd been svelte lying down but now her stomach has rolls. Dirt and grass are on her back, she has tangles in her hair, and she must have gotten bitten while she slept—there's a welt.

The pond feels deeper when she starts swimming back. She's afraid of going under and afraid of getting out, treading water till her limbs can barely keep her up. Then she's planted in the mud again. Something jabs her heel. She fishes out her bathing suit and tugs it on fast, drying off quickly with the damp, cold towel.

Her nipples and her navel are apparent through the fabric and the suit keeps riding up the middle of her seat. It's a long walk back and she's obsessed with poison ivy, every little insect buzzing in her ear. At last she finds her things where she left them with the web. She retreats several steps but he isn't here to meet her.

Ava notices his chisel and his rasp near *The Weaver*. His sanding cloth dangles off the middle of the arm. She snap-folds her chair, takes her cooler and her bag, and carries all she has toward the cabin and the trail. When she makes it to the clearing, Sam's sitting on a stump, head down, feet apart, hands clasped between his knees.

The chair's metal armrests cut against her ribs.

"You're leaving?" he asks.

She checks her bag to find her keys. Once she's certain that she has them, she continues on her way, never breaking stride until she's made it to the shade. She pauses at the trail, daunted by the long walk out to reach the car, and when she turns around, expecting he'll be standing right behind her, he's very far away—still watching from the cabin.

"Will I see you?" Sam asks, with an undertone of *ever*.

She notices his boot, darkened from the water.

"I don't know," she says. "Henry's here tomorrow. He's been talking about you all week."

Sam takes a step, like he did beside the pond. She can almost feel the ripples moving in the air.

"Thanks for letting me come," she says. "I'm glad I got away."

"Ava . . ."

"Don't."

"I'm sorry," Sam says.

For an instant she imagines dropping everything she has, but then she readjusts her load and says, "Accidents happen. It's what I've been telling Henry all summer."

A band of sun cuts her eyes and then she's fully in the trees, following the ruts and looking for the first real bend along the trail. The ice inside the cooler rattles off her hip. Even here she feels the motion of the water all around her and the suction of the mud when she tried to move her feet, and she doesn't look back because she knows that he'll be standing there, watching her the whole way out in case she stops.

She makes it home long before Henry. The house looks quiet from the middle of the street, but right inside the door, Wing scampers up around her, barking out loud and coiling like a slinky. But he's nervous and his ears pin back around the kitchen where he's pooped on the floor, two feet from the paper.

"Close enough," Ava says. "It's okay . . . you're okay!" and then he's puppyish again, nuzzling at her leg. She lets him out, cleans the floor, and balls the paper into the trash. She gives him food and fills his water dish, and when he comes back in to eat and have a drink, she watches him and smiles.

"You're a good dog. *Good dog*," Ava says.

Suddenly she's crying, and she kneels to let him kiss

her on the cheeks and on the eyes. He waits at the top of
the stairs when she goes to the basement, where she quickly
undresses and drops her clothes directly into the washer.
Upstairs she takes a two-minute shower, dries her hair, and
stands in front of the mirror. There's color in her skin
where there should have been a suit, and when she slathers
it in lotion, praying it'll fade, the burn starts to tingle from
the friction of her hand.

She picks a dress Henry bought her that she never really
liked—a housewife's dress, square and oversimple. Wing
leads the way downstairs, seeming to believe they're up to
something good, and everything she does satisfies him fully.

Ava marinates chicken: better late than never. She cleans
the table outside, carries silverware and plates, shucks
corn and watches Wingnut gambol in the yard. He sniffs a
holly bush and finds an old ball near the roots. Ava throws
it for a while, and once they both tire of the catch, she opens
a beer and they go to the front porch, where the sun's like
nectar on the columns and the floor.

She thinks of how relaxing it'll be this fall, how she's
missed the lazy weekends of board games and television,
ironing his uniform every Sunday night. They'll eat at res-
taurants again. Share a hobby. Go to movies. With the Finns
finally gone, they can rearrange the house. Buy a woodstove. Maybe get a brand-new bed.

She looks at Wing panting in the sun and tips her bottle. He waggles up close and licks a dribble of the beer. They
sit erect, hip to hip, and watch the grackles and the finches,
Wing feeding off her eagerness and looking up the street.
Henry's coming home any minute, any second. It's his favorite time of day, the hour of reunion, when the family's
all together and it's perfect, just perfect.

21

He hadn't gone to swim. That was all he knew for sure.

The week had seemed a month and then he'd felt it passing, standing there alone when she departed for the pond. Like his finger, barely healed whenever he examined it, notably improved the day that he forgot. Five days, forty hours—she had only just arrived, and then before he knew it she was leaving him for good.

He'd found her towel on the ground beside a small heap of cloth, familiarly blue but not immediately obvious. There hadn't been a rustle or a splash, not a sound. He'd picked the garment up, startled by its delicacy and form, like when he comes upon a snakeskin and wonders where the snake has gone.

He thinks of telling Henry—we were both so embarrassed!—and he's sure to get a laugh: what a gas, Ava skinny-dipping. What if it's a secret, though, and Ava doesn't tell him? What if Ava *does* and Henry waits for him to mention it?

Any way it goes, he may have cost himself the Coopers. After this, weeks alone. Sporadic visits. Maybe none. Sculpture after sculpture after tree after tree. There'll be frost in October, dead leaves, frozen weeds. Too cold to sculpt outside, too dark and unremitting. Then the true cabin fever of a season in the snow. He sees it coming in the dusk and the long slant of light, the void that opens up whenever he gazes at the stars before bed and sees directly into space, directly into nothing. Even summer's like an accident, a meaningless reprieve.

"Oh my *God*," Sam says, clutching at his head.

He can't imagine staying here, can't imagine not. He's standing with *The Weaver* when he notices the chisel. It's the one he cut his finger on, the one that shaped her leg. He picks it up without a thought and almost chucks it at the trees, and then he hacks *The Weaver*'s face until it's hideously blank.

He hears a siren in the distance. He's been hearing it awhile. It's not unusual for sounds to carry from the town—the whistle of a train, certain motorcycle engines—but it's rare to catch a siren so distinctly. Must be close. Maybe on Arcadia, he thinks. Then it stops.

Henry reaches Arcadia Street and slumps. Despite his summer exercise, delivery's worn him out. His shoulder throbs. He tries keeping pressure off the blisters on his feet and he's as liable to cry from yawning as he is from seeing the Bailey lot. Ava's car isn't here. He's been hoping every day he'll catch her going out but she and Sam have holed up solid in the woods, and who can really blame them in a week like this?

The temperature and sunlight, the hint of wood smoke seasoning the air . . . he almost feels nostalgic for the hour of the fire. The stillness has a late-day ripple of mirage, as if the summer is evaporating right before his eyes. He

thinks about the Finns—the floral lace curtains, Joan's
figurines—and he can't help smiling when he thinks about
Nan, how she hit him with the dryer when he carried her
to safety. He misses Sam now, too, and thinks of visiting
tomorrow, but he can't imagine getting out of bed and
driving off, not with Ava staying home, lounging in her
gown with her caramel-cream tan. They'll fry some bacon
and eggs, sit in the yard with Wing. He'll surprise her with
a restaurant date, let her know with just enough time to
get dressed. Maybe hit the drive-in. Maybe just park.

He spots a yellow football stranded in a maple tree,
high above the road in front of the Carmichaels' house.
Danny and Ethan meet him at the screen. They've gotten
haircuts that make them look a full year older and they're
confident around him, like he's actually their uncle.

"Hey, guys," Henry says, handing in the mail.

"Hi, Mr. Cooper."

"Your football's stuck."

Danny nods and says, "We know."

"Dad threw it up and couldn't knock it down."

"We tried everything."

"Just monkey up and grab it," Henry says, and then he
smiles with a wink and adds, "You gotta be the best climb-
ers in the neighborhood now."

Danny's freckles seem to fade. He glances at his brother.
They're a well-matched team, sharing thoughts without
words, but they're not quite masters when it comes to keeping secrets.

"What's the matter?" Henry asks. "Something wrong
with the tree house?"

"No."

"It's fine."

Henry hunches till his mailbag's resting on the step.

"What's up?" he asks.

"Mom says we can't use it."

"We're sorry, Mr. Cooper."

"Dad's trying to change her mind."

"She really hates you," Ethan adds. Danny whacks his arm.

Henry lifts his bag. He stands erect, every muscle in his body grown taut, and then the brothers straighten, too, inspired by his posture.

"It's not your fault," he says. "I'm sure she has her reasons."

"Yeah, crappy ones," Danny tells him.

"Come on, now," he says. "She loves you more than anything."

They listen to her heels clacking up the hall.

"Who are you talking to?" Peg asks, worried and annoyed, and when she sees him at the door her face snaps tighter than Saran wrap. "Get inside," she tells the boys.

"We are inside."

"Ethan."

"Mom."

"*Ethan*," Peg says.

"Fine. See ya, Mr. Cooper."

"Later, boys." Henry waves, ignoring Peg and smiling at the twin set of cowlicks—the unaffected mosey of the brothers heading off.

Peg claps the door and locks the hook and eye, glaring with her head dark and hazy through the screen.

"I've already filed a complaint that you're delivering my mail," she says. "If they don't listen, I'll have to live with that. But when you're here, you keep your mouth shut. You put the mail in the box. You walk away. Got it?"

"Why don't you let the boys use the tree house?"

"The only reason it's intact is that I promised Sam Bailey."

"What do you care about Sam?"

"I pity him," she says, proud of her emotion. "Has it ever occurred to you, while you're out playing Boy Scout, that instead of all these useless gestures you could think of how other people feel? You gave the Finns a room, bravo. I got them a *house*. And this is *my* house, and these are *my* children. You want to drive someone nuts, go home to your wife. I pity her, believe you me."

Henry looks down, the only thought in his head how flimsy that aluminum looks around the lower portion of the door, how thunderous it would sound with a good hard kick. Instead he walks down to the tree, gives the trunk a pat, and lays his mailbag gently on the ground. He grabs the lowest branch and pulls himself into the crook, ten feet tall and agile as a boy.

"What are you doing?" Peg asks. "Stop it."

"I'm getting that football."

"Oh, no you aren't. Get down," she says, stepping out as if to forcibly remove him. "That's *our* tree."

"It's past the sidewalk," Henry says, pointing at the roots. "It's a public tree."

"That doesn't mean that you can climb it."

"Sure it does. I'm a public servant."

"I'm reporting this," she tells him.

"Go ahead," Henry says.

The branches crowd around him but it's easier to climb,

offering a better set of footholds and handles. It's a healthy tree, well-pruned and cabled in the middle, and he wonders what Sam would make if he could sculpt it. Henry relishes the smell, the flickers of the sun, the vibrancy and busyness of several thousand leaves. He feels elated after days of flat-footed burden, gravity-defiant and relieved of obligation.

Higher up he takes a rest, considering his options. The ball's ten feet out, high above the road, wedged tightly in a fork so he can't shake it down. But the branch feels solid and he crawls out lengthwise, bellying along until he's close enough to reach.

"Are you trying to impress me?" Peg asks him from the sidewalk.

"No."

"Good, because you aren't."

He wonders how he'll justify his recklessness to Ava. Maybe Peg's right: who's he trying to impress? But that's a good yellow football stranded in the tree. There's simply no reason why a man wouldn't try.

"You're going to kill yourself," she says.

"Better me than someone else."

He's thinking of the boys, who might be brave enough to try it. Then he stretches too far and slips around the limb, swinging upside down and clamping with his thighs. Suddenly his heartbeat's thumping in his head. It takes a second for his brain to reinterpret his position and it's dazzling and alarming when the sun's above his knees.

He reaches for a long sturdy branch to his left, its crookedness reminding him of Wingnut's tail. Peg's shouting and her voice sounds scissory and bright. He can almost reach the tip—it scratches at his finger—but he needs a bigger lunge to grab it where it's strong. The head rush is equally distracting and refreshing, heating up his ears and speeding up his thoughts. He hasn't tried an *ordinary* sit-up in a decade but he tries one now, tightening his gut. Here it comes, the extra reach to get his hand around the branch, and then he has it and he smiles at the power in his arm. He's looking at the sky beyond the dark green leaves, and the football's there, right there, like a fruit.

Then he's falling headfirst. Henry doesn't understand it. He can still feel the texture of the branch when he hits.

Sam stops the ATV and runs around the trailer, looking for Ava's car amid the tumult in the street. There's an ambulance, a paramedic, and a cop car right in front of his property. A policeman is talking to Peg, who hugs herself and looks to be in tears, and Sam continues jogging, thinking, *No, not the boys.*

But there they are, safe and sound in the window of their house. They stare at him. He lifts a hand but neither waves back. The fear it seems to indicate disturbs him more than anything.

Billy's on the sidewalk, staring at the road. A couple more neighbors stand across the street. The ambulance is leaving but the siren and the lights are off. If not for the policeman, he'd be thinking false alarm.

There's blood in the road. It's shaded by the tree—at first he took it for an oil stain—but closer to the curb it's unmistakable and fresh. Billy turns around, looking stunned and even ashen, and before Sam has to ask he says:

"It was Henry."

He's explaining what he knows—the climb, the broken

branch, Peg shouting in the road—and pointing at the football above them in the tree.

"... dead," Billy says. "... didn't move and then ..."

Dead.

Sam hears him but it's cottony, a rumble in his ear. The grass along the road shifts tint, turning blue, and he can see the bits of the gravel in the concrete walk.

Billy keeps him up and says, "Whoa, take it easy."

"I'm all right."

"You want to sit?"

"I'm all right," Sam says. Hot-cold, up and down, trying not to heave—he takes a hold of Billy's arm and says, "A phone."

"What?"

"I need your phone."

Next thing he knows he's sitting on he ground, limp and hyperventilating, head between his knees. He has a cell phone now and can't remember how he got it, can't remember any numbers, let alone who to call.

PART THREE

22

Late October, four weeks after Henry's death, Nan and Joan sit in their kitchen with Bob Carmichael, drinking tea and sharing a plate of ladyfingers. They talk around Sam's housewarming table, and the kettle steam and radiator ticks give the room a sleepy, twilit atmosphere even in the middle of the day. Outdoors the weather's overcast, colored by the still-warm smolder of the trees, and they can see Danny and Ethan raking in the yard, red-cheeked with yellow leaves clinging to their corduroys.

"How have they been?"

"They're doing all right, Nan. Doing all right," Bob says. "School came at a good time. They're out of the house, staying busy with their friends. The funeral helped a lot. They insisted on going and they both seemed calmer next day."

"They didn't shy away."

"That's right, exactly right."

Joan pours them each another cup of tea and offers the cookie plate to Bob, whose timid manner, so ingrained he won't eat without permission, makes him like another of the boys instead of an adult.

"I drove them to the church without telling Peg," he says.

"She thought it was morbid, like when they wouldn't stop harping on the fire. But they're resilient this age. Flexible, you know?"

Nan's seen a similar resilience in her sister. In their months of living with the Coopers, Nan came to rely on Ava's teamwork more profoundly than she realized, and she found herself overwhelmed with housekeeping in the early weeks of living on their own. Joan stepped up in unprecedented ways, learning—and remembering—how to wash delicates, how to sauté, how to clean grout and use the cable DVR. There were hours Nan discovered they had nothing left to do and they could sit, Joan with a puzzle, Nan with a copy of *Vanity Fair*, for two or three hours of a pleasant afternoon. And it was Joan who first remembered Danny and Ethan, doubly shaken by the fire and Henry's death, and suggested that they hire them and grossly overpay them.

"She had me nail the trapdoor of the tree house shut," Bob says. "She'd been saying all along that climbing wasn't safe, then Henry came along and proved her right. I'll tell you a secret, though," he adds, with such a tantalizing look that the Finns lean forward in their chairs. "Danny and Ethan must have climbed up and gotten that football. I don't know when, and I haven't told this to Peg, but I found it in their room. How about that? Even I was scared to climb that tree."

They ponder this awhile, looking outside. They've been here for over an hour, but with the leaf bombs, jumped-in piles, and nonstop shedding of the maple, the boys have cleared very little of the lawn and only a handful of bags are twist-tied full. Nan's delighted with their progress. At this rate, they'll have to come next week, too.

"How are you two bearing up?" Bob asks, giving Joan particular attention.

Joan's flustered by a question that pertains to herself. They've been focusing on Ava every day since the accident, rarely giving thought to any struggles of their own. Henry's death is still a shock, needle-bright when it stings, and she hasn't found any consolation in her prayers.

"I don't understand it," Joan says, looking down. "He was such a good man."

"That has nothing to do with it," Nan says. "We had a good house. That didn't make it fireproof."

"I think about that," Bob says. "We're all afraid of heart attacks and car wrecks, and then it's something like a ball or a fifty-cent cigar. Mysterious ways ain't the half of it. And then the article they wrote . . ."

"I sent a letter to the editor," Nan says, referring to a story in the *Waterbury Times*. The writer hadn't openly declared that it was fate, but there had been a line—he had used the word "logic"—that had almost seemed to justify Henry's dying on Arcadia. "A journalist's *opinion* doesn't suddenly explain it."

"Where's the meaning in it, then?" Joan whispers to herself.

"*We* give it meaning if we really need to have it. What else can Sam and Ava do? What did *we* do?"

"I don't know," Joan says.

They talk awhile longer and the boys come inside with a clatter of doorknobs and hinges, flooding the kitchen with cold air and daylight and leaves, the color in their faces unbelievable to Nan, Joan, and Bob, who've grown accustomed in the gloom to one another's pallor.

"We're done," Danny says.

Incredibly it's true: the yard's raked clean and all the bags are in a row. They join the company and talk, swallow cocoa and cookies and remind the Finns powerfully of Henry, how his appetite radiated more than it consumed. The boys are comfortable today, a far cry from their shyness in the supermarket, not only answering questions but asking about the Finns' house, the framed puzzles on the wall, the other kinds of work—like snow shoveling and spring cleaning—that the sisters might hire them to do.

They stay another thirty minutes, well beyond requirement. Finally the sisters make excuses to release them. Bob cleans up and stacks the dishes on the counter while the boys get their coats and struggle with their laces.

"It's good you're learning knots," Nan says. "Too many kids are growing up with Velcro on their shoes."

Joan hands them each a twenty and a brownie for the road. The brothers say thanks and then, unprompted by their father, Ethan shakes hands and Danny hugs them at the waist. The hugs are delicate and quick, lacking any strength, but they're enough to give the Finns a noticeable lift.

The woods are stripped except for the pines and a few late-season maples, and the fallen leaves make the ground intimate and warm, as if the trees have come down to Sam's level and he's close, at last, to learning some elemental secret of the place.

He's eaten twice a week in Nan and Joan's kitchen, and he finally has a cell phone and never turns it off. They call each other often, sharing news, trading notes, talking constantly of Ava: how she is, what she needs. He saw her every day following the funeral, less frequently of late and yet prepared at any hour, like today when she just needs company for lunch.

He's built a fire in the clearing, a welcome light to greet her, and he sees her on the trail through the bare-bone trees. She looks petite walking in, almost like a Finn. He would have met her at the street but she asked him not to come, preferring to hike the quarter mile alone—an urge he understands and hopes will do her good.

Wing runs ahead and Sam claps him over, where he's treated to a handful of Canadian bacon. He's been clingier of late, not as openly rambunctious, but he's glad seeing Sam and being in the woods. He's on his own during workdays and waits for Ava's car, and he's always disappointed when she comes home alone. Every morning he's convinced that Henry's in the kitchen, in the yard, in the bathroom, right around the corner.

"Gone," Ava tells him. "Daddy isn't here."

And with all the repetition, he's begun to understand. Waiting at the window doesn't bring him anymore. Maybe Henry's *here*, Wing suddenly decides, and he's off like a shot, round the cabin and the trees. He returns, panting hard with a dullness to his fur, and then he settles in the leaves and shivers near the flames.

Ava, knowing better, has the same intuition, and she looks around the clearing like he really might appear. Sam hugs her and they set a couple chairs by the fire. He's appraising her; she knows it when he doesn't really look.

Her tan's worn away. She's lost weight without trying and she looks like a widow when she sees herself in mirrors. Have her breasts always sagged? Has her hair always hung this bodiless and drab? Her appetite's gone and sometimes, hours after dinner, she wakes up feeling like she got herself drunk. She spent a while last night dry-heaving at the toilet and the bathroom lights made her panicky and cold. Eventually she curled up fetal on the bath mat, Wingnut vigilant and breathing at her side.

Other nights she cries incessantly or doesn't cry at all. She feels the stupor of exhaustion lying wide awake, or grows incredibly alert and can't perform the simplest tasks, like reading a magazine or brushing her teeth. In the nights she really sleeps, she dreams of everything but Henry. When she wakes she likes to fool herself, pretending he's alive, fleshing out stories and entire conversations. She's admitted this to Sam. He's told her that it's normal and they've fallen into sharing their imaginary lives.

"We had an argument today."

"What'd you fight about?" he asks.

"I don't remember. It was one of those fights. He put his dirty socks in a basket of clean laundry," she decides on the spot. "He apologized and gave me that grammar-school frown. But I couldn't let it go after getting so mad, so I scolded him some more and let him suffer for a while."

The overcast sky makes the fire twice as colorful. Ava puts her foot right against the flames. Her shoe begins to steam but she doesn't feel the heat; it fascinates her, watching it and toeing at the log.

"I pretended I caught Laura cheating on me," Sam says. "She'd gotten home from work and fallen right asleep. Her clothes were on the floor, and there was something in the way she'd left them on the rug . . . they looked, I don't know. *Used*. Like someone else had handled them. I fished through her pockets and found a note, signed with another man's name. Ridiculous." He smiles. "Digging up proof."

He adds a fresh-split log and waits for it to catch, the wood impervious at first, two splinters flaring up but all the rest of it intact. Then the bark curls off, white-yellow when it burns, and the fire dims orange and the log turns black.

"I imagined him, a doctor at the hospital," he says. "Salt-and-pepper hair, really fit. He had a silver watch and perfect hands, a surgeon's hands, and he did something outdoorsy on the weekends, like kayaking. He and Laura had coffee in the cafeteria. She admired him. He was a great guy, really decent, and he appreciated Laura somehow— made her feel good in some necessary way. And one night they went in a room, some little office in the hospital, and held each other close for two or three minutes. They didn't talk and didn't kiss. All they did was hug, and when I pictured it, she looked so beautiful and small. Holdable," he says. "I've thought of it a lot."

Ava takes her foot from the fire, and it's only when she plants it on the ground that her shoe feels dangerously hot. Overhead, where the canopy had been so full, the sky feels enormous with its high white clouds, and the light looks pale—more factual than warm.

"I think about the morning at the pond," Ava says, watching very closely out of the corner of her eye. He seems both rigid and entirely relaxed, as if he's dreaded this but long ago resigned himself to facing it.

"I'm sorry it happened," Sam says.

"I'm not asking for an apology."

"*You* didn't do anything wrong."

"Of course I did," she says.

Sam presses on his temples, leaning forward in the chair. Ava slumps and her tears start drying from the fire, stiffening her cheeks and reddening her eyes. He reaches over the arm of her chair, prying through her interlocked fingers in her lap, and she doesn't pull away when he takes her by the hand. Wingnut stands, noticing her tears, and there's a decency about them, in the way that they surround her.

"We loved him," Sam says. "He would have liked us here today."

She loops her hair around her finger, absentmindedly at first but continuing to twist until her fingertip's white and strands begin popping at the roots.

"I started making half-pots of coffee," Ava whispers.

"I don't even drink it anymore," Sam says.

She contracts toward her knees, still clutching at his hand, pretending that it's Henry's and they're sitting in the yard.

"Listen," Sam says. "Why don't we have Thanksgiving here at the cabin. We'll invite Nan and Joan . . . see if my new stove can cook a little turkey."

"I'd like that," she says, warming at the thought. "I've been scared of Thanksgiving all month."

"So have I."

23

Ava's in the produce section of the supermarket picking potatoes. The air's ripe with too much off-season vegetable and fruit, and the feel of the potato makes her think about the burial. She puts it down and wipes her hand, and when she leans against the cart for a moment of support, it rolls a few feet and forces her to walk. She turns the corner into the pharmacy aisle and there's Peg Carmichael carrying a basket full of yogurt. They're at opposite ends of the aisle, Peg reading vitamin jars, Ava drawn forward by the natural momentum.

The market turns brighter, almost clinically fluorescent, and the floor has the high bright luster of a hospital. Peg sees her coming and clutches a jar of chewable iron. She doesn't look away or feign familiarity but waits, inexpressively, to gauge the situation. Ava steers the cart directly at her hip.

When they're close enough to talk, neither woman speaks but there's a mutual appraisal, instantaneous and sharp. Peg's professionally minted—pantsuit and heels, hair immaculately bobbed—but she's exhausted and her makeup's thick to hide a zit.

"I don't know the right thing to say." Peg sighs. "I wish

it hadn't happened. From the bottom of my heart, I wish that none of it had happened."

Ava nods, hearing nothing she can rightly contradict. Peg wasn't at the funeral but her family had attended, and Danny and Ethan had sent her a drawing of Henry standing in the tree house. She keeps it on the fridge and sees it every day.

"How are your sons?"

"Shaken up," Peg says. "Between the fire and . . . the accident. They really aren't themselves. I'm calling different therapists."

Ava twists the handle of the cart until it squeaks. She needs a bathroom soon and hopes the burbling isn't audible.

"Please thank them for the picture and the card," Ava says. "Henry spoke of them a lot. He was always thrilled to see them."

"Mm," Pegs says. She puts the iron in her basket.

"If there's anything I can do," Ava finds herself saying.

"No," Peg says. "No, you've all done enough."

"I'm sorry?"

"I appreciate the offer—"

"What do you mean we've done enough?"

Peg frowns condescendingly, summoning her tact, as if responding to a question any child might have answered.

"I've tried to move my family past the fire," she replies. "I even compromised, against my better judgment, when I let Sam Bailey and your husband build that fort in the yard. But I didn't want help. I never asked for it at all. I wish to God he hadn't climbed that tree . . ."

"You could have stopped him."

"How?" Peg asks, almost chuckling at the thought.

Ava moves around the cart, cornering her in, pressing

up tight until they feel each other's breath. Peg backs away
as far as she can manage and her heel taps hard against the
bottom of the shelves.

"I'm not going to have this conversation. Out of respect for your loss—"

"Shut up," Ava says. "Shut your mouth before I slap it."

Peg trembles like a windowpane ready to explode.

Ava thinks about the boys, the civil suit, the tree house.
She thinks about the football stranded in the tree. They
listen to a cart pass behind them in the aisle and she wonders what it looks like, two grown women close enough to
kiss. It seems to her that Peg has the same self-awareness.
She glances over Ava's left shoulder with a blush and then
she murmurs something short and difficult to hear.

"What was that?"

Peg pales until her zit glows red.

"What?" Ava asks, menacingly now.

Peg firms up, taller by a head. She pushes out her breast
as if to say, "Who are *you*?" and scowls like it's all been the
raving of a widow. It's terribly effective—she's imperious
and beautiful, rising like a woman who's been boorishly af-
fronted. She pushes Ava backward with the corner of her
basket, walking off with a sniff and a haughty recomposure.

Ava can't think, can't move or look away. It's as though
a kind of paralyzing fear has come upon her. Then she
fixes on the jar of iron supplements and says, "I hope you
have anemia."

But Peg has turned the corner.

"What happened?" Nan asks.

Ava clomps up the hall with her hands like *Wait*, as if

the Finns have come to *her* house and stormed through the door. They've never seen her this way, so furious and raw. She can't quit moving and her eyes skit around. Joan's shaken by her force, unsure of what to do, waiting in the living room for Nan to calm her down.

"I saw Peg."

They've been dreading this for weeks, the inevitable run-in, praying that it wouldn't go as badly as they feared.

"Where?"

"At the market, just now. I left my groceries in the cart and drove straight here."

"What hap—"

"She isn't even sorry that he died!" Ava yells. "It was all fake sympathy and bullshit and that was just the start. She talked about her boys, how hard it's been for Danny and Ethan, but she didn't even care about *them*. She made it sound like one more problem on her plate, like Henry dying at her house was bad enough, and now her kids are giving her a headache about it. And she didn't want to talk out of *respect* for my *loss*. She's furious her siding got burnt, but I'm the one dragging things on, still complaining that my husband died . . ."

Ava's dripping from the rain, scarlet at the neck, everything about her scalding and alarmed. She continues this way for several more minutes, repeating herself, embellishing the scene, growing wilder and less and less coherent till she finally sputters out and shivers in the damp.

"Come and sit," Nan says, drawing her inside.

By the time they reach the kitchen, Ava's sobbing on her arm, trembling in the warmth and indescribably petite.

Joan helps her jacket off, hangs it up to dry, and guides her to a chair with a hand-knit cushion. Ava huddles with her hands pressed between her knees. They've had the oven on today; the kitchen's warm enough to sweat. Nan drapes a blanket from the sofa on her shoulders. Joan starts a kettle and prepares a pot of tea and no one talks until it's brewed and steaming in the mugs.

Ava picks one up and holds it by her chin. She cradles it and sips when the boil simmers down.

"I'm sorry," Nan says, worn with disappointment. "This kind of thing is like a heartworm. You have to let it go."

"I can't forgive her," Ava says.

"I regret never saying it to Henry," Nan admits. She swallows and her wattle has a noticeable quake. "I thanked him but I never really told him I forgave him."

"Henry tried," Ava says. She grips her mug until her knuckles pale. "Why does Peg get a pass? Why does *she* have a husband? She shouldn't be a mother after everything she's done."

Nan's chastened by her vehemence and has to look away, seeming feebler than her sister and reluctant to respond. Ava stares out the window to the lawn behind the kitchen, where the grass has a smattering of new red leaves. The blanket and the tea begin to soothe her anger and she's thoroughly cocooned, past the point of moving.

"It keeps getting worse," Ava whispers to herself.

Joan holds her arm with a liver-spotted hand. "I used to be afraid," she says, "especially in winter. There were months when I would worry that the spring wouldn't come."

"She was clinically depressed," Nan quietly explains.

"I was living on my own. I was terribly alone."

With the passing of the rain, the yard shifts hues—amber when the sun nearly penetrates the clouds, pewter in the shade, dimming and suffusing. The effect makes its way through the windows of the kitchen, altering the colors of the table and the walls.

"I remember one night," Joan says. "It must have been in February . . . maybe early March. PBS ran a show about the climate and the glaciers. They said another ice age could happen anytime. It was such a hard winter, I was worried it had come. I didn't feel safe until the crocuses were up."

The light keeps fainting and reviving all around them. Ava shuts her eyes, thinking, *Crocuses* and *Ice*.

"It frightened me for years before I came to live with Nan."

"Even then," Nan says.

"Even now," Joan agrees. "I hated all the dark. It seemed to last forever. After Christmas came and went, it would start to wear me out. But I remembered that the first day of winter was the shortest, that it started getting better right then, right away. I began to log the times of every sunrise and sunset. I keep them in a journal right beside the bed."

"It's true," Nan says. "She starts it on the solstice."

"Now whenever I get scared, I pick it up and read the numbers. Just the few extra minutes every day mean the world."

Ava watches them and wonders how it feels being old. She hasn't really listened since she heard the word *Christmas*, but the voices are a comfort. She's afraid of going home.

24

Billy's browsing ointment in the drugstore when he sees Ava passing at the far end of the aisle. He wipes the oil off his forehead and breathes through his nose, trying to calm himself but frazzled by the various scenarios he's memorized—conversations, introductions, everything a scramble now.

Be sensitive, he thinks. *Don't fuck it up.*

He reassesses what he's piled in his basket: acne wash, tanning cream, Max Muscle bars. He leaves them on the floor and grabs a heavy-duty cord, like a man who has power tools littering his workshop. She probably remembers that he worked at True Value and he needs to reinforce it, now that he's been fired.

They caught him taking money from the drawer, less than two hundred bucks over six or seven weeks, and then his manager accused him of stealing a pack of lightbulbs. Out of work ever since, insurance money spent, unemployment not enough to pay the credit cards down. He's being hassled on the phone about his mortgage and his debts. No one else calls. No one comes around. Mid–last week, troubled by a dream, he took a paring knife and cut a straight line along his forearm. Now it looks infected and he needs a tube of ointment, which is better than a doctor that he can't afford to pay.

The night he crept around the Cooper house, he'd seen her in the bathroom, almost like the glass had been a television screen. Then *snick*: Henry's death had unlocked the window. He's seen her at her lab, in the bank, in the market. All he has to do is saunter up and say hello. He finds her in the dental aisle, takes another breath, and goes to meet her with an inadvertent bounce in his step.

"Ava?" Billy says, louder than he wants.

She spins around, spooked by the nearness of his voice.

"Hey, it's Billy. Billy Kane," he says, offering his hand.

She shakes it automatically with faraway eyes. Her expression goes bright, then dark and then illegible.

"*Hi*," Ava says with a mini-step back. "I didn't recognize your name at first."

"Yeah, no, it's fine," he says. "Listen, Ava. Hey. I'm sorry for your loss."

Ava nods, smiling tightly as if to clench back tears.

"I was there," Billy tells her, not sure if she's aware of that. "I'm the one who dialed 911." He waits for her to thank him but she doesn't say a thing. Maybe she's assuming Billy didn't like him. "I met him at the store one day. We had a good talk. Even after the fire, I wouldn't have wished it on him in a million years." He lets her take it in and says, "How you holding up?"

Ava blinks twice, very far apart.

"Not too well."

"I hear that. It's been a hell of a year. Between the damage to the house and, well . . ." He trails away, pausing with a frown. "My wife left me. I guess I wasn't a perfect husband, but I don't know. It knocked my wind out. We had some arguments—every couple does, right? Then poof. All a sudden she decides that's the end. I keep trying to figure out exactly what happened. She must have bottled things up, let a lot of little problems seem bigger than they were."

"I'm sorry," Ava mumbles after waiting several moments.

"I'll be all right," Billy says. "Still, it's tough going home to an empty house, eating meals alone. Some nights I barely want to cook."

She puts a toothbrush into her basket, starting up the aisle like she's comfortable enough to shop while they talk.

"I make a pretty mean steak," Billy says. "If you ever want a home-cooked meal, someone to listen—"

"Oh," she says, gasping it and sounding like *Ugh*. Billy rears back to measure her reaction and she looks at him and says, "I'm not the best company lately."

"Nah," he says. "I wouldn't let you be a downer. Pick a night."

"I prefer to be alone at this point," Ava says. She faces him and stares, crisp and diplomatic. "I have to go. Good luck with everything, okay?"

"Sure, yeah. You too," he says, watching her leave and wishing he could catch her by the hair. He starts to say *I'll see you soon*, changes it to *See you around*, jumbles up the two, and hollers out, "I'll see you surround."

He retreats to the back of the store, still holding the extension cord and passing every aisle till he sees her up front by the registers. As soon as Ava leaves, he drops the cord and follows her out. She sees him from her car and briefly meets his eye, and what can Billy do, having trailed her into the lot without so much as a grocery bag?

He leans against the wall until she's fully out of sight, and then he hits his own arm, directly on the cut, and hurries to his car without the ointment that he came for.

Thank God for Wingnut right inside the door, greeting her with barks, snuffling in her hand. She leads him onto the porch and looks for unfamiliar cars and then she kisses him, relaxing at the odor of his breath. A crawliness has lingered in her body since the store, one of unwashed hair and germs beneath her nails. She thinks of how the Finns used to harden at the name, how the wire he'd been carrying reminded her of cellars.

"Don't be stupid," Ava says, and yet she can't forget his face, how he greeted her and spoke as if he knew her awfully well.

"Want Sam to come and eat?"

Wing wags, hearing *eat*.

Ava makes the call—she's memorized the number—and he answers straightaway. He'll be there in thirty minutes.

She clips up her hair and dresses for convenience, just a sweater and a soft pair of jeans, like pajamas. When Sam arrives, they hug at the door and eat in the kitchen: salad and spaghetti and a ten-dollar wine. He's very much at home with a Henry-size meal, lean despite his appetite and groomed as if they're eating in a restaurant. Ava's still adjusting after setting back the clocks, glancing up mid-meal to find the yard's disappeared. It makes the house feel small, not cozy but confining, like a two-person capsule at the bottom of the sea.

They take their coffees into the living room and Wing lies between them on the couch. Sam knows about Peg—

Nan and Joan filled him in—but he lets her tell it anyway and doesn't interrupt. They talk about the news and books they ought to read, the possibility of flurries in the hills around town. He talks about the snowmobile he's buying for the trail, smaller sculptures he can do when it's too cold to chisel outside, and while he's telling her his plans, Ava thinks about hers: emptying the drawers, filling boxes up for charity.

She often tries remembering the graces of the marriage: steamed creases when she ironed Henry's uniform at night. His whiskers when he kissed her on the cheek and on the neck. The time he hummed the o.b. tampon jingle and Ava, surprising herself, had known it well enough to sing along. How they'd laughed at that.

When Henry used to snore, she'd get a breathing strip and sneak it onto his nose. She liked the wrappers, how they opened with a little glow of static, and she always took her time and never woke him up. She smoothed the edges with her fingertips and listened to him breathe, and he'd be totally surprised when he found it in the morning. When the box ran out, she didn't bother getting more. It was easier at night to jab him in the ribs.

"I hate myself sometimes," she says without passion.

Wing's hind leg twitches in a dream. Sam pets him and eventually the leg settles down. Ava cries without covering her face—just a little—and the tears run smooth and tickle to her throat.

"I feel so scared all the time."

"I know," he says.

"Does that go away?"

"At first I wouldn't get up in the morning. I'd see the daylight and shiver," Sam says. "Early summer and it looked like March. Later on it felt required. Out of bed, eat some breakfast. Keep myself preoccupied and battle through the day. Now I'm up before dawn without a clock, like it's normal. I have mornings where my first thought *isn't* missing Laura."

They sit awhile, listening to Wingnut sleep. When Sam gets off the couch it feels both quick and overdue, and after he's taken his coffee into the kitchen, rinsed the cup, and returned to the living room, the night feels deeper than before and she can tell, even with her eyes shut, that he's considering the hour and the dark drive home.

"I hate that you're alone out there."

"I'll be fine," he says. "I have owl vision now."

"Why don't you stay in the guest room? The bed's already made. You'll have your own bathroom."

He pauses, seeming casual but reasonably wary.

"I ran into Billy Kane this afternoon," she says. "He introduced himself at the drugstore and offered his condolences."

"He was always really *friendly*," Sam says, sitting down. "Waving from his yard, staring just a little too long. Laura didn't like him. She compared him to the calls we used to get from the police benevolent association. They'd politely ask for money, we'd politely say no, and then they'd almost seem hostile, like we didn't like cops. That's the way it is with Billy—like you *have* to wave back. We always felt sorry for his wife."

"She left him," Ava says.

"I haven't seen her car around. We used to hear them arguing. I'll bet the Finns have quite a few stories."

"He said he felt lonely, like we had that in common. He invited me to dinner."

"What?"

"It sounded like he'd worked himself up to finally asking. I've never even seen him before. And then he followed me out of the store and watched me drive away. I know it's stupid," Ava says, "but I kept checking the street before you came, making sure he wasn't parked outside."

She hugs herself and stares, seeing patterns in the rug. Sam's quiet for a minute, really thinking by the feel of it, looking back and forth at nothing in particular. He flexes at the jaw and squeezes on his knees.

"You want me to say something to him?"

"I don't want to make things worse."

"I'll stay if it makes you feel safer."

"It'd help knowing someone else is home," Ava says. "No offense to the guard dog."

He waits with Wing on the couch while Ava finds an unused toothbrush, a clean towel, and a pair of Henry's sweats. When she goes into the kitchen to prep the coffee for tomorrow morning, Sam changes in the downstairs bathroom. Wing follows him in, bleary-eyed and yawning, exactly as he did when Henry was around, the sight of the old sweatpants comforting the dog like a blanket he remembers from his youth.

Quiet falls around the house, a special mildness of movement Sam associates with life before the fire—cups and plates clinking in the dish rack, footsteps going upstairs, the hiss of faucets and the hum of the refrigerator. He hears a clock tick but doesn't see the clock. It's been so long since he cleaned up for bed in a regular bathroom, he pauses with the towel, unsure of where to put it when he's done. There's a light above the mirror, hot water on demand, and the tiles feel warm, almost silky, underfoot.

Ava comes down to say good night. She's washed her face; her cheeks are rosy and her hairline's damp. He adores how sweet and unsexy she's become, a grown woman in pajama bottoms and an oversize shirt. She smells like peppermint and hand lotion, reminding him of Laura on the rare nights their schedules aligned and they were able to fall asleep together, and he hugs her like Henry would have hugged her, full of health, and it's something neither one of them is liable to regret.

25

Sheri finally made contact two days ago, and however much Billy had steeled himself, however many conversations and scenarios he'd dreamed, he hadn't been prepared for the sleep-soft nearness of her voice, or his buzz, or the calm, almost tender way she told him she had filed for divorce. This was it, a simple heads-up, and she was maddeningly patient start to finish. She wouldn't tell him where she was—"You don't need to know"—and so he naturally assumed that she was staying with a man.

He apologized and listed all the trials he'd been suffering—his joblessness and bills, the imminent foreclosure on the house, how he never spoke to anyone and slept on the couch and used her old shampoo, remembering her smell. How he'd cut his arm and now it wouldn't heal and he was sorry, every day, and Sheri listened like she knew it to the last little detail.

"Henry Cooper died," he said.

"You're exhausting, Billy."

"Tell me you don't love me. I need to hear you say—"

"I don't love you," Sheri said. "I don't like a single thing about you. My favorite memory of us is when you choked me on the floor because it finally, *finally* kicked my ass into gear."

She made it sound as if they'd separated seasons, even years ago.

"I love you," Billy whispered. "More than anything. You have to know that."

"Go to hell," Sheri said, cutting off the line.

He cried a few minutes following the call—the very tears he'd tried to summon when he had her on the line—and then he threw the phone and hit the television, fracturing the screen, and flipped the coffee table over. He stumbled in his rage and landed on the upturned legs, shouting at the floor and then collapsing into bottomless sobs.

Two days later, Thanksgiving morning, Billy wakes up paralyzed. It's happened often in the last few weeks and yet he panics every time, conscious of the room and certain that he's suffocating. If only he could roll or twitch a finger he'd be fine, but he can't, no matter what, and he can't draw a breath. He tries surrendering to sleep but his fear won't let him and he lies there, frantic, wishing it would end. He finally kicks a leg and spasms in the blanket. Then his fear seems foolish and he's horribly exhausted.

He looks out the window, guessing at the time. Late morning, by the sun, maybe early afternoon. A fine light snow has fallen overnight, and the room feels colorless and typical and cold.

He lifts the sheet and finds the bandage dangling off his arm. There's a damp gray stain where he placed it on the wound. The cut's crusty at the edges, jellied in the slit, and his forearm throbs without his touching it at all. He slathers it in ointment and applies another bandage, then remembers it's a holiday and pops a can of a beer. He drinks it with his coffee and a bowl of Rice Krispies, watching a smaller, cheaper TV until he finally has the energy to carry out his plan.

He hangs his khakis and shirt in the bathroom during his shower so the steam will get the wrinkles out. The bandage gets wet and needs another change, but he shaves without a nick and likes the style of his hair, newly cut, when he parts it with a soft-hold gel. His clothes are good to go and he knots his tie correctly first try, and after spitting out his mouthwash and cleaning up his shoes, he grabs a twelve-pack of beer and takes it to the car.

Straight to Ava's. She'll be lonely—major holiday alone. He can walk right up, ring the bell, and say *Hey*. She'll be thrown at first, hanging back and patting at her gown, embarrassed by her looks in front of Billy and his tie. *Come on*, he'll say. *Get yourself dressed. You shouldn't be alone today, not for Thanksgiving.* He'll take her out to eat and ask about her life and then she'll start to understand, maybe with dessert, that it doesn't have to be so hard for either one of them.

Her car is there, exactly like he figured it would be. He parks across the street and loses his nerve. He planned to save the beer in case she asked him inside after dinner, but he breaks open the box and chugs half a bottle, thinking it'll seem more natural anyway, less a plan to get her drunk than just an extra box he happened to have in the car.

He scans the radio. A station's playing "Jingle Bell Rock" and the chime of the guitar is like a warm winter balm. He finishes the beer and opens another, imagining the mall decked for Christmas in the morning with the shoppers and the smell of baked cookies in the food court. He thinks of going out with Sheri last season, splitting up to

buy presents, meeting at Applebee's for lunch. Hot choco-
lates on the road, fresh-cut tree. They strung the lights after dark and cuddled on the couch, drinking rum out of
mugs and listening to music. He plays it all again, putting
Ava into Sheri's role—lying on the guest-room bed, sipping rum, watching her undress very slowly at the mirror.

He drums the wheel and kills the car and says, "Come
on come on come on," and then he walks across the street,
dizzy from the beer and from the bright rush of air. His
heart's beating strongly when he creeps up the porch. He
rings the bell and backs away—he doesn't want to crowd
her—but the bell just hangs. She doesn't come. He rings
again.

He cups his hand against the door and tries to see inside. The lights are out. He doesn't hear a television on,
and then he thinks about the dog and wonders where it is.
It would bark if they were home—she must be at the Finns'.
Of course she is, of *course* she is. They wouldn't have
abandoned her.

But neither of them drives and Ava's car is right behind
him. He leaves the porch and drives around the neighborhood, taking his time and checking every side street and
alleyway, hoping to see her walking the dog and finding
nothing but a lot of sleepy lights in all the homes. It's the
time of afternoon when people settle in. Roads empty out,
meals are under way. You can stare in every house and no
one notices or cares.

She isn't here. She must be *there*—he must have picked
her up this morning. Billy squeals a three-point turn and
speeds away. He drives across town, skipping red lights
and stop signs, pounding back a beer and picturing the
cabin. She'd have walked right past when he was shower-

ing or sleeping. That's assuming that she didn't spend the night. He has to know. If he doesn't, he'll obsess about it, sitting home alone, thinking *right this second* Sam's cutting her a second piece of pie, giving her a neck rub, saying everything—and more—that Billy meant to say.

Sam collects the Finns in his new pickup, a twelve-year-old Ford he purchased after selling his healthier but far less practical car. He mostly drives for groceries and supplies, the latter of which are often so big—his cast-iron cookstove an obvious example—that he's usually forced to rent a truck anyway. The pickup has a cap and Wingnut's behind them in the bed, free to roam and ludicrously happy, sniffing at the windows, pacing unsteadily and hip-checking walls.

A day of ecstasy for Wing—first a supermarket trip, then a morning out at Sam's, where he ran around the cabin in the inch-high snow and marked a dozen trees, master of the woods. He ate a liver, not quite frozen, when Ava dropped giblets on the floor, and the smell of warm turkey's had him ravenous for hours. Then he got to ride again to go and get the Finns, and now they're all together, driving back to Ava, and he's starting to believe that Henry might appear.

The Finns are wearing slacks and cashmere sweaters, Joan brown and green, Nan brown and orange. They've had their hair done and smell very faintly of salon. It's overcast today, spiritless and pale with the roads wet-black and slushy in the gutters. They make it to Arcadia, where Sam's prepared a flatbed, covered with a blanket, for the Finns to ride behind him on the ATV. Wing's leashed between them and they have to take it slow, but despite the bumps and dips, Nan and Joan are happy on the passage up the trail, reminded of years they used to visit Christmas-tree farms, smitten with the woods' spare beauty in the snow.

They give a heart-deep sigh when they come upon the cabin, admiring its tininess and firelit glow. Ava's at the door and waves when they approach. She's rosy from her work and wearing a blue vintage housedress, and even though she's quite a bit thinner than she used to be, she doesn't look drawn or malnourished anymore. She takes a pie from Joan and leans forward at the waist, giving each of the sisters quick little kisses on the cheek. There's a smell of burning oak and turkey in the stove, newborn ice and frostbitten leaves. Sam frees Wing, who gallivants about, biting at a few stray flurries in the air.

"How's the bird?" he asks.

"I don't know." Ava laughs. "We have another hour if you want to walk around."

"You want to see the sculptures?"

"Of *course*," Nan says with the tender irritation Henry used to prompt.

It won't be easy for the Finns—the way is poorly beaten and the ground's grown slippery—but they're both wearing boots and winter coats and look determined. He offers each an elbow and glances back at Ava, guiding them along beyond the clearing, nice and easy.

He starts them at *The Reacher*, still grasping for the bough, the oldest of his work and so familiar to him now that he's affected by the genuine amazement on their faces. It happens all the way without diminishment or talk, and every time another figure comes into view—partially ob-

scured or suddenly appearing—Joan makes a sound, like
an in-drawn "oh," and points it out to Sam as if to savor
his reaction.

Each of them is blanketed in fine clean flakes, delicate
enough to scatter with a breath.

The Pusher at the rock, now holding up an ice floe.

The Strongman burdened with the extra weight of fall.

The Lover like a sepulcher in some forgotten graveyard.

The Prisoner with his heart-hole mended by the snow.

The Field of Limbs, like a terrifying vision of the spring.

The Gazer at the brook, water frozen to a trickle.

The defacement of *The Weaver* is concealed by a veil,
and the great white web sparkles when it moves. They see
the others he completed in the warmer weeks of autumn.
There's *The Carver* at his work, sinewy and twisted, in the
process of sculpting out his own hidden legs. Then *The
Fire*, which he shaped from a gathering of logs. He finished it in stages all throughout the summer, adding to
the ripples and the ribbons of the flames. Now it stands
enormous, sinuous, and dense before an evergreen bush
representing smoke.

They reach the final figure that he carved before the
freeze. It's a freak growth that awed him when he found it:
two giant oaks, one dead and one alive, fused together at
the trunks and sixty feet tall. He carved a woman in the
deadwood but didn't cut the green. It'll foliate in spring,
unaffected by his work, and be a fully living sculpture with
a canopy of leaves.

She's climbing with a bare foot lifted off the ground,
her other leg buried in the dirt, mid-calf. Her only clothing
is a long, sheer gown, fine as silk, and her hair unspools
down the middle of her back. She's looking at the sky with

a radiant expression, but her limbs have weight—there's a gravity about her—and the roots around her ankle are inflexible and cruel.

By the time they come around and see the clearing just ahead, the woods feel numinous and gracefully alive. Joan's reminded of her long-lost set of figurines, and even at the cabin she expects something more, certain that another strange marvel will appear. Even Nan feels hypnotized and doubtful of her senses. They're reliant on his arms, glad of his support.

Back inside the cabin, Ava takes their coats. Nan stands frozen at the stove, her hands so numb they barely register the heat, until her fingers start tingling and her joints begin to thaw.

The table's fully set and dominates the room. Wing's underneath, watching everybody's feet and waiting for the next dropped morsel on the floor. Turkey saturates the air, along with cinnamon and yeast, coffee and a myriad of spices and aromas. Nan helps Ava with the meal, organizing bowls and discussing the reliability of meat thermometers. Sam and Joan talk about the cabin, and the Finns' own home, and the use of black pepper in a good pumpkin pie. A pair of deer pass the window and they all stop to watch, admiring the quick white flickers of the tails. Wing naps until Sam starts sharpening a knife. They heap the plate with breast meat and fill a bowl of stuffing, set the carrots and potatoes out, pass around rolls.

Nan says grace. It's traditional and brief, a single-sentence prayer, but she almost starts crying when she says the word *bounty*. She watches Sam and Ava all throughout the meal. They sit together, opposite the Finns, a widow and a widower that look too young, too alive to play the roles. A stranger coming in would see them as a couple, with the nearness of their chairs, the automatic way they hand each other food, the subtle touch of elbows that neither seems to notice.

It worries Nan, thinking they'll be devastated later when the night sets in and they remember who they are. *Let it go*, she decides. *Let it breathe for a while*. All five of them deserve an hour of reprieve.

26

The Carmichaels are due at the restaurant in less than an hour. Peg wants to leave early in case there's holiday traffic but Danny's been sitting on the toilet for the last twenty minutes when he ought to be tying his shoes.

"Get off before you give yourself a rash!" she hollers through the door, with the same breaking-point tone she used on Bob when he left his whiskers in the sink, and on Ethan, moments ago, when he groused about putting on a belt.

"I want to hear a flush in ten, nine, eight . . . ," she says, faster than actual seconds, and when she gets to three and hasn't heard the toilet paper roll, she opens the door and walks right in.

Danny's wide-eyed with fear, tears streaming down his cheeks, standing at the sink in his little shirt and tie. His pants are on the towel rack over the heat vent and his underwear is hidden in a ball behind the garbage. He wet himself and panicked. He's been trying to correct it and he cries without a sound while his mother looks around and registers the scene.

Peg hugs him so abruptly that he sobs even harder. His

fingers on her back make *her* cry, too. She contains it with a sniff and reassures him with a smile.

"It's okay," she says, closing the door before Bob or Ethan happens to wander by. She gets him undressed and puts him into a quick warm shower. Once he's toweled off, she helps him with his shirt and tie, kisses him twice, and checks his pants. Even in the dryer they'll retain the smell of urine so she folds them up and says, "You'll have to wear your jeans."

Danny almost starts to cry again.

"It'll be cool," she says, assuring him it's really very stylish. "You'll look like a teenager. If Dad or Ethan ask, we'll say the slacks didn't fit."

She gets the change of clothes and he's immediately calm, and then she sneaks his pants into the washing machine and follows him up to the boys' shared bedroom.

"I want to talk to you two," she says, and whether it's her mildness of voice or Danny's lack of worry, Ethan comes to her with confidence—a slightly bigger version of his brother, handsome in his dress clothes and old, so much older than she comfortably admits. They look at her together and she kneels on the carpet, holding hands with each of them and turning face-to-face.

"I'm sorry for everything that happened this year. I wish I could have kept you from it all," Peg says. "I know you think that I was mean to Mr. Cooper. I know you're mad about the tree house and all my other rules . . ."

They shake their heads because they're young and she's their mother, not from honesty. She understands the difference and continues all the gentler.

"It's okay," she says. "I don't expect you to like every

one of my decisions. But I worry you're afraid of me . . . afraid to disappoint me. And you shouldn't be afraid of that. I love you more than *anything*."

They hug her, both at once, in an awkward clutch of arms.

"Does this mean we can use the tree house again?" Ethan asks.

"No."

"Can we order two desserts?"

"Yes," she says.

"Why does Danny get to wear jeans?"

"I peed my pants," Danny says, smiling in his shame.

Peg tenses when they openly discuss it, very crudely, but instead of redirecting them she watches them together, how they laugh and seem to instantly forget her in the fun.

"Okay, enough," she finally says. "I want you at the door in ten minutes, not eleven, and we're all going to have a wonderful Thanksgiving if it kills us."

She walks downstairs, weary and regretting her decision that they eat away from home. Bob has occupied the bathroom so she waits before the living room window, looking at the neighborhood and thinking it was only last year, incredible but true, that the Baileys and the Finns were hanging decorations.

It's lovely, she admits, with the fresh coat of snow, and even the trailer has a cleanness and a tidiness about it. But she can't abide the cabin, a thing too *Deliverance* to have behind her yard, and though she's known of its existence since the week of Henry's accident, it stuns her all the same whenever she remembers.

Now they're gathering for *dinner* there. It's almost like a cult. Earlier today she heard the ATV and saw him driving up the trail with Ava and the dog. She heard it once again and saw the Finns riding out, as if they don't have a kitchen in a very nice home.

She's surprised when Bob's behind her, asking what's the matter.

"Just the holidays," she says.

She hugs him like a girl.

He rubs her back and she remembers how strong he really is, despite the softness of his muscles, and his paunch, and his manner—how he used to pick her up and she was happy when he did.

The boys are coming down—she can hear them on the stairs—but instead of pulling free she lingers in his arms, wishing it were easier to hold them all together.

"Look at that," Bob says. "Billy Kane's going, too."

That's the capper, she decides. At least they didn't ask her.

The eight-o'clock dark feels like ten, especially in the woods, where dusk falls sooner and the night is more insistent, right beyond the glass and underneath the floor. Everybody's overwarm and overfed and just about dozing mid-conversation, and the Finns begin to dodder and discuss going home.

Sam helps them with their coats and thinks of Laura after parties, how her skin smelled of cocktails and hours-old perfume. The outdoor air has a mentholated freshness. Nan and Ava spend another five minutes snapping up Tupperware and organizing bags. Sam walks Joan toward the middle of the clearing where the cabin light ends and they can better see the stars. He teaches her a handful of major constellations, all that he can show her in the space between the trees. Nan and Ava meet them at the ATV, following their eyes and looking at the sky.

Ava doesn't have her coat.

"I'll stay and help you clean," she says. "You can drive me home later."

"Don't worry about it. You don't want to be here alone," he says, knowing how the dark yawns out around here, all the world growing distant in a heartbeat of quiet.

Ava draws him closer with a gravity of will, speaking quietly as Nan and Joan shuffle off behind him.

"I can't go home yet," she says, eyes moonlit and wet. She almost leans her forehead right against Sam's. "I need a little more time. I want to know you're coming back."

"All right," he says reluctantly. "Wing'll stay, too."

Ava shakes her head and motions off behind him. Wing's sitting on the flatbed, leashed between the Finns.

"We can't disappoint him," Ava says. "I'll be fine."

He doesn't like it but relents, unwilling to deny her and relieved, truth be told, to have another hour of her company tonight. They hug each other tight. Ava walks inside the cabin and he watches her the whole way in before he goes. The Finns are unsurprised. He's embarrassed when he passes them and doesn't bring it up, and then he starts the ATV, verifies that Wingnut is properly secured, and smiles at Nan and Joan before proceeding onto the trail.

Right inside the trees, Wing jerks against the leash. He's caught an unfamiliar scent, something worth attention, but his high-pitched yelps are taken for excitement. Nan shortens up his leash before he tries jumping off.

They rattle through the dark. For the first time in months, the woods feel perilous to Sam, and his attention is divided as he tries to focus ahead, navigating the trail and hoping they don't get stuck, and glancing back at the Finns, especially Joan, whom he expects to be alarmed by the wilderness around them. Once they make it out, he drives the ATV straight across the lot—it's noisy but the Carmichaels seem to be out—and then he helps them into the truck, puts Wing in the back, and lets the engine warm up before driving away.

The asphalt's pleasant after bumping on the trail. No one else is driving. Even in the center of town, the parking lots are empty and the cars sit cold. A soft electric sheen warms the edges of the road: streetlights, gas stations, neon signs reading CL SED, CLOSED, LOSE.

"How'd she seem to you?" Sam asks.

"Healthier," Nan says.

"It makes me nervous leaving her behind," Joan adds.

"She insisted."

"Oh, we know," Nan says, waving absolution. "Joan predicted it this morning."

"What do you mean?"

They idle at a traffic light, redder in the glow.

"I thought of being her," Joan says, sounding smaller than before but with the confidence of having been correct. "Holidays can be so short. I used to cry every year after Christmas."

"And your birthday," Nan says.

"It must be worse for you and Ava."

He's thought of Laura all morning, all day, and all night, imagining her fingers in the flutes of the piecrust, her mittens in the snow. But the memories have given him a lungful of air, not the slow suffocation he's been witnessing in Ava. He was conscious of his strength and often thought of Henry—when he split a load of firewood, and loaded up his plate, and smiled, with conviction, when she needed him to smile.

"I don't know how to help," he says. "I hear myself giving her advice and can't believe how meaningless it sounds."

"What helped you?" Joan asks.

"I don't know. Seeing people helped. Other times it didn't. I've got to wonder how much of it actually worked, how much of it was time."

Their faces pale and darken with the intermittent streetlights. He'd like to crack a window but the Finns look cold and so he tolerates the heat, wishing he were home.

Joan asks him if he prayed.

"I'm pretty sure *that* didn't work. Nothing ever swept in to save me."

"Henry did," Joan says.

"I mean that God didn't help."

"Like a big warm hand reaching from the sky?" Nan asks.

"Right," Sam replies, unsure of how to read her.

Joan fidgets with her hands, a habit she's developed as a puzzle builder, playing with imaginary pieces in her lap. They finally pass a car driving in the opposite direction and the road looks darker when it's gone, hard black between the curbs.

"I'm eighty-three," Nan says. "A lot of people, even people my age, think I'm foolish for believing in God. It's fear of death, consolation in the night . . . I ought to know better, especially after this year. They tell me look at how cruel the world is, like it's nonstop fire and disaster. Look at how primitive religion really is. They never think I might

believe in something richer, or stranger, or more sophisti-
cated than whatever they *assume* I believe."

Sam holds a breath, eyes bolted to the road. He's
ashamed that he's offended them and wants to smooth it
over, but before he has a chance, Nan continues, very calmly.

"Any idiot can know there isn't a wise old man with a
bucket of lightning, but a lot of people stop right there.
Their grammar-school beliefs weren't enough. They think
it's more adult to throw them off. And they're right. You
can't keep thinking like a child when you're grown."

"I hate it when you talk this way," Joan says.

"I didn't mean you," Nan whispers.

"I don't see what's so complicated about it."

"I wish it *weren't* complicated," Sam says. "It'd be so
much easier if God were obvious."

"He is," Nan says. "It isn't."

"I'd like to talk about something else," Joan decides,
and then they're briefly at a loss, staring at the traffic lines,
following the last few turns toward their neighborhood.
Wingnut's finally relaxing in the back. Sam sees him in the
mirror, panting from his earlier excitement on the drive,
his crooked tail seeming more broken than deformed.

Snow glitters in the headlights, hours old but still pris-
tine, eddying in fine blown patterns on the blacktop. The
cabin feels lost, far behind them in the dark, and the meal
is like a memory from early in the week.

"So what do we do for Ava?" Sam asks.

"Whatever we think is right." Nan sighs.

"But how do we decide?"

"Sam," Joan says, with an air of disappointment. "How
often in your life do you really not know?"

27

Ava cleans dishes in a black rubber trug. The water from the pressure tank is painfully cold—she wonders how long Sam can keep it unfrozen this winter—and she heats it by the kettleful and adds boiling water as she goes. She lays the washed dishes and utensils on the table, emptying the trug at intervals and starting with a fresh round of suds. Her hands are raw but it's satisfying work, reminding her of holidays with Henry when the dishwasher filled and they would stand together, elbow to elbow, finishing the rest with a towel and a sponge, Ava washing, Henry drying and asking every ten seconds: "Where's the ladle go? Where's the yellow pie dish go?"

She notices a hairline fracture in a plate. The quiet and the nearness of the fire make her woozy. Thirty minutes, he'll be back, then . . . what? She thinks of riding out in the dark—unfair of her, she knows, forcing him to make a whole second trip—and how she didn't leave the porch light on, didn't leave any of her lights on at home. She'll make a lot of noise opening the door, sending Wing in first to run around the rooms, but turning on the lights will only make it emptier.

She takes her shoes off, rubbing on the arches of her feet.

Embers settle in the stove and the windowpanes tick. In the drafts from the walls, she can almost smell winter. But tomorrow she can start to plan Christmas with the Finns.

There's a knock. Ava jolts, more inwardly than outwardly. She would have heard the ATV along the trail and it was definitely a knock and not an animal or branch. The door is unlatched. Ava tenses on the chair. Then she's up like a shot, reaching for the lock, but the door swings open and she moves back fast.

"Hello?" a man says, hesitant but clear.

Billy Kane steps in, twisting at the knob.

The cabin has a fluttery reality about it, like a film with a gap in every other frame. Billy looks at her and grins—sheepishly, it seems. He's wearing boots and a barn coat, corduroy brown, and his knuckles and his cheeks are cold-bitten red. Ava doesn't move, doesn't blink, doesn't speak. Billy stands at the threshold, patient and polite, as if he wouldn't dare cross without a formal invitation.

"Ava?" Billy says. "Hey, it's me. It's only Billy," waving at her face as if he's found her on the floor. "I didn't mean to scare you."

"What do you want?" she asks, dampening his smile.

Billy says, "I know it's weird showing up like this," as if it isn't really weird and she'll forgive him just for saying it. He's talking too slowly and enunciating words.

"I didn't expect to find *you* here," he says. "Where's Sam?"

"He's around. He'll be back in a few minutes. Wingnut's here . . . my dog. He's right around back."

"Your dog was with the Finns. Maybe Sam didn't tell you," Billy says, leaning on the doorframe and blank behind the eyes. "I just wanted to check on him. Holidays, you know? I'm sitting home alone—my wife's divorcing me, I told you some of that . . . I figured we could all use some company tonight. I stopped at your house, too. You weren't home. I mean *oviously*," he slurs.

"This isn't my house," Ava says. "I can't invite you in."

"Ahh," Billy says, dismissing her excuse. He bumps the trug with his boot, splashing water on the floor, and the door falls shut behind his back. "I know Sam. He's my *neighbor*."

"Please go. I don't mean to sound rude. I just . . ."

"I'm not a burglar," Billy says. "I could steal a piece of that, though," looking at the pie half eaten on the table and appearing to remember some better Thanksgiving. He looks at Ava's body with the same dull gaze, moving up slowly from her knees to her stomach.

All the while she's remembering the time before he came, how many forks and plates she washed, how many minutes since Sam drove away.

"Remember at the drugstore?" he asks. "I think you took that wrong, like I might have asked you out. I'll be honest, I was nervous. I didn't want to say the wrong thing, you know? And afterward I thought of what to say and it's been sticking in my head ever since. Listen . . . being honest, right? So you can trust me? I didn't come to see Sam. I came to see you. I figured you were here. I know you come here a lot. See it's this," Billy says. "We're the *same*. We're a fit. You don't see it yet, the crazy kind of sense it all makes. Listen for a minute, let me talk it out. Your husband wrecks my house, right? Everything's a mess. My marriage falls apart. All because of him. And then he dies, and neither one of us can see it for a while. One day Henry owes me everything, more than he could ever pay me back, and then"—clap!—"he leaves it all behind."

Billy shuts his eyes and wobbles very smoothly.

"I understand what you're doing out here," he says. "I *understand* it. But with Sam—and I don't mean anything against him—but sometimes a person's too broken up. If you're taking care of him, who's taking care of you? You see what I mean? You're gonna make me say it." Billy smiles at her, timidly but acting like he's doing pretty well. "I understand what you're going through. You lost your husband. I lost my wife. But Sheri didn't die. I'm not a wreck like that. I'm standing on my own two feet. Not like Sam. Not like Sam. All I'm saying . . . I don't know," he says, pausing in a swoon. "We're like a phoenix from the ashes. You and me. We're a *phoenix*."

He watches her reaction, shivering and tense. When she doesn't say a word, he looks deflated and confused.

"I'm rambling like an idiot," he says. "I've never been good at this sort of thing. You can think about it. That's cool. I don't need a major answer right here. Just know I'm always here. I'm *always here*. Come on, come here," he says, summoning her over with his hands.

"Please leave," she says.

"Ava . . ."

"Get out!" she yells. "Get out of here, go!"

"Hey hey *hey*."

Billy staggers up and hugs her round the waist. The stubble on his chin catches in her hair.

Ava flails, hitting Billy with an accidental uppercut. He grunts and backs away, feeling at his teeth, and then he grabs behind her neck and says, "What's the matter with you?"

Ava falls against the stove and scalds her arm, crying out and shoving at his jaw. Billy pulls her down and kneels on her stomach, pinioning her wrists and twisting at the burn. His eyes look swollen and his cheeks billow out, everything about him melting and disfiguring. A thin line of spit dangles off his lip. It glistens there, stretching down closer to her mouth.

"I'm sorry," Billy pants. "I'm sorry. Calm down. Take it easy, calm *down*."

Ava glances at the door but doesn't hear a sound.

"I want to let you up," he says. "I want to talk this out."

"You're hurting me," she whispers.

"Where?" he says. "How?"

"My wrist. I burned it on the stove."

Billy lets her go but keeps kneeling on her gut. He takes his coat off and throws it on the floor, rolls a shirtsleeve up and peels a bandage off his arm.

"I'm hurt, too," he says. "You want to squeeze it? I'll let you do it if you want to."

Ava doesn't move.

Billy stares at her and says, "I'll let you up. We can talk. I'm trusting you—I wouldn't trust Sheri like this. Just stay calm, all right? Everything's okay."

Ava lies there, looking at the shadows in the rafters. Eventually she stands, shaky on her feet. As soon as Billy turns, she shoves him over a chair. He falls sideways, reaching out and swatting at the floor, and hits the corner of the stove right above the ear. His neck goes rubbery and awkward when he slumps.

Ava runs out, looking for the ATV, and when she doesn't see a thing, she pauses in the dark. Her phone is in the cabin but she hears him getting up, vigorous and guttural,

knocking into chairs. She doesn't trust herself to run the
quarter mile to the street, not with Billy right behind her,
following the trail. She darts across the clearing to a thick
stand of trees and hides behind a trunk.

Ava sees him at the door, working things out, a crooked
silhouette leaning on the frame. He notices her prints in a
line across the clearing, but he totters and he still seems
addled from the fall. Eventually he'll find her—even now
he's looking over—so she runs to keep ahead of him and
heads toward *The Reacher*.

She's freezing in her dress and isn't wearing shoes but if
she concentrates, remembering her way around the sculptures, she can lose him in the dark, circle back, and get
away. She hurries through the snow. Billy crackles up behind her. He can follow but the woods are all hers, so familiar, and the statues seem to look at her and guide her
on the way.

Billy's vision blurs. He tries to walk and finds he's already
moving, tries stopping and he can't for several seconds.
Whenever he falls, it's a banged knee or scraped knuckle
that alerts him. It takes him too long to get back up, and
when he does, he finds the footprints and wonders what
they are, where they're leading him, and why it's so important that he follow.

He keeps touching his head. It isn't bloody but he
checks every time, sometimes remembering the fall against
the stove, other times feeling only pressure and a pulse.
Thoughts stab through, causing him to wince, until eventually it comes to him—Ava in the cabin. Only where's the
cabin now? He doesn't see it through the trees. Something

dark pools in, confusing him again, and so he staggers on ahead, frantic and afraid.

There's a body right before him. Billy jumps backward in the snow, legs kicking wild, staring at the figure with its arm raised to hit him. It's a man, or rather *half* a man, rising from a trunk. He isn't real, Billy thinks, and yet he isn't quite sure—it's skeletal and twisted as a long-dead corpse and yet it *looms* there and really seems to menace when he flinches.

He escapes and rushes on, crashing through the branches with his hands out before him, and he's scraped, jabbed, and tangled up from unexpected angles, almost like the woods are reaching out to get him. He can feel her up ahead, barely out of sight, and then he comes upon another dark figure in the trees. Bearded and colossal with its arms spread wide, it tries to grab him and he pushes it away, saying "No," feeling dizzy and surrounded, reeling as he goes.

He sees a log near a brook and swears it has a mouth. He sees an arm in every branch, things swaying overhead, congregations in the shadows and a hundred other forms. Little creatures out the corners of his eyes and at his ankles, faces in the bark, faces in the snow. A man with crooked antlers, and a serpent, and a bear, all with human features and a snarl, and a leer. He finds a woman on her back, beautiful and nude, writhing in the feathers of a terrifying wing. He thinks of Sheri on the bed and Ava on the floor, lepers in a cave and bodies in the ground. There's a figure with a blade, carving at his thigh, and a girl with no expression being eaten by a spider. Now the forest is evolving into fire, into webs. Billy huddles in the dark to overcome his nausea but he vomits and the night feels infinite around him.

He sees her up ahead, clinging to an oak. The footprints lead directly to the trunk. He's caught her mid-climb and yet she freezes when he comes, her only covering a dress and the glitter of the snow.

"Ava," Billy says, crying when he sees her.

He's tired and his body feels gray and unclean, as if the cut along his arm has putrefied his veins. There isn't any motion in the pines or on the ground, but the quiet's like a rumble in the bottoms of his feet. He stands awhile, panting and admiring her hair, wishing he could touch her but afraid, too afraid.

"I'm sorry," Billy moans, ears building to a roar.

He charges headfirst directly at her back. At the moment of embrace, there's a great black flash.

He lies for several minutes, bleeding in the snow. Then he rolls and lurches off, forgetting who he is until he stumbles to his hands, puzzled by the blood, and starts to worry that he's done something very, very wrong.

Ava pauses in a thicket, straining for the faintest sound or movement in the dark. Her shiver's gone deep. She has spasms in her core. The burning in her lungs has settled to an ache, and she can't feel her feet or move her toes anymore. Her adrenaline matures to a wiser kind of fear, an awareness of her ever-growing distance from the cabin. She can stay here barefoot, assuming that he's quit, or she can hurry out now and hope he isn't waiting.

Ava runs, looking hard for the gully of the stream, the clearest way to go without getting lost. She finds her tracks from earlier on and freezes at the sight. She meant to loop around but now she's here where he can find her, fifteen yards from *The Climber*. There's a second set of prints covering her own; the prints veer away and Ava gasps. There he is.

Billy's shadowy and slumped, just a body in the snow. At first she can't determine if he's lying down or crouching. Several steps more and Ava sees blood. It gives her energy to run, watching Billy all the while, and he doesn't even twitch when she crashes through a shrub.

She's elated that he isn't getting up and yet it worries her. The ease of her escape, so strange and unexpected, makes it feel as if he's tricked her—like she's running into danger. And the blood . . . is he bleeding from the stove? Is it new? For a moment she's afraid, looking all about, scared that something else is prowling in the woods.

She pauses at a pine in the shadow of a bough, enlivened by the strong green odor of the sap. If she runs and he recovers, if she flees and Billy dies . . . she can't just leave him there bleeding in the dark. She creeps toward him slowly, growing bolder as she goes, following a need to help him if she can.

Billy's unresponsive, lying on his face. The blood around his head has melted through the snow. Ava prods him with her foot and says his name. He doesn't move. She rolls him on his back and marvels at his forehead, dented in the center with a wide flap of skin. Blood's slicked through his hair, down his cheek, and to his throat.

She checks his breathing with her hand and verifies a pulse, and then she tears her own hem to make a bandage for his head. It's delicately tied but enough to stem the flow. Billy moans when she starts to say his name more insistently. She tugs off his boots and puts them on her feet, leaving Billy in his socks and buttoning his coat. She lifts him by his armpits and drags with all her strength, and when his head lolls back he sees her upside down, glassy-eyed and slurring, wholly in her care.

"That's good," she says. "Look at me. Focus on my face."

Billy garbles, shuts his eyes, and grows heavy in her arms, passing out at intervals and waking up dazed. She hauls him backwards, rarely looking but convinced of her direction, passing by *The Gazer*, and *The Weaver*, and *The Fire*.

"Billy," Ava says. "Billy, look at me, come on."

"Am-sa," he says. "Am-sa."

"That's right. I understand."

"I'm-sa. I'm-sa. I'm *sai*."

"We're almost there."

She recognizes trees and looks beyond her shoulder. There's the cabin, gently lit. She smells the chimney and his blood. Billy stares at her and gapes, head dangling to the ground, with his mouth above his nose and his eyes long gone. When she struggles in a tight-fit passage in the briars, it's a feeling of defiance that rejuvenates her will.

She sees a pair of headlights coming up the trail. Billy gazes at the cabin—accidentally, it seems—and Ava's saddened by the lantern hanging in the window, his only consolation when she leaves him in the dark.

She has her coat and phone when Sam drives into the clearing and sees her there, bloody in the headlights. He jumps off the ATV, unable to hear most of what she's saying now that Wingnut's barking from the flatbed. He hasn't yet seen the body near the cabin and he stumbles running over, falling to a knee. Ava meets him halfway and

Sam's afraid to touch her, holding her as gently as he dares by the shoulders.

"What happened, where are you hurt?" he asks, panicked by the blood.

"It's Billy, Billy Kane," she says, pulling his arm and pointing at the ground.

"Billy . . . what, he hurt you? Did he hurt you?"

"No, his head—he hit his head. He chased me out of the cabin . . . no, Sam!"

She physically restrains him when he lunges down at Billy, worried Sam will harm him more severely in his anger.

"He's dying," Ava says. "We have to get him out."

Sam looks at her with crazed incomprehension, seeming to believe her levelheadedness is shock. He may be right—she isn't shaken, isn't crying or relieved, only wired to the moment with a clear-cut goal. One look at Billy's wound and Sam understands: whatever happened doesn't matter now. They have to act fast.

He brings the ATV right beside the cabin and they lift Billy up, as smoothly as they can, onto the flatbed. Wing stops barking, neither wary nor aggressive, comforted that Ava's near, and sniffs Billy's arm. Once they're all secure, Sam drives them out, more careful on the trail than when he'd driven with the Finns. Along the way, he calls an ambulance to meet them on the street.

Ava sits with Billy, holding his head in her lap and saying his name, gently but distinctly, like a mother with a child waking from a nap. Billy looks at her. He moves his lips but doesn't really speak. Wing keeps watch, instinctively subdued, knowing something serious and intimate is happening.

28

Billy lapsed into a coma after surgery for a depressed fracture of the skull. He woke the following week, and though he tried to understand when people asked him questions, he neither spoke nor followed instructions and spent the bulk of his time gazing at the television or the blank wall of his hospital room, incapable of feeding himself or possibly unwilling. Much of his life came to light—his unemployment and his debts, his self-inflicted cuts, Sheri's testimony of abuse throughout their marriage—but despite being charged with trespassing, unlawful restraint, and aggravated assault, to name a few, no one expected a full enough recovery for Billy to stand trial. No one visited. His long-term care was undecided, assuming he'd survive the hospital at all. He was still losing weight and fighting off infection. He'd begun to stare obsessively at trees out the window.

Ava was treated kindly throughout the investigation, and the police who examined the woods were careful at the cabin and respectful, almost reverent, when they searched around the sculptures. They questioned Ava, Sam, the Finns, and even the Carmichaels, who had witnessed Billy entering the woods that day, and although the injury at the tree was ruled accidental, some suspected that the act had been intentional—a suicide blow resulting from panic, drunkenness, or the deeper instability that brought Billy to the cabin in the first place.

Sam blamed himself, both for leaving her alone and for neglecting her concern after Billy had approached her in the drugstore. Ava spent a week with the Finns after the attack. She found herself scrutinizing people at the lab, growing leery when her patients seemed a little too friendly. She went shopping only if the Finns went along. She yelled at Sam for not having a fire extinguisher, scolded him for climbing on his one-story roof, and even tried leashing up Wing so he couldn't run wild in the woods.

One night the telephone rang and Ava picked up, thinking it was Sam. It was Sheri Kane, who introduced herself twice before the name made sense. She'd gotten Ava's number from the phone book; she'd had it for a while, since the week of the attack. She hoped that even now she wasn't calling too soon.

Sheri spoke about herself, how she'd felt both shock and horror at the news, and she apologized repeatedly, convinced that she was partially to blame.

"It's not your fault," Ava said.

"I'm sorry about your husband," Sheri told her. "I watched him build that tree house for the Carmichael kids. He was a good guy."

Ava thanked her, crying into the phone and trying to hide it. Sheri let her go, saying "Anything you need" and giving her a number, not that either woman honestly believed she'd ever use it.

Ava sat awhile after, petting Wing and thinking how little the phone call had clarified, and yet it calmed her more and more, seeming to atone, in some small way, for the darker types of randomness that had, of late, seemed the only kind left.

There's a blizzard coming: gale-force winds, two feet of blown snow, the storm's outer bands several hours off. Sam's spent the morning stacking wood, filling kerosene lanterns, getting batteries in order, and reading the owner's manual of his new snowmobile. He's come to the street to wait for Ava and has his cell phone charging in the truck when she eventually pulls up, unannounced and yet expected, so much so he's brought her hot chocolate in a thermos.

She called him yesterday and earlier today, giving him the latest forecasts and telling him he shouldn't ride it out. He can stay with her and Wing—they'll order food and rent some movies—yet he's flustered her by saying no, gratefully but firmly. She clapped the phone down this morning when he wouldn't tell her why, and when he tried calling back and Ava wasn't there, he knew that she was coming to confront him here in person.

She stands before him now, buttoned up snugly in a pea-coat, little brown boots, thick brown mittens. She's cut her hair shorter and it suits her, rounding out her cheeks and giving her a softer, more adorable effect. Sam studies her expression, and her mood, and her mittens, and the way she moves her chocolate so it swirls around the thermos cup.

"Where's Wing?" he asks.

"I don't understand why you're staying."

"I wish you wouldn't worry."

"I wish you wouldn't stay."

He's sold the trailer and the lot looks emptier without it, but he's placed a pair of sculptures at the left and right of the trailhead. Ava saw them at the cabin but they're new to her again, standing in position where he placed them, only yesterday, so everyone could view them from the street. They're simpler than the others, more impressionistic. Each of them is life-size, the woman slightly taller than the man, dignified and graceful with their arms at their sides, unposed and unadorned, standing in memoriam.

"I just think I ought to stay and keep an eye on things," he says. "I'll be all right. The snowmo—"

"What if something happens overnight?"

"I have a phone."

"Disposable," she says, "with nonexistent coverage. You barely get a bar *without* a blizzard."

"It isn't that bad," Sam insists.

She makes him get the phone and, sure enough, one bar. He holds it higher to the east and says, "Look," certain that a second bar flickered for a moment.

"Sam . . ."

"I have firewood and food. I've got a flashlight, lanterns, a crank radio . . . I'm better prepared than people in town."

The Carmichaels' realty sign rattles in the breeze. They moved across town early in the month, but the house is overpriced by twenty thousand dollars and no one's showing interest. Now, with Billy in foreclosure, the entire section of the block is formally abandoned, all except the cabin and the sculptures in the trees.

"It just seems crazy running off," Sam says. "I spent the whole summer scared of being alone. I can't do it anymore. This is where I live now. This is home."

She pours her chocolate on the ground, wearied by his

answer, and he wonders if it's selfish to refuse her invitation. She'll be safe, strictly speaking, from the menace of the storm, but blizzards have a way of building in the night, of fostering a special kind of panic in the dark.

"I miss him," Ava says, staring up the trail.

He hugs her and her hands lock tight around his back.

The clouds are heavy and depressed with the incoming storm, and there's an air of something great and unstoppable in motion. He thinks of being trapped inside the cabin when it starts, whiteout squalls darkening the woods, snow blowing up and mounding at the door. He'll listen to the branches cracking in the wind. He'll think of Ava miles off and wish that he were there, reconsidering his choice and lonely in his fear.

He smells her hair and feels her coat, how familiar she's become. How they argue into hugs, how comfortably they fit. He knows when she arrives before he even hears her coming, simply by the way his nerves unwind. For now he's satisfied to hold her for as long as it'll help, following her breath until she needs to pull away. In the morning he'll be up, discovering the snow, awed by the drifts and the newness of it all, and she'll be glad he isn't with her when she wakes and thinks of Henry. They'll have made it on their own. After that, who can say.

Back at home, Ava calls the Finns to see if there's anything they need before the storm.

"Everything's in hand," Nan says. "I'm making a roast. I have candles and a basketful of unread magazines."

"How's Joan?"

"Her puzzle came an hour ago," Nan says, referring to

a two-thousand-piecer of *The Last Supper*. "She won't even notice there's a blizzard outside."

They talk about Sam. Ava works herself up again, looking out the window and thinking this is it: the final hour he can leave before the snow packs him in.

"He'll be fine." Nan sighs.

"He's stubborner than Henry."

"But a little less impulsive. He'll be ready. He'll be smart."

They talk awhile longer, going over plans for Christmas next week. The Finns are having dinner at their house after Mass, and the vision of the holiday, all of them together opening gifts and eating sugar cookies, feels like proof that Sam'll make it through.

After the call, Ava finishes her own preparations for the storm. She gets a shovel from the basement, walking past the pegboard of Henry's old tools: screwdrivers, hammers, the power drill she bought him on his thirty-fifth birthday. She takes the shovel upstairs and props it on the porch. The sky's darker in the west, ironclad, dense, and a cloud bank spreads out wider than the town.

She scatters salt down the steps and up the sidewalk, then twists the top of the bag and rubber-bands it shut. The mail's here. She glances up the street but the postal truck's gone. They have a new carrier, a redheaded woman named Dawn. She laughs a lot and talks too loud and lets Wingnut kiss her on the mouth, and while she's built very similarly to Ava, she's firmer all around and quite a bit younger. Henry would have liked her, and it's possible that Ava would have secretly resented her, especially her breasts and the color of her hair. It's precisely this reason Ava's warmed to her now. She'd have liked being jealous. She'd have liked being wrong.

She walks through the house and calls Wing toward the yard.

"Come on," she says, getting him to pee one more time.

He lifts a leg near the elderberry shrub and trots off, sniffing at the crust of last week's snow. Ava looks around from the center of the yard. She sees flurries near the roof and suddenly the air's full of flakes. She catches one; it's bigger than a quarter in her palm. The yellow of the kitchen has a quietness about it, like another lit room from another afternoon, but it's not quite a memory and not quite a wish. It's something either side of what she has now, a sense of having just seen Henry moments earlier, a feeling that he'll pass by the window any second.

Wing laps the yard, snow clinging to his back. He thought of Henry, too, when Ava got the shovel and the salt from the basement, reminding him of going out in last year's storms. But he's past that now, standing in the cold, dazzled by the flakes and the sparkle of the wind. It's almost time to eat. He can tell by his stomach, but he's panting and disoriented, blinded by the squall. He shivers there alone, narrowing his eyes until he sees Ava's blouse, bright and reassuring, and greets her with a bark, wholeheartedly alive.

ACKNOWLEDGMENTS

I thank my parents, first and foremost, for nourishing every creative impulse I ever had, and for giving me all the love and support I needed along the way. My writing abilities fail me here. I love them too much, and have benefited too deeply from being their son, to properly evoke how great they are.

Stephen King once attributed his success to good health and a good marriage. I've had both. My wife, Nicole, is the woman I hoped to marry long before I met her. Even if I could have written this book without her encouragement, I would have been sadder, and lonelier, and yes, probably unhealthier. The best and brightest colors of marriage in this story are inspired by her.

I thought that becoming a parent might hinder my writing. The opposite is true. Our son, Jack, changed everything for the better. He's enriched my appreciation of stories; they matter more now. And although I believed I knew about love, optimism, fear of loss, and adulthood before he was born, the kid reeducates me daily. I love him like crazy, and although he's currently too young for this particular book, his future self is my ideal reader.

Our cat, Max, and our dog, Bones, have been my daily company, keeping the solitude at bay.

My aunt Catherine is more than anyone can reasonably ask for in an aunt. She's bolstered me nonstop since I was born. I love her dearly.

My original agent, the amazing Zoe Fishman Shacham, was the first to believe in this book and introduced me to my editor. When Zoe retired midsubmission, I was lucky enough to find my current agent, the capital Jim Rutman, whom I will not allow to retire. Additional thanks to Dwight Curtis at Sterling Lord Literistic, Inc.

When you're an unpublished writer fantasizing about the passionate, whip-smart, delightful editor you'll eventually work with, you're imagining someone like Emily Bell. I can't thank her enough, though I'll continue to try. This book is immensely stronger thanks to her brilliance and commitment. She's not allowed to retire, either.

I want to thank Sean McDonald, Charlotte Strick, Annie Gottlieb, Wah-Ming Chang, Jonathan Lippincott, and everyone at FSG for their talent and care. Big thanks to Ellen Pyle at Macmillan.

Matthew Pendergast was there at the very beginning, when we were Serious Teenagers. Tony Corina and Maureen Marion of the USPS offered invaluable postal information. Paul Burke, John Faragon, and Scott Boardway also provided helpful expertise. Stanley Hadsell, Susan Novotny, and the entire staff of Market Block Books in Troy, New York, and The Book House of Stuyvesant Plaza in Albany, New York, have been my extended family for years. Tony and Dolores Abbott have given me much more than I deserved. Kevin Guilfoile kindly answered my many, many questions with great generosity. I played a lot of the National while writing this book.

Thanks also to Henrietta and Richard Larcade, Christopher and Saundra Larcade, Larry and Marie Ellen Smith, Kurtis and Melissa Albright, Rosecrans Baldwin, Andrew Womack, Joshua Allen, Kevin Fanning, and Fr. Daniel C. Nelson, O.F.M.

And thanks to my readers. I blog at Giganticide.com. Feel free to e-mail me using that site's contact page. I'll do my best to answer quickly.